THE TRAVELLERS' LIBRARY

★

VIENNESE MEDLEY

A selection of the volumes included in
THE TRAVELLERS' LIBRARY

A complete descriptive list will be
found at the end of this volume

VIENNESE MEDLEY

by

EDITH O'SHAUGHNESSY

LONDON

JONATHAN CAPE 30 BEDFORD SQUARE

FIRST PUBLISHED 1924
RE-ISSUED IN THE TRAVELLERS' LIBRARY 1927

PRINTED IN GREAT BRITAIN

CONTENTS

VIENNESE MEDLEY

" 'S giebt nur a Kaiserstadt,
'S giebt nur a Wien."

(There's only one right royal town,
There's only one Vienna.)

I

THEIR AUNT ILDE

Adagio assai   'Sorrow's crown of sorrow
                                 is remembering happier days.'

                                 ★

War and Peace had stripped Frau Ildefonse Stacher, born
von Berg, of everything except her physical being, leaving
her quite naked in another but certainly not better world.

As the widow of a Viennese Kommerzienrath, dead
after thirty years of service in the Finance Ministry, she
had enjoyed a comfortable pension. She had been considered rich herself at the time of her marriage, for she had
had as dowry some shares in a beetroot industry in
Bohemia; but when the Republic of Czecho-Slovakia was
formed she found herself mysteriously and without appeal
separated from those shares, which had been as much a part
of her life as her hands and feet, and the separation though
swift was to prove fatal, at least to her use and dignity.

During the long, pleasant years of her widowhood she
had had a little house at Baden near Vienna, where her
only brother, an official in the Northern Railways, and his
various wives and many children had been in the habit of
spending holidays and convalescences. If any child were
ailing it was promptly sent to Tante Ilde, who could
always be counted on to receive such gages of affection
with open arms.

When her brother, accompanied by one or the other of
those quickly succeeding wives, went off on his annual
walking tour through the Semmering, as many as could be

got into the little house were deposited there for safe-keeping. The family Christmas and New Year's dinners took place at Tante Ilde's, and on the 18th of August, the Emperor's birthday, they were all to be found again sitting about that well-laden table.

She was the first to know their joys and griefs, and 'I'm going to tell Tante Ilde about it,' was a familiar expression in the family.

A pleasant lady to look at, too, with a bit of lace flung over her shining white hair, a bit of it always about her neck. Her skin had a lustrous smoothness, the many tiny wrinkles no more disfiguring than the fine crackings in old ivory. Her nose was delicately arched and her lips kept long their agreeable red. But it was her eyes, more than all of these, that caught the attention. They were very large and were set quite flatly, shallowly, in her face, pale blue lakes of indefectible innocence, and while time had wrought some changes in the areas surrounding them, — a wrinkle, a dent, a falling in or away, — their placidity had gently endured. They opened widely, and though some-times they had been obliged to gaze upon one or the other wicked spectacle of a wicked world, no shadow of its evil remained upon them. That wide, blue, child-like gaze from that ageing face was what was first noticed about her and last forgot. The startled expression that appeared upon her countenance at the beginning of her misfortunes, to-wards the end was changed into one of almost formidable submission.

She had always been slender and graceful with a way of

holding herself that verged on elegance, and her clothes
were put on with a pleasant precision. She had worn a long
gold chain around her neck since any of them could
remember, holding a little gold watch tucked in at her neat
belt; she always wore, too, a pair of round gold bracelets
that successive baby nephews and nieces had grasped at,
leaving fine marks of little teeth upon them. Tante Ilde
loved those tiny dents. There was often a gentle tinkle as
she played with her chain with the hand bearing her wedding ring and a quite inconspicuous one of amethyst and
pearls. Just as inconspicuous was Frau Stacher's being, her
situation and her works, as that pale stone, those little
lustreless pearls. None save a doubly blindfolded Fate,
striking recklessly about at millions, would have found so
unimportant a mark.

Corinne, her best-loved niece, always called her 'my
Dresden-china Auntie.' There was between them some
natural affinity, as well as special affection; though Tante
Ilde loved them all, Corinne was the true child of her
heart, what the best of daughters might have been. She
had never had any children, and her life had revolved beneficently about the family of her brother, – only her half-
brother to be sure, but then they never thought of that.
When he married for the third time, quite superfluously
the family considered, the ostensible reason he gave was
that it would be a pity to leave no one to enjoy the pension
due whoever was fortunate enough to be his widow. His
sister had smiled at this, her fine, soft smile, and even
Heinie himself had been obliged to laugh, though he cared

little about jokes concerning his somewhat solemn being; and he had married the bright-cheeked, shining-eyed, full-figured, not over-intelligent young Croatian of his desire, Irma Milanovics, and they had had three sons in the four years he lived to be her husband. It made him the father of eleven children, all living at the time of the outbreak of the war, together with an adopted daughter, the child of a dead friend – (one more, it couldn't matter where there were so many). He had always enjoyed the patriarchal feeling which would come over him as he sat at that big oval table, serving the most generous of portions, or when out buying objects by the half-dozen or dozen. In many other ways, too, that numerous, good-looking family had flattered his persistent paternity.

Two sons had been lost in the war, one last seen at the fall of the Fortress of Prszmysl, then traced to a prison camp in Siberia. After two years a card came through the Red Cross informing them of his death from typhus. The other had been killed in the last mad scuttle across the Piave. A daughter, too, had died of a wasting malady in the winter of 1915 after the death of her lover at the taking of Schabatz from the Serbs that first August of the war. But there were still eight of them in the thick of the fight for survival in post-war Vienna. Irma's three boys, nine, eleven and twelve years of age, were not yet ready for the combat, but all the others were in it for victory or death.

To return to their Aunt Ilde. The first two years of the peace had not been so bad. With some difficulty she got

through and succeeded in keeping that roof that showed
such unmistakable signs of collapse from falling about her
head. Still in a small way she received them all on New
Year's Day of 1921. For the customary roast pork was
substituted a less expensive 'Rindfleisch garniert,' the classic
boiled beef and vegetables, and there had been an Apfelstrudel, delight of all Viennese. Tradition maintained itself in a world now obviously composed of wreckage. But
Frau Stacher had had an uneasy feeling as she sat, for what
was indeed the last time, at the head of her table surrounded
by her nieces and nephews. A week later she found, quite
suddenly, that never again would she get anything from
those Bohemian investments handed down from her father,
the revered von Berg. She made some desperate, useless
efforts, but she was always brought up round by the fact,
once so pleasant, now disastrous, that she was the widow of
an Austrian, and herself an Austrian. That sudden cleaving of things that she had supposed indissoluble opened a
gaping void in front of her, into which she was inevitably to
fall. Behind her, far behind her, lay the shining, solid, comfortable years, like another person's life, when she was Frau
Kommerzienrath Stacher, born von Berg. That provi-
dential 'von' had incredibly embellished her life. There
was, indeed, all the difference in the world between being
born a 'von' or not a 'von.' She had always regretted that
her mother's somewhat hasty second marriage to handsome
Heinrich Bruckner, some years her junior, had not had the
more sustaining qualities of a 'von' – then all Heinie's
children, too. . . .

15

Now it appeared that nothing made any difference. Every landmark was gone. Authority was gone. Gone beauty, reverence, faith. All that warm, imperial lustre in which the middle classes had burnished themselves, proud and content that such things were, had faded into the night with Vienna's setting sun. Sweet things were gone not only out of her life, but out of the nation's, leaving black misery, or a crushing commercialism which, though it lent money, lent neither beauty nor honour.

It was all symbolized to Frau Stacher in the ruin of her own life, epitomized in the blank, useless loneliness of her downlyings and her uprisings. Life, once dear life, had become quite simply a monster that threatened to devour her and then spit her into the grave.

.   .   .   .

One warm, golden January Sabbath set like a jewel in the silver of the Baden winter, Frau Stacher had sat hour after hour at her window in chill, stark dismay, watching without seeing the soft afternoon light sift through the bare velvety branches of the chestnut tree in front of her door. She was waiting for Corinne; but the moon had already risen and its silver glimmer had taken the place of the gold of afternoon before she heard a light step on the gravel. That light step carried the heaviest of hearts, for Corinne had come out to discuss baldly matters till then not even thinkable. . . .

But whichever way they turned and twisted and tried to avoid it, they were always finding themselves back at a certain dark spot. Finally, they very quietly owned to each

16

other, even saying the unthinkable thing aloud, that the
Baden house would have to be given up. Then Corinne
braced herself to meet those pale eyes, out of which the
colour had been suddenly washed.

'You can get quite a sum from the sale of the furniture,'
she ventured after a long silence in which she had looked as
through a blur at the familiar appointments of the room.
They sat knee to knee, holding each other's hand tightly;
Corinne felt as if she were watching her aunt drown in the
Danube; she wanted to cry 'Help,' but she only said:

'Of course you must keep enough of your best things
for a nice room near us all – if we can find one.'

The housing problem was beginning to loom up blackly,
overshadowing quite a number of things already dark
enough. She leaned closer and pressed her aunt's head
against her loving young heart. There Frau Commercial
Advisor Stacher, born von Berg, wept her only tears. She
had a fine spirit which even then was not broken, but hurt,
bent and vastly astonished. During the long hours that
followed they mingled their pity and their love, which bore
in the end a thin hope that 'something would happen'; but
all the same, when early the next morning Corinne went
away she knew that the first stone had been cut for the
sepulchre of her aunt's existence.

. . . . . .

That 'nice room near us all' proved indeed unobtainable.
In a city that had once offered every imaginable sort of
pleasant shelter, there didn't seem to be a single 'nice
unfurnished room' to offer a homeless old lady, – and it was

said so many had died in or because of the war, – no, Frau
Stacher couldn't understand.

A few bits of furniture left from the sale were finally
distributed about among the various nieces, and Frau
Stacher went to board, just as a makeshift – 'till things get
better' Corinne had assured her, at the house of an acquaintance, who in the palmier days had partaken of her
easy bounty. There, nights of aching, sleepless homesickness followed days of empty, useless longing for all that had
once been hers, for her little situation in life that had
enabled her, childless as she was, to be a centre of pleasure
and comfort to the only beings she loved. It was finished,
done with, that was quite clear. She sat more and more alone
in her room. The clack of Frau Kerzl's tongue and her
invectives at Fate, quite justified though they were, got
finally and intolerably on her nerves. She thought she
could not bear to hear another time that things were as
they were because the Hapsburgs had taken all the gold out
of Austria when they went, and left the 'others' sitting
with the paper money.

Frau Stacher was no intellectual, and had attempted no
mental appraisement of the national calamities. Even in
the good days her most enjoyable reading had been the
Salon Blatt, where what the Imperial and Royal family
and the 'Aristokraten' did, said, wore, and where and how
they showed themselves was duly recorded for the delecta-
tion of an appreciative people. A morning paper had always been brought to the house, it is true, but she would
only run quickly over world-events which had never so

slightly modified her life, whereas the doings of the First Society lent it both lustre and interest.

She knew that Frau Kerzl, whose grief had dyed her political feelings a deep red, was going on in a stupid, even wicked, manner, when she so unjustly and blasphemously spoke of the Hapsburgs, but she had no satisfactory answer to make, so after her way she was silent, spending the long evenings alone in her room. She couldn't see to sew in it, nor indeed to do anything more complicated than move about. The single light was placed high up in the centre of the ceiling and was reflected but dimly from the dark walls, the pieces of heavy furniture and the brown porcelain stove that was never lighted.

Fortitude was, seemingly, the only virtue that Frau Stacher, gentle, easy-going, unheroic, was called upon to practise.

But the thing couldn't last for ever. Often she was glad she was seventy. It made the outlook easier. There couldn't be more than twenty years of treading up other people's stairs. The instinct of home was almost as strong in her as the instinct to live. No, there couldn't be more than twenty years of it. . . . Then, too, in a month, a day, an hour even, it might all be over. But one evening sitting in the shadowy room, her little white, knitted shawl drawn about her shoulders, her hands crossed under it on her breast, she was suddenly and terrifyingly aware of the beating of her heart – almost as if for the first time. She found she was as much afraid of death as of life – and that was a great deal. . . .

19

Sometimes one or the other of 'the children' remembered to come to see 'poor Tante Ilde,' and often Corinne, in her moonbeam way, would slip in and out, still and pale indeed like a ray of reflected light, and every Sunday after dinner she and Corinne would meet at Irma's. She went frequently to Kaethe's, too, that is, whenever she had anything to take to the children. It wasn't a place where one could go empty-handed.

But all, in one way or another, were caught up in the struggle for survival. In a starving, freezing city, not starving, not freezing, took the last flow of everybody's energy, so she was mostly alone. But solitude, for which nothing in her life had prepared her, had no charms for her. She had an almost unbearable longing to be in crowds, in happy, busy crowds, where people jostled each other as they went about little, pleasant errands.

But there was another thing beside being certain – vaguely – that she wouldn't live for ever, which had come to make her sojourn at Frau Kerzl's not only endurable but desirable . . . a cold, creeping premonition concerning the not distant time when even that measure of independence would be denied her. The money from the sale of the furniture was going, was gone.

One morning in that terrible 'little hour before dawn' when anxiety had done its worst, she got up and counted and recounted the thin packet of crowns left in her purse. Then in panic she made a mental survey of her other remaining 'values,' of those things her nieces were 'keeping' for her. The result had sent her shivering back to

20

bed, where, frightened by a fear beyond any she had ever known, even in nightmare, she had pulled the bedclothes up over her head. She was afraid, afraid. It was grinning at her. . . .

She dozed finally. But she only knew she had been asleep when she found herself throwing the sheet aside with a start, thinking she heard Corinne's voice calling up the stairs in the house at Baden. . . . Perhaps something would happen.

But little can happen to women of seventy except more of the same, whatever it is. . . .

When in that chill December twilight she first found her way to the pawnshop, to 'Tante Dorothea's,' familiar to her all her life as a sure object for humorous sallies, and left there her gold bracelets, that old life dropped finally and for ever from her almost as if it had never been, leaving her unticketed, unbilleted, between time and eternity. Truly she found that there is no greater sorrow than in adversity remembering happier days.

She hadn't spoken to any of the children about that fatally impending visit to 'Tante Dorothea's,' though she had thought of consulting Pauli; Pauli who always gave the impression that nothing human was foreign to him. But he would have given her the money. Humbly she deplored the burden of her existence on that younger generation, that dead wood of her fate among those green trees, bent themselves in the blast of misery that swept over the city. Every day, every hour, one had to look out, or one was quite certainly blown over. But Pauli was away. Corinne, dear, lovely Corinne, she couldn't bear to think of her pale light flashing in through the door of that pawnshop in the Spiegelgasse, that fatal 'Tante Dorothea's,' whom the mention of in the good old days had always raised that ill-considered laugh. Once or twice her thoughts had played glimmeringly about Fanny instead of 'Tante Dorothea' — to go out in a sudden, chilly little gust blowing from the *terra incognita* of Fanny's life. In the end it was her business, not another's, that was in question. She realized for the first time the solitariness of her fate, of everybody's fate, so long hidden from her under the pleasant details of her daily existence which had seemed to bind it in a thousand ways to other lives.

When she finally slipped out, looking fearfully and guiltily about her long before she got to her destination, as if her shameful errand had been stamped in red upon her face, she was further intimidated rather than reassured to discover, as she turned into the Spiegelgasse, that she was by no means alone of her kind. All the human scrapings and combings of the Inner Town seemed to have been blown there, too. Old women like herself with arched noses and deeply circled, tearless eyes; thin, wan women, in once-good, now threadbare, clothes, whose gentle mien, like her own, recalled unmistakably happier days – how many of them there were! Pale spectres of that middle class whom the War and then the Peace had stripped of everything save their sorrows. The war loans they had invested in had gone up in the smoke of battle, or down in the bitter waters of Peace; the thousands, the tens of thousands of comfortable little incomes, left them by fathers, by husbands, had soundlessly, untraceably disappeared, and they were learning the way to 'Tante Dorothea's.'

. . . .

The Dorotheum, if one's business there is not vital, is one of the most interesting buildings of its kind in Europe. Five of its seven stories rise above ground, the other two are in deep subterranean spaces, reaching to the old catacombs, and where household and personal effects of the Viennese middle class are now stored so thickly and so high, once Roman mercenaries of the Xth Legion lay buried. . . .

But Frau Stacher knew nothing of the Dorotheum in its historical aspect, and had she known, it would have been of little interest to her.

A motley, miserable throng was pressing in at the doors, for many, like herself, chose the dusk for such an errand. She found herself pressed close to a young mother with an anxious, withered face who had a pallid baby sleeping on one arm, while under the other she carried a small bundle of linen, that last of all possessions to be offered to 'Tante Dorothea.' Behind her stood a former officer. It was easy to see what he had been. He was still erect, but he was very thin, with deep pits under his cheek-bones, his coat was buttoned up to his chin and he kept his hand in his pocket.

The pale baby on the woman's arm waked up as they stood in line, and began a wretched wailing. The mother tried to quieten it as she passed up to the counter, where a being, necessarily without bowels, looked quickly at the poor contents of the bundle, gave her a ticket and a few

23

bits of paper money. Silently she received them and made way for Frau Stacher, who in a distress that moistened her brow and dried her mouth, tremblingly produced her bracelets. She was brusquely pointed to another counter for precious objects, as also was the officer. There she found herself behind a woman selling a worn wedding ring, not much heavier than the money she got in exchange.

The bulging-eyed man, giving Frau Stacher a quick, circular look that further chilled the thin blood in her veins, proceeded to weigh the bracelets in the little scales on the counter. On their last golden gleam was borne in a flash by Frau Stacher those bright, warm years in which she had worn them. The dull ticket she received was the true symbol of her state. The money would soon be gone and she would have neither money nor bracelets, just nothing. As she turned away she saw that the officer was offering a small medallion and a miniature. Again she thought of the foolish jokes about 'Tante Dorothea.' This stark, final misery was what it really was. . . . This doom-like end of everything.

Two short weeks after, Frau Kerzl again showed signs of nervousness and talked loudly and significantly, or what Frau Stacher, who had got timid even about leaving her room, thought was loudly and significantly, concerning the price of food; and how money, even an hour over-due, represented in those days of falling currency a fabulous loss. That afternoon she took out her watch and chain and her amethyst and pearl ring. It was less frightening the second time, but she felt much sadder, and she was unspeakably depressed by the old man just ahead of her who fainted as he stood waiting.

By January Frau Stacher's situation became finally and visibly desperate. She could obviously no longer pay to remain in Frau Kerzl's house, and quite as obviously Frau Kerzl could not keep her just for the pleasure of it. The link in their lives got thinner day by day until it broke squarely in two that morning of the sixth of January when Frau Kerzl plainly hinted at the possibility, nay probability, of being able to wrest from the black heavens that star of first magnitude — a foreign lodger. No trouble, out all the time, solid, certain pay. She didn't cease to paint the foreigner in ever brighter colours. He stood out attractively, even flashily, against the grey tenuity of her present boarder. Though she had feared that something of the kind was impending, it fell on Frau Stacher like a blow on a bruised spot; indeed, she found she was one vast bruise. Anything that touched her nowadays was sure to hurt unspeakably, but being 'turned out,' as she called it, had about it an ultimate ignominy, not at all befitting the day. She had always loved the sixth of January, that noisy feast of the Three Kings, and though she had been wont to complain that she hadn't been able to sleep a wink because of the tooting of the horns, the blowing of the whistles, the beating of drums and countless other noises announcing their arrival, that racket had really appealed to her sentimental soul, heralding as it did three royal beings bringing gold and myrrh and frankincense. As she lay awake through the cold, dark night, though there had been no noise at all in the streets, she suddenly remembered that it was Epiphany; a few thin, salty tears moistened her cheeks as she realized that in a world once seemingly full of gold and myrrh and frankincense she now possessed naught save the breath in her body and the remnants of raiment covering it.

She was clearly, unless 'something happened,' among the serried ranks of that middle class fated to disappear. Thousands, hundreds of thousands, of them had disappeared, been absorbed in one or the other appalling manner into something nameless and then lost from the ways of men. The 'aristocrats' were vaguely 'away,' economizing and waiting in their castles, living, as well or as ill as might be, from their lands. The working-classes, much in evidence, were not at all badly off. Brawn had still some market value. But the middle classes, upper and lower? They could not all have died, the streets would have been heaped with bodies. There was some painful absorption of them into the life of those persisting, and this is what, for a very little while, happened to Frau Ildefonse Stacher, born von Berg; but one variation on the ubiquitous theme of genteel old age and sudden penury in post-war Vienna.

On the wet, black afternoon following the wet, black morning of which we have spoken, Frau Stacher and her niece Corinne might again have been seen, discussing whisperingly in the chilly room at Frau Kerzl's, the evident extremity of the situation. The eye in the ceiling that saw rather than was seen by, revealed them sitting even closer together than usual. Frau Kerzl had developed out of her former friendliness and respect, strange, spying, keyhole ways. She was as well aware of what Frau Stacher had done with her bracelets and her watch and chain and her ring as Frau Stacher herself. She hadn't noticed the disappearance of the bracelets, but when she no longer saw the gold chain and when her boarder incautiously asked her the time of day she knew the Stacher jig was up, and she wanted to know, further, to just what tune she herself was stepping. She had her own troubles – the son who had gone off to the war, fat Gusl he was then called, so jolly, so full of Wiener quips and quirks, always humming about the house or playing his zither. He had been invalided home that last September of the war and was now coughing his life out in the room that was supposed to be to the south, but that the sun was really unacquainted with. A dark room in a dark side-street, one among hundreds of dark, windy side-streets in Vienna where consumption has its breeding-ground: the 'Viennese malady,' it is sometimes called. . . .

The light had found and gleamingly mingled the pale gold of Corinne's hair and the silver of her aunt's; their hands were tightly clasped as they considered ways and means. There seemed to be few of one and none of the other.

'I've lived too long,' Frau Stacher said at last, and in her heart was distilled a sudden but final grief that found its stinging way to her so-long untroubled eyes.

Corinne leaned swiftly over and embraced her.

'Why, I can't think of life without you!' she cried suddenly and so glowingly that for a fleeting instant her aunt found herself warm in the fire of that love. The salt was even dried momentarily out of that bread and water of charity which was now so evidently to be her only nourishment.

Corinne had come with a scheme of existence, the barest draft of a scheme of existence, she knew it to be, for her precious Tante Ilde. For all she looked elusive, shadowy, with that one light hanging uncertainly above, her hair the brightest thing in the room, she was, in accord with a strangely practical streak in her make-up, considering the matter that engaged them in its true aspect. The sight terrified her, but she was there to give courage, not to get it. . . .

She sat quite motionless in long, slim, graceful lines (the family liking more substantial contours didn't know how handsome Corinne was, 'flat as a pancake' being no recommendation to them). Familiar with those fireless, post-war rooms and their creeping paralysing chill, she was still wrapped in her sheath-like black coat. Her little grey fur-trimmed hat had been laid on the bed, for Tante Ilde always liked to have her take it off, it made the visits seem less hurried; her dripping umbrella had been placed in the pail near the iron washstand with its diminutive bowl and pitcher; its handkerchief-like towel was folded across the little rack above it. With a disturbing, child-like confidence her aunt's wide full gaze had followed every movement. Apparently mistress of herself and of the

28

plunging situation, Corinne had been conscious of the most horrible feeling in the pit of her stomach when she finally met it full as she sat down and began to caress that thin hand in the uncertain light which seemed, however, bright enough to reveal the next step in all its horrid indignity.

Corinne was a tall, small-headed, blonde woman with a finely-arched nose and shell-like ears lying close to her head. Between her very blue eyes with a recurring oblique look that could veil her thoughts more effectually than dropped lids, was a slanting line that of late had perceptibly deepened. 'Very distinguished,' was always said of Corinne in the family; always, too, that she was 'different,' not quite indeed of their own easy-going, somewhat irresponsible Viennese kind which knows so well, in a somewhat un-analytical way, how to get something out of life – with half a chance, with a quarter of a chance. So little was really needed for happiness with a basis of enough to eat. Humming a new waltz, remodelling a pair of sleeves, getting hold of a bit of fat or sugar for the women; for the men sitting in a warm café drinking beer or black coffee, turning over the *Lustige Blätter*, smoking a Trabuco or a Virginia – joy was still as easy as that when momentarily far enough from the abyss not to be dizzy and sick with the fear of falling in. Corinne had had in common with Fanny, a North German grandmother, and though that explained, in a way, a lot of things, still there remained something about her that the family hadn't been able to label satisfactorily. Sometimes they called it cold, some-times hard, they had all come up against it in one way or another in those days of elemental issues, but terribly clever, they conceded that. She could generally be counted on to find some little door in the thickest wall.

Since their father's death and the consequent breaking up of the home, Corinne had been safely, solidly and enviably, it seemed to the rest of them, employed in the Depositen Bank, whose personnel even in those uncertain days was not doing badly; an expanding wage as the times demanded and at a place run by the bank an eatable midday meal at a possible price.

If it had been a matter of her Aunt Ilde alone, Corinne could have managed, after a fashion, to keep that existence, so dear to her, from falling to pieces, though what she earned was not yet enough for two; but all whose heads were above water had not one but many drowning persons clinging tightly, stranglingly, about their necks. Corinne was conscious of a finally sinking sensation as she proceeded to unfold the plan which appeared to her more and more what it really was – a last monstrous attack on her aunt's existence – pushing it nearer and nearer to the fatal edge. She had no single illusion as to what she was doing, and her voice was very soft in contrast to the hard, stark meaning of her words.

'I've spoken to them all, darling; you don't have to do a thing about it. To-morrow you are to move to Irma's. It will be a sort of combination arrangement. You'll be paying, of course. It's a way to help Irma and the boys as well.'

Now the famous pension on account of which Herr

Bruckner had charitably made that third marriage, had shrunk in buying properties to such pigmy-like proportions, that they didn't count it any more when Irma's needs and necessities were being discussed. Yet Irma and the boys had to live, that establishment in one way or another had to be kept up a while longer.

'But I don't see where Irma can put me,' Frau Stacher answered after a long silence.

Corinne flushed:

'Dear treasurekin . . . the alcove. . . . It'll only be till I can look about, perhaps something will turn up; it's to get you out of here and remember you'll be paying Irma for it, you'll feel perfectly independent. I've talked it over with her. She's glad enough to be helped out. Don't forget the alcove has got that plush divan of yours that we've all slept on at Baden. It's upholstered, thick and soft, with happy memories. I think you've had a beautiful life,' she ended tenderly, desperately.

Her aunt smiled, a ghost of a smile, at the mention of Baden, and the upholstery of the divan, and then her thin, broad lids closed flutteringly over the expanse of her blue eyes to keep the tears from falling, but she made no answer. There wasn't really anything to say.

'I felt of the curtains yesterday when I was there,' continued Corinne in a voice that had quite lost its resonance, 'they're good and thick and Irma sewed a big hook and eye on right in the middle, and when they're fastened you'll be almost by yourself,' she ended but with a sudden quiver of her lips, as her aunt continued to look at her with her soft wide, pale eyes in which the distaste she felt for the alcove in particular and the arrangement in general was clearly mirrored. She had never cared for Irma. Irma had something hard and strange, almost rough about her, that had never fitted into their own easy, pleasant ways. She did her duty, yes, but they were used to a pleasanter fulfilment of duty. However, it was too true that she was the only one of them having a living-room with an alcove. . . . Life was like that.

'It won't be for ever,' pursued Corinne, 'and I'll be there on Sundays for dinner.'

She spoke cheerfully but she felt as if she were pointing her dear treasurekin to the winter road instead of to shelter. Could she but have lodged her really in her heart!

'I've been thinking about you all this week and planning ever since that hateful Kerzl woman' . . . here Corinne was pulled up short by the sudden flush on her aunt's face; she couldn't bear to hear of *that* even from Corinne. . . . Frau Kerzl, who once had been grateful for a smile or even for advice, to whom she'd sent broth a whole long winter.

Corinne continued gently as flowing water – but as inevitably as water seeking its own level:

'Darling – and this is how I have arranged for your dinner every day,' she spoke even more gently and her touch was soft, the softest touch that thin, trembling hand had ever known. A brightness beyond tears was in her eyes. What was she offering really to her precious, her fragile, her Dresden-china aunt?

'On Mondays,' she proceeded, striking the simplest

32

chord at first, 'Liesel wants you to take dinner with her. She said she'd love to have you.'

This wasn't quite exact. What her sister Liesel, married since two years to a young official in the Finance Ministry, Liesel who was very happy, had really said was:

'Of course, I don't mind Tante Ilde coming once a week; we certainly ought to do what we can for her . . . but when Otto comes in he does like to find just me. However, we've got to look out for her, poor dear – she was always so good to us.'

Otto was one of some half or three-quarters of a million government employees in Vienna and was doing fairly well, that is well enough for two. He was an expert accountant and as prices went up, so mercifully did his salary. They got along very comfortably in the tiny, three-roomed apartment that Liesel in her smiling way had conjured up out of the abyss of the housing crisis. It sufficed amply for their needs. They lived almost in the style that would have been theirs had they lived and loved a decade earlier. Sometimes in the evening they even went to the theatre, or to a moving picture. What use in keeping money when the next day's fall in exchange made it act like ice in hot water? So with many shrugs of her plump handsome shoulders Liesel continued to wrest an immediate happiness from the miserable city, and with a special sapience born of love pursued her daily and absorbing round of making her Otto and herself comfortable. They cared a great deal for each other, though the family thought Otto rather a stick and wondered how he had come to find such favour in Liesel's soft, dark eyes. As a husband he had turned out to be vigilant and exclusive as well as loving, a sort of little Turk. Having small natural faith in men and still less in women, from the first he had set about guarding his treasure. It somehow suited Liesel. 'But jealous!' she would boast, casting her eyes up delightedly, a finger at her red lip. They were so young too, that they could hope that something, in the many years they expected to live, would happen to place their upset world on its proper feet again, and while awaiting that miracle they were very happy.

Otto sometimes remembered Galicia. . . . When a certain look came into his face it was because he was hearing those terrible machine guns. He limped slightly, his right knee having been smashed by a ricochet bullet, and he had had his feet frozen in an Italian prison camp and lost the toes of the left foot. . . . Oh, that mountain camp, that terrible cold, that tiny blanket! If he didn't pull it up about his shoulders he shivered and shook with that deadly central cold, and if he did pull it up his feet froze. Sometimes he dreamed of it in that warm bed with Liesel and would awake with a start to find her there, and drawing the feather-bed up higher would sink again into a blessed slumber. He knew that he had been lucky.

It was because Liesel was so happy that to her Corinne had first gone with her plan for Tante Ilde. Liesel had spent summer after summer in the house at Baden. Her aunt had always spoiled her. Everybody spoiled Liesel, so evidently made for happiness. As a little girl she was for ever rummaging in the attic for bits of silk and lace for her

dolls, and would turn out the nattiest things. Now for herself she did the same. She was round-faced, fresh-skinned,
and smiles played easily about her somewhat wide, very red
mouth – she would have been attractive in rags. But she
had that peculiar Viennese talent for wearing clothes, a
jaunty manner of pulling her belt in snugly that made the
observer conscious of her very small waist under a full bust,
above broad hips, a way of pressing her hat down upon her
head at the most becoming angle; and her high-heeled
shoes were always bright and neatly tied. These and a lot
of other details of an extremely feminine sort added undeniably to her natural charms. Pauli said that though her
soul was but a centimetre deep, you looked to the bottom
through the clearest of waters. If in her happiness she
sometimes forgot other people's miseries, it was but natural,
and when she was reminded she was all solicitude and self-
reproach.

'That will be nice,' Tante Ilde was saying slowly after
another long pause, and she was gladder than ever that she
had added the knife-rests and napkin rings to the spoons
when Liesel was married. Then as a sudden thought came
to her, she quite brightened up, 'I can do the dishes,' she
cried, 'Liesel always used to hate to do anything that would
spoil her hands.'

' Well, she doesn't seem to mind spoiling her hands for
Otto,' answered Corinne rather dryly.

'They're in love,' returned Tante Ilde gently, glimmeringly.

A shadow fell over Corinne's face at the answer as if a

ray of light had been interrupted, or as if something had been muted for a moment. Her aunt, who was not one to break into silent places, waited patiently, though she was wondering who and what was coming next.

'Pauli,' the shadow was followed by a light in Corinne's face as she spoke the name lingeringly, 'Pauli,' she repeated, 'wants you to go to Anna's on Tuesday. It's one of their meat days – when they can get it.'

'Perhaps I better not go there then. It looks,' she hesitated, and there were sudden tears in her eyes, 'so greedy.'

'Not at all,' cried Corinne. 'Pauli wants you to go on Tuesday just because of that. He said he'd try to be there himself, that first time anyway. Anna and Hermine are quite worked up about it and wondering what they can give him to eat.'

'Poor Anna,' said her aunt very gently.

Corinne flushed. Again they were silent.

Frau Stacher, bewildered at her own fate, felt quite incapable in that moment of picking up the threads of any other life, even of Corinne's. But her confidence awakened warmly at mention of Pauli. Pauli had a heart and was always showing it. Pauli understood, she felt sure, anything, everything. . . . Even poverty-stricken old aunts by marriage who had lived too long. Even to such Pauli was kind.

.   .   .   .

Pauli Birbach, the husband of her eldest niece Anna, had got through the war without a scratch or an illness – of an unbelievable luck. When a bomb burst where he and his comrades were sitting or lying, he was certain to be unhurt and soon to be seen carrying the wounded in gently or burying the dead deeply. Typhus and dysentery alike avoided him. He was naturally a debonair and laughing soul, and his easy resourcefulness had endeared him to both officers and men. 'As lucky as Pauli Birbach' was a phrase among his comrades. And even in little ways. Wasn't he always turning up with a handful of cigarettes or a bottle of wine or a chicken, got heaven knew how, in a country picked bare as a bone? An excellent cook, too, he could instruct the warrior presiding over the pot how to make the very most of what little he had. Hot water and an onion under Pauli's direction became a delectable if not nourishing soup.

And the way he played the zimbalon he discovered in a castle they were quartered in during an interminable winter in the Carpathians, the Russians, millions of them it seemed, just opposite – only half hidden by the snowy hill that some dark morning they must charge. . . .

He had seen terrible things, terrible things to a laughing, soft-hearted man, things that knocked the laughter out of him like a blow on the chest. . . . The time he went out with a patrol at daybreak, the thermometer 40 below, and they thought they were coming to a tent or a little hovel in the grey half light. . . . But it was a dozen Cossacks huddled together, frozen stiff, their heavy boots sticking out. . . .

And other things that had turned his pleasure-loving soul black with horror. . . . Christian Zimmermann, they'd been at the High School together. . . . Christian, his comrade, three days in agony, hanging on that barbed wire and no one able to get at him, and when Pauli finally did bring him in . . . oh, no, you didn't think of such things.

And the Peace that stuck in his throat and lay on his chest, and the fierce angers it aroused, beyond, far beyond the blood-angers of the War. . . . Five years to repair the damages of the War – a century those of the Peace. . . . Still Pauli often laughed, even in that cold grey Vienna, scarcely recognizable ghost of what had once throbbed and glowed, that funeral urn among cities; for he was naturally a man of hot hope, in spite of the fact that Fate at her most capricious had married him to Herr Bruckner's eldest daughter, a horse-faced, quite inarticulate woman, all of one colour, with a solemn, brooding look in her eyes. She was so different from the glowing-eyed, sparkling-faced damsels about him that marriage with Anna Bruckner came to seem like the solving of some deep mystery. What lay behind those heavy, brooding eyes, with their curtain-like closing? She had rather fine broad shoulders, something long and big about her body, built in majestic proportions, or so it seemed to him. He got into a state where he had to know what it all meant – or die. He had been inexplicably mad about her all through his lyric years. . . . Anna his Sybil. Anna had been conscious of a flattered wonder, and her chill, slow blood had known its only warmth and quickening when she married Pauli Birbach. Then so soon. . . . Yes, Anna had gone through every hell, and there are many, reserved for stupid, jealous, ugly, virtuous women. She loved him more year by year. She was obsessed by the thought of Pauli, doggedly, uselessly obsessed, for early Pauli had passed to the contemplation of other mysteries.

It was a tribute to his humanity, however, that Tante Ilde felt not the slightest distaste at going to his house . . . even in 'that way' as she called it to herself. He gave more freely than he received, and he did both easily. Probably for all his good intentions he would not be at dinner on Tuesday, he had an airy, dissolving way with him, akin to atmospheric changes — brightness into cloud, cloud into sun — and you never knew. . . . But Anna with her joylessness and her one ugly daughter as like her as the eighteen years between them permitted, Anna was her own flesh and blood, and she had been at Baden with her aunt during innumerable infantile illnesses. She was always catching something and when her hair came out after the measles Tante Ilde had faithfully brushed it back to a shining, brown abundance. It was even now Anna's one beauty. They had, after all, so many memories in common — she couldn't have forgotten all, everything. . . . On Tuesday then.

'On Wednesdays you're to go to Mizzi's,' Corinne was saying.

'To Mizzi's!' exclaimed her aunt in astonishment, throwing back her thin shoulders and sitting up very straight.

'Yes . . . Fanny,' here Corinne made the habitual pause that followed any mention of Fanny in the family —

39

'Fanny has arranged it. You know Mizzi's anxious to please her.'

Again Frau Stacher showed no especial enthusiasm for the arrangement. It was getting into quite another category. After all Liesel and Anna were her own brother's children, but when you went into houses – in that way – kept up by nieces-in-law, it was quite a different matter. Mizzi was the family dragon too. Mizzi with a look or a word could quite ruthlessly devour aged aunts, superfluous children. A monster really, with a mouth and stomach, but no entrails. They all had come to know about Mizzi – in one way or another.

'Perhaps I better go without dinner on Wednesday,' Frau Stacher suggested with a slight quiver of her lips, though not because of the food.

'You could perfectly well if you had too much or even enough at other times. But we've got to keep your strength up through the winter. You've just got to live,' Corinne repeated sweetly, warmly, 'and then think of poor Manny – he'll love having you.'

'Oh, Manny,' her aunt responded, 'poor Manny's got nothing to say,' but her voice had a note of loving compassion.

'Poor Manny, dear Manny,' repeated Corinne slowly in the same tone, adding, 'It isn't any of it for ever – next year I'll be making more money, and perhaps we can get a tiny, tiny apartment somewhere.'

Now the 'tiny, tiny apartment,' even as she spoke, seemed to Corinne the mirage it truly was. People had been known to die of joy on getting a tiny, tiny apartment. That very morning in the newspaper she had read of a man who had fallen dead when he heard he was at last to have a certain apartment he had long needed for himself and his family, and a rich man, too. Everybody was talking about it.

'I can't leave Elschen,' continued Corinne, 'it's a miracle anyway sharing that pleasant room with her while her sister's away.'

'It makes me so happy to know you're there,' said her aunt warmly, for Corinne was of the race of homeless ones, and her address apt to be uncertain. Then for all her patience, she couldn't help wondering about Thursday.

'On Thursday,' continued Corinne, having got to the fourth of her slender fingers, 'you're going to dear Kaethe's.' Kaethe and Corinne were half-sisters by Aunt Ilde's brother's first and second wife.

'To Kaethe's!' she interrupted, 'but they're all starving. I couldn't eat a mouthful there.'

'It's just because of that, that it's easy. When you go there on Thursday you are to take the whole dinner — for all of them. It'll be quite like old times when you always brought us things.'

Though delicacy was an essential attribute of Frau Stacher, she could not, at this point, restrain a slightly inquiring look at her niece Corinne, who answered after the thinnest of pauses:

'It'll be all right. . . . Fanny's going to see about it. She does everything for them anyway that *is* done.'

41

Frau Stacher closed her eyes rapidly once or twice, but made no remark. It was, undeniably, Fanny which ever way you looked. . . .

The contemplation of the Thursday arrangement, however, induced a long silence. They had a sort of hopeless, trapped feeling when they thought of Kaethe.

Some thirteen years before she had married a brilliant young professor of biology at the University, who now, as he accurately and baldly stated, earned far less than the women who kept the toilets at the railway stations. . . .

They had seven children – lovely, white-skinned, pansy-eyed, golden-haired children, or glowing-faced, starry-eyed, brown-haired. Kaethe's was indeed a terrible situation, one that made her relatives sad or angry according to their various temperaments and philosophical reactions to life. Three of those children had been born, ill-advisedly, during the War, and another since the Peace. Mizzi had soundly aired her opinion of that last arrival, ending with her usual 'dumm, but dumm!' and casting her eyes up.

Out of the thick fog of his practical inexperience Professor Eberhardt had gropingly tried various and mostly unsuccessful ways of providing for his family, ways unrelated to his brains and his technical skill, which suddenly seemed not of the slightest value. Time apparently was the only thing he had and he was directly, unpleasantly aware of its useless passage. He'd lived mostly in a blessed, timeless world of theory and experiment. Courses were only intermittently held at the University, in half empty aula reached through dusty, echoing corridors. There was no money to keep up the laboratories and the few students were apt to be as listless from under-nourishment as the professors themselves, or fiercely, disturbingly, redly subversive of everything and everybody; and anyway the struggle to keep life in the body was so terrible that it quite chilled any desire to know how it came to be there in the first place. Nature's secrets, except of the harvests, were at an entire discount.

He had duly tried several forms of those manual labours that alone seemed to be worth money. The summer before he had helped with the crops on a farm in Styria that a brother professor of geology, whose case somewhat resembled his own, had told him about. At first he had dreadful backaches and his long, delicate hands that could hold a microscope or a retort so steadily, would shake after the day's work and his thin palms were one great blister. Horrified he would hold them out at evening and watch them tremble and wonder would they ever be steady again for use in the laboratory. He had, however, made what seemed to his inexperience quite a lot of money for that sort of work, and he never knew what the peasants really thought of him. Some of the money unfortunately had been stolen from him that last Sunday when he had been incontinently dreaming about a certain theory that could always, if he didn't look out, captivate his attention. . . . Still, he brought home enough to get them through the autumn . . . and with what Fanny would do. . . .

But suddenly, or so it seemed to him, the crown began to fall. He would sit flushing and paling as he read the

43

descending quotations of the national currency and the
rising prices of food. In a few weeks that money was gone.
The Eberhardts had, relatively, gorged when they saw it
shrinking – next week it would be worth only half, and the
week after only a quarter. They laughed a good deal, too,
Kaethe and the children. Kaethe even taught Lilli and
Resl to waltz, humming 'The beautiful blue Danube' as
they spun around. The professor allowed himself to think
again of certain combinations . . . once quietly back in the
laboratory. . . . Then came the collapse.

In desperation he tried street-cleaning. A late November morning, on looking out of the window, he saw that it
had snowed heavily during the night. In spite of himself
the beauty of the little crystals lying against the panes
entranced him. He shook himself free, however, of such
luxurious and wasteful thoughts and decided to try for a
chance to shovel off snow. He said nothing to Kaethe
about it as he went briskly out. But it proved not to be
much of an idea after all, for he got a heavy chill late that
afternoon waiting in line to be paid, and when he passed by
his brother-in-law's office feeling very ill, Hermann had
administered a potion to him and told him to go immediately to bed and stay there.

About Christmas time he was put wise by another col-
league, a professor of botany, to a certain address near the
Stephansplatz where a midday meal of a sort was provided
by foreign benevolence for starving university professors.
A cup of cocoa, rice, and a slice of bread; a cup of cocoa,
beans and a piece of zwieback. It was not designed to

fatten any of them; it was only meant to keep as many of them as possible above ground . . . keeping the sciences alive. . . . The calories were carefully marked on each menu and the men of learning could take their choice without paying.

Professor Eberhardt went there every day, but with his own physical necessities ever so meagrely provided for, it was pure agony to go back to those rooms where seven hungry children and a pale wife awaited his return. He was always asked what he had had and how it had tasted. He was often able to slip the bread or the zwieback into his pocket, but there was no way of handling the cocoa and beans and rice except to eat them.

Kaethe kept his only suit brushed and darned. Indeed, it was getting to be one large darn with areas of the original cloth making patterns. She kept him in clean collars, too, for a long time, but even at the last, with his coat collar turned up, he had the unmistakable air of a man of learning and a gentleman.

He loved his wife and children greatly. But it was a terrible life, a cold, damp, under-nourished life, the things of the brain and the spirit slipping further and further from his sight. Brawn was indeed what was wanted. . . . Unless one had that strange, mysterious but apparently essential thing called money — that some had and some hadn't. Professor Eberhardt had never been fanned, even gently, by any breeze of commercialism. . . .

They had all been so proud of Leo and Kaethe in the old days; sometimes Leo's name was mentioned in the newspapers, and though they cared little and knew less about the congresses held in Vienna, they would quickly run their eyes over names and subjects, hunting for Leo's and 'as proud as dogs with two tails,' according to Hermann, when they discovered it.

The plight of Leo and Kaethe and their lovely children kept the two women silent a long time. Just as the thought of Hermann had made them very still. . . . In fact, viewed from any angle, the family fortunes were now apt to engender silence.

'Oh yes . . . if Fanny . . .' said Tante Ilde at last, picking up the thread where they had somewhat charily dropped it, 'if Fanny . . .'

She had to concede that going to Kaethe's with something of the old familiar gesture of giving to those she loved rather than receiving from them, when obviously, they had none too much, put Thursday in quite a different light.

'What do you think I could get to take them? How much do you think,' she paused musingly, 'Fanny will send?'

'I don't know, but it will be enough. You can look around and see what you can get the most of for the money. There are so many of them,' she ended, the familiar phrase losing itself in a sigh.

Too many of them, doubtless, and yet those lovely children — each one a treasure, looking at you so confidingly with their big eyes in shades of blue, except Resl's and Hansi's darkly flashing — which one of them would you not want? Not want Elsa, who had a way of snuggling close and seeking your hand as she looked up with those heaven-blue eyes? Not want Carli, that gold-and-white angel of three summers, who couldn't yet walk, his little legs would crumple up under him when he tried to stand up, but he could smile in a way that went to your heart; and as for the baby, a thing of such sweetness that one wanted to eat her up. She was still at pale Kaethe's breast; rosy and fat, though heaven alone knew how or why; and all the others. Lilli, whose beauty made you hold your breath; Resl, to whom something nice was always happening, and Maxy, with his plans for supporting the family when he grew up. Any one of them would have been the pride and joy of a childless home. . . .

Tante Ilde felt herself pleasantly excited at the thought of Thursday – relieving want – no matter how – instead of adding to it. Her eyes got quite bright.

Corinne, seeing the change, continued gaily, almost:

'And Friday, now guess,' she paused, 'Friday you'll have dinner with me. I'll let you know where and we'll talk everything over. What fun it will be! Saturday, I haven't arranged for Saturday yet, but I'll tell you in time. Sunday we don't have to plan about. I'll come as usual with the meat for the boys' stew, and we'll have a nice time all together. Perhaps in a few months we can arrange something quite different. It's only to get you over the winter . . . and you'll have courage,' she ended entreatingly. Courage, that angel, she was thinking miserably to herself, as the unalterableness of her aunt's doom became more and more apparent.

47

But suddenly it all seemed quite possible, even easy, to Tante Ilde. Yes, she would, she *could* be brave. She had Corinne . . . as long as she had Corinne. . . . Corinne was so clever, too, anything might happen when Corinne took the reins in her slim, elfin way, guiding life quickly, lightly along over the roughest spots.

'Now, dearest, don't worry about a single thing,' Corinne repeated faintly, the iron very deep in her soul as at last she got up and stood lingeringly by her aunt's chair. She had again that horrible realization of something irreparable being in progress. It sharpened her features and muffled her voice. 'I'll see Frau Kerzl on the way out and pay her up till to-morrow morning, and you can leave early.' For all her glimmering smile and close embrace she was increasingly consternated at the collapse of her aunt's existence, not even slightly concealed behind their words. She loved her more than ever in her final and inevitable rout, for pity was swelling abundantly her love. But the world! It cared little for old ladies in flight before Fate. . . .

That courage momentarily imparted to Frau Stacher by her niece's loving nearness fell heavily with the dragging hours in which more and more miserably she went about the dim, chilly room, emptying the bureau and wardrobe of their scanty contents and laying them in her shabby valises. The very old brown leather one dated from her wedding trip, for Frau Stacher had never been a traveller; it had always been pleasanter to stay at home or go only to very near places for the day. Now strangely she was become a pilgrim, and when she was hungry she was to eat of other people's bread and she must go up other people's stairs for shelter. The realization of the power of those nieces over her life terrified her. It was complete if they chose to exercise it. Withdrawal of their protection, she starved, she froze — just the not having those few thousand crowns a year put her at the world's mercy. . . .

Even Frau Kerzl's quite unctuous attentions at that last supper of cabbage-turnip soup failed to dispel the deepening gloom of her heart. Frau Kerzl was obviously though politely rejoicing. She had indeed through an incredible bit of luck secured that foreigner, an Englishman, too, who would pay in shillings, in the magic 'Devisen,' for that room in which the very next night he was to sleep — as soon as that; Frau Kerzl already basked and expanded in the approaching light and heat of those shillings. The long Englishman, strangely, hated short, square feather beds and was bringing his own blankets. It appeared, too, that he was in the commissary department of a certain relief society. Anything could grow out of such a situation — condensed milk, butter, oatmeal. . . . The arrangement was undeniably of a marvellous fertility.

Though Frau Stacher was truly glad of Frau Kerzl's good luck, it but emphasized her own impending homelessness. She had been quite miserable there, but at least her living-space had been provided with a door, and blessed with a key, — ultimate desirabilities as she now saw, — and to-morrow she would move into the uncertain privacy of the alcove. Then, too, in some way that she couldn't define, Irma, her young sister-in-law, terrified her.

Yes, homeless, in a new sense, she realized herself to be when she went back into the luxury of her solitude for the last time, and as she closed the door she knew, indeed, that she had 'lived too long.' . . .

In that bed, abundantly salted by the tears of her uncertainties, so soon to know the deep slumbers of a care-free Englishman, Frau Stacher lay long awake thinking of those homes, over whose thresholds, day by day, week by week, she was to step. . . . She would love them so much, she would be so grateful, she would hold so sacred the joys and sorrows which might be disclosed. . . .

But they seemed to her tired body to live, those nieces of hers, at the ultimate points of the Viennese compass. Her feet and back ached at the bare thought of those endless, cobbly streets, wind-swept, wet by rain and snow. All roads led to Calvary. Those once charming streets of the Imperial City were now but so many ways to the hill of charity, and it was a hill that old age crept up timidly, anxiously. The cross was so surely at the top. . . . Then she bethought herself how the days of the week came only one at a time, the way, after all, that life was tempered to mortality, one day, one thing at a time. . . .

But it wasn't only troubles of food and raiment, of shelter; Frau Stacher had grave theological difficulties as well, encrusted confusingly about the admonition: 'not solicitous for your life, what you shall eat or for your body what you shall put on . . . for your Father knoweth that you have need of all these things.' No, she had no slightest understanding; and faith was but the dimmest of night-lights, flickering so uncertainly that the dark masses of her difficulties alone were apparent. She seemed to be caught terrifyingly between her needs, reduced though they were – really only a bed and enough food to keep her alive, and the Divine withholding of those things. No, she couldn't understand, and all through that last long night at Frau Kerzl's she hung shiveringly over the dim puzzle of her life, which once had fallen so easily into its bright and pleasant pattern. . . .

For the dozenth time she pulled the little, hard, square feather bed, disdained of the Englishman, about her shoulders and drew her knees up under it. At last out of her chill bewilderment she began to think of Kaethe, of taking her the Thursday dinner, of what she could get, in a world now filled mostly, it seemed, with inedible substances. The thought of giving, even vicariously, lighted in her a glowing eagerness. She found herself suddenly quite warm, even to her ankles and feet, and as the late January light began to filter in through the cracks of the brown rep curtains she fell, mercifully, into a deep slumber.

.   .   .   .

II

LIESEL AND OTTO

Allegretto amoroso   Sorgen sind für
                                        Morgen   gut.

*

WHEN belated and hurriedly Frau Stacher finally got
away from Frau Kerzl's, it was somewhat as a little war-
barque after its time is up, leaves an unpleasant port, but
still a port, and puts out to sea in sure signs of rough
weather.

The once fat and merry Gusl had had one of his worst
nights; spasms of coughing were coming through the
open door of the so-called south room as the two women
stood together for a last time in the sombre little hallway,
sadly stencilled in terra-cotta on dark blue. The haggard
agony on that mother's face gave Frau Stacher a deep stab
accompanied by the first and only realization in her
childless heart of the pain mothers know for doomed
children. It was something so sudden, so poignant, as
she stood saying a somewhat lifeless good-bye (she hadn't
yet pulled herself together after being abruptly awakened
out of that timeless, death-like sleep by Frau Kerzl's loud
knock), that had it remained with her an instant longer
she would have fallen in a heap. It seemed to her that
now she was always running full tilt into griefs she had
never even suspected in the veiled and pleasant years.

The ring of the hungry colonel, only incompletely
disguised as a porter, who came to get her folding straw
basket and her two lean valises, broke in on the distress

52

of the two women. Frau Kerzl forgetting for a moment
the blessings that would so surely follow the Englishman
into the house, embraced her, suddenly regretful, in a
rush of hot tears; Frau Stacher's sympathy was so immediate, so real, that it seemed to stand there with them.
They hung a moment lip on cheek murmuring to each
other 'courage,' and again and again 'auf Wiedersehen';
then turned to their now separate paths, Frau Kerzl
running back to her son's room at a faint and gurgling
sound, and Frau Stacher to continue what she called
(though no one knew it) her 'March among the Ruins,'
walking close behind the porter, sweating a neurasthenic
sweat, in the raw January air under his unaccustomed load.
She felt safer quite near him, for those once cosy, familiar
streets seemed now to converge to the unknown, to infinity
even, and the proximity of her valises somewhat steadied
her. With genteel, restrained little steps, her elbows
pressed to her sides, her hands clasped in front holding
her umbrella and her shabby little bag that always came
unfastened if she didn't look out, and somebody would tell
her it was open, she proceeded to the street off the Hoher
Markt where Irma, her brother's widow, half starved
with her three boys on the famous pension, together with
what various members of the family gave her and what
she herself made by her beautiful 'petit point,' dimming
every year a little more those once hard bright eyes.

Irma, knowing that hunger stalked just around the
corner, yet desiring to live alone with her boys, had been
immensely relieved and at the same time almost uncon-

trollably irritated at the thought of the arrangement by
which Tante Ilde was to be given the very relative freedom of the alcove. She had gone about the simple preparations for her taking possession in the best obstructionist
manner. The alcove already contained the old brown
plush divan, relic of the house in Baden, but Irma had
shown an amazing unwillingness to clear out a certain
little green-and-yellow chest of drawers which had 'always'
been between the windows in her living-room and contained an unrelated accumulation of objects.

'But she's got to have something to keep her things
in!' Corinne had cried, at the time the fatal arrangement
was being made.

This was so obvious that Irma had made no further
demur than to say: 'I didn't think she had that much left.'

'You've never heard about the lilies of the field?'
Corinne asked with her most oblique look; but it was lost
on Irma, who said:

'What?' as she noisily dragged the chest of drawers
into the alcove.

'How these little pebbles hurt my feet,' murmured
Corinne further, and when Irma answered: 'What hurts
your feet?' she turned aside. Irma was clearly imper-
vious. But she had emptied the drawers — all except the
top one — quite ostentatiously. Various blessings flowed
from Corinne, who brought their Sunday dinner and who
could be counted on to get the often expensive materials
for her needlework; she knew, too, that Corinne from
time to time gave Mizzi a finely-pointed thrust of truth

about what Irma called 'jewing her down' in her prices.
Corinne could quietly cut to the bone. Irma had been a
skilful needlewoman even in the old days, now through
Mizzi she kept abreast of the latest styles. That season
the rage was for motifs of 'petit point' which were being
inserted in suède handbags, making one of the famous
Viennese leather novelties. She had once received 80,000
crowns, when 80,000 was something, for a tiny medallion,
so fine that she had only been able to work on it on warm
summer mornings with the window open, even the glass
panes seemed to blur it somewhat, though that north
window up those five flights of stairs was certainly as
good a place as one could have for working.

Irma being without sensibility, unconnected with her
boys, had said further to Corinne on that same occasion:
'Business is business,' at which Corinne had ineffectually
protested that it was just what it wasn't, – business.

'You know how I am situated with the three boys,'
Irma had answered, in the same tone she would have used
to give new information rather than to discuss a situation
already threadbare, 'so much for a cup of coffee in the morning, and you know what bread costs, then the soup in the
evening – a plateful – she won't need the thick part of it,'
she proceeded baldly, 'the boys are growing and so hungry.
She'll only need something to warm her up, and when you
think that she will have eaten well every day at noon,
she'll get on all right.'

The family had never been able to accustom themselves
to the shock of certain unexpected thoughts appearing

quite unclothed and without the least shame from Irma's most intimate being. A chill visited Corinne's backbone at the reference to the thin part of the soup, and a white point appeared in her eyes, glacial as an iceberg in blue water, which, however, did not attract Irma's attention nor reduce her temperature. She was, anyway, a woman who easily got red in the face and was always saying how hot she was when others were half frozen.

Having thus delivered herself of her inner thoughts she had proceeded to draw, not uncheerfully, two nails out of the kitchen wall and drive them neatly, loudly, deafeningly into two light-grey roses in the brown wallpaper of the alcove, near the curtain, where they wouldn't be seen, and just a little too high to be reached comfortably. She had then duly sewed the hook and eye on the curtains under Corinne's very gaze and zealously, inexpensively flicked away any possible dust from the gilt-framed engraving of Haydn leading the young Mozart by the hand, and the flat white-and-gilt vase on the little bracket underneath, sole embellishments of the alcove. But all the same in order to feel the least bit amiable about it Irma had to keep reminding herself that her sister-in-law would be paying for that same alcove. Indeed, with a second bare, arctic look also lost on Irma, Corinne had put the money for it for a whole month in advance into her hand. She had felt like snatching her treasure up in her arms, conveying her a hundred, a thousand, miles and setting her down in some warm and pleasant spot. And this, this was what she had prepared for her, this quite evident place of tribulation. She made no answer to Irma's last words beyond drawing her lips thinly together. They had all learned that they couldn't get at their father's widow except through her sons, but just as soon as she could turn around she'd get another niche for her Dresden-china auntie. . . .

No one, not even Corinne, was ever to know what Frau Stacher's thoughts or rather feelings were, as soundlessly, in the narrow confines of the alcove, she unpacked her few possessions. When those designed for the lower drawer of the little chest were laid in, it stuck obstinately in a three-cornered way as she tried to close it. The upper one had proved to be still full of old letters, post-cards and photographs. A faded reminder of Heinie and Irma with knapsacks and alpenstocks, off on their honeymoon in the Dolomites, caught her eye, which was further held by a likeness of her unsuspecting self staring at her from under an oak in the Stad-park at Baden, with Anna's baby, the first-born grandchild, on her knee. And *this* was to what it was all leading up, she thought, in unaccustomed irritation, as she gave another push to the lower drawer, which went in with a jerk that left her breathless. When she wanted to hang up her coat she found that she had to stand on the divan to reach the nail. Her eyes taking in the details of that very evident tent of a night were at their palest, scarcely a trace of blue left in them. She was quite alone. Irma waiting impatiently to open the door for her sister-in-law's belated arrival had almost immediately departed to engage in the protracted and militant operation of marketing. The three boys were at school. Irma's welcome had been hasty and without warmth. The room itself was cold with the insidious chill of a room in a damp climate that has not had a fire in it since the day before. The white porcelain stove, as Frau Stacher stepped shiveringly over to it, possessed not even a reminder of heat, though she put her hands knowingly on certain tiles, hoping possibly to find one still warm from the previous evening. Irma never lighted the fire till the boys got back in the afternoon. She herself would sit at her embroidery frame with a round, grey, stone bottle of hot water, wrapped in a piece of old flannel, in her lap. Frau Stacher tried to think that the place would be warmer in many ways when the boys came home.

Then the cuckoo clock struck eleven hollow strokes and hurriedly she began to lay out her very best things to wear to Liesel's. Liesel adored good clothes and always noticed what people wore. A large part of her conversation was about making over old things or the possibility of getting new ones, and the discussion of what was being worn that season and might be worn the next could induce in her sensations bordering on rapture.

Frau Stacher was still wearing for 'best,' with a measure of decency, some stancher remnants of the years of plenty. She now proceeded to put on her black cloth suit with the embroidered black-and-white lapels, the last thing she had bought before her 'crac,' arranging softly about her neck, which was already encircled by a bit of narrow black velvet, a certain piece of oft-washed and much-mended old lace that she had worn for twenty years, pinning it with an oxidized silver bar pin on which was stamped 'Karlsbad,' unlosable, valueless relic of a journey in the happier days. She carefully brushed her black hat, with its purple velvet knot faded into grey, giving it a few supplementary pinches and pats before putting it on, instinctively at an angle that was dignified, even becoming; then she rolled tightly her black cotton umbrella and drew on her neatly darned black gloves. She paused on the threshold to give a strange, pale glance about the familiar room become suddenly not only unfamiliar, but odious. The cold north light lay whitely upon it, bringing out every thread in the worn spots of the old rug, by the door, under the table, as you went into the kitchen; she remembered that Heinie's feet had had their part in wearing them threadbare, Heinie now seven years in his grave. There by the window was the unwieldy, red upholstered armchair that he had sat in all through that last winter of his life, with smooth, shining, dark spots on the arms and at the top. She shivered again, but this time it was not from the cold of the room. As she passed out, her arms held more closely than ever to her sides, her head very erect, her little pride all indeed that she had left to her out of a whole life full of things, she still looked the Frau Commercial Advisor Stacher, born von Berg. Her gentility was ineffaceable.

. . . .

Liesel was busy in the tiny kitchen when her aunt rang gently, apologetically. As she opened the door an entrancing smell, unmistakably of fresh noodles in fresh butter, was wafted on the air. It wasn't the sort of scent that hung around Frau Kerzl's apartment nor about Irma's. Frau Stacher found herself sniffing it up eagerly, and certainly Liesel's warm welcome fittingly accompanied it. Where on earth did Liesel get the butter? she was thinking as she felt her niece's bright cheek against hers and her soft breast warmly near. Her spirits began to rise. She was momentarily out of sight and hearing of the combat for food, enveloped sustainingly in that delightful union of scents – above lilies and roses – fresh flour, fresh warm butter! Her heart was suddenly flooded with an immense gratitude, not alone for the food, as she returned the soft embrace.

It was a comfortable little living-room into which she then stepped, crowded with furniture, mostly Biedermayer, that had belonged to Otto's mother and his grandmother before her. Mellow, pale brown furniture decorated here and there with a black motif. A writing-desk, with high shelves and glass doors destined for books, now held a mauve-and-white tea-set in old Vienna ware. A green porcelain stove stood in one corner and was beginning to give forth its gentle heat. Liesel lighted it about an hour before Otto returned, and then all day long into the evening it could be depended on to give out generously its pleasant, even warmth. Between it and the window were Otto's arm-chair and his special stool for his lame leg; near it a little table with a rack for his pipes, his wallet of tobacco and a box of Trabucos. Otto *had* to have his cigar after supper, and when luxuriously he had smoked it he would pull at his pipe and read the *Wiener Journal* or perhaps get out his flute. They talked of renting a piano when things got better and then Liesel could play his accompaniments. After busy days, pleasant evenings. Liesel's deft fingers were always at work salvaging something old, – her darning was famous in the family, – or smartly fashioning something new. She had a way of standing in front of him and asking him if the stripes were more becoming across or up and down, or she would sit in his lap and ask him if his treasure could wear her dress as short as *that*, only so much stuff, every centimetre counted, that enchanted his uxorious soul. He would pinch her ankles and say that anybody who wore a 35 shoe could do as she liked, or as far up as the police permitted, and Liesel would be delighted and laugh and laugh. After hearing what had happened at the Ministry, she would tell of those even more vitally interesting visits to provision shops, where evidently the tradespeople liked to see her, and as far as was wise she would let him into the secret of her ways of ferreting out the little that was hidden; her ready smile, those two soft dimples and her even softer brown eyes counting for much in such operations. Once, but that was in the very beginning, she had started to tell Otto of the quite fresh remarks of the cheesemonger – a good-looking fellow – but he'd pouted for two days, and though secretly Liesel was gratified by these signs of jealousy – once in awhile, like that – in the end she wisely kept the not at all displeasing personal attentions she received while marketing to herself.

Liesel had no books and never dreamed of opening the newspaper – world-events were nothing to her. After supper, as she sewed, Otto would sometimes read her amusing bits under the caption 'Around about the Globe': 'A dangerous Don Juan,' 'The most useful tree in the world,' 'The Adonis of the American film world,' 'Solemn mourning for a cat,' and such-like. Liesel adored cats. She wanted a cat, a piano and a baby; otherwise she had really little left to wish for.

Occasionally they followed a case through the criminal courts, especially if it had an amusing side. Liesel loved to laugh, and laugh she often did in the weeping city. . . . And a jewel robbery made her eyes shine. But Liesel's real use for newspapers was to soak them in water, then roll them into tight balls and set them to dry. They made excellent fuel, one or two, put knowingly into the porcelain stove with a couple of briquettes. There were always a few drying on the window-ledge in the kitchen.

Otto's own reactions to the problems of the Fatherland as set forth in the Press were not much more vigorous than his wife's. When he read of a new difficulty he would in his mind straightway blame some far-off, unreachable individual or circumstance for the national misfortunes in general and particular. He had then done all that could be required of him; effort was ended and he was quits with the situation. He didn't blame openly the Republic, he got his living and his Liesel's from it as from the Monarchy, and he rarely used the now familiar expression 'Dos homma von da Republik' (that's the fault of the Republic), but he

thought it. It was, further, a source of evils, that he, Otto
Steiner, could not be expected to purify. What, indeed,
could he do about the Republic, about the Jews, about the
Freemasons, about the exchange? Nothing, quite evidently nothing, and it let him comfortably out of all
responsibility. He just kept on at his work, came home to
his Liesel, who in turn pursued her agreeable and busy
round of making him happy. So endless were the combinations and strategies involved in this once simple matter
that she had her hands and time full.

She felt very sorry for her Tante Ilde, losing her money
and being old and alone, for Kaethe and her children, for
Irma and the boys, and sometimes she took them things
to eat. Quite often she found her way to Mizzi's shop,
where she was always sure of a warm welcome, for undeniably Liesel understood the niceties of Mizzi's business.
She sometimes even thought of going in with her, but she
felt that she was, momentarily at least, better employed
in using Otto's salary to the fullest advantage, and 'with
things as they are' (which was Liesel's nearest approach
to intellectual participation in the national misfortunes),
that took all her time and thought. Standing in those everlasting queues, running as she said, 'from Pontius to Pilatus,'
bringing everything home herself, though the aged porter
at the corner of the Kohlmarkt and the Wallnerstrasse
always helped when it was a question of coals, glad to
serve once more a handsome woman – handsome in the
traditional way he so thoroughly understood. Liesel would
listen, quite truly interested, as they walked along, to his

tales of other days when gentlemen were 'cavaliers' and
ladies hard to win; of whilom young attachés at the not-
distant Foreign Office, that imposing Ballplatz, who had
been wont to send him with love-letters and flowers and
bon-bons. The telephone had given the first blow to such
romantic expressions of love; and as for the War and the
Peace, they were equally and finally calamitous. . . .

She could well afford to greet her aunt lovingly, and
her 'dearest aunties' and her 'how sweet you look' and her
'I'm so glad to have you,' came gushingly out of the
abundance of her heart. She was so happy that she could
add cheer to her food without the slightest effort.

The table was already spread. Aunt Ilde's involuntary
though delicate glance showed her three places set, just
the same for all; three wine-glasses, three plates, three
knives even (on those knife-rests that she had so fortunately
added to the coffee spoons and napkin rings when Liesel
was married), knives meant meat, but she then and there
made up her mind not to take any – perhaps a little wine.
The carafe stood on the table filled with a Voslauer, a
pleasant, light, open wine, gently quite gently warming to
the stomach. It grew on those very slopes about Baden.

Then she bethought herself cheerfully of the moment
when she would say to Liesel: 'Now you stay with Otto,
I'm going to do the dishes, but I must have an apron.'

She had taken her things off and hung them up on one
of the pegs in the little hallway. She had wished even as
she did so that she didn't have to leave them there. They'd
be the first things Otto would see, and perhaps . . . But

such misgivings and some others had given way before that delicious odour and Liesel's warm welcome. She looked so pretty, so appetizing, in that big pink apron. As she went back into the kitchen her aunt could hear her singing an old waltz from the 'Graf von Luxemburg,' 'Bist meine liebe, kleine Frau.'

Frau Stacher had for a moment the illusion that she was still living at Baden and that she had only come in for the day. There, too, was her little inlaid work-table that had belonged to her own mother and that Liesel had taken for safe-keeping when the house was given up. She'd always kept her wools and her fine darning in it and Liesel did the same.

'Can't I help?' she asked, as she continued to look at it, rent by a sudden, terrible homesickness, that made her voice quite weak.

'No, you just sit quiet and rest. Everything is ready. It's time for Otto to come, anyway,' Liesel answered with a look at her wrist-watch. 'He's always to the minute. He only has an hour for dinner and must find everything ready.'

Indeed as she spoke the rattle of a key was heard at the front door. She flew to it. There were the unmistakable, immemorial sounds of embracing and then a whispered word from Liesel.

'Ach, yes, yes,' Tante Ilde heard him answer.

He had hung up his green plush hat with the little grey feather at the back on its own invariable peg, had divested himself of his overcoat, with its rather high, tight belt and hung it up on the next by Tante Ilde's hat and coat, just as she had known he would, but without the inhospitable thoughts her humility had attributed to him. As he entered he was combing his hair and moustache with his little pocket-comb and smiling his somewhat fatuous smile.

Otto Steiner was the son of a small Government official and the grandson of one. He had gone into the Ministry of Agriculture when he was eighteen, and had been there seven years, when at a certain hour the war found him, in a certain room, at a certain desk, bending over a certain big ledger. And out of that secure and dusty routine, as natural to him as breathing, he had been thrown to the Russian front, then to the French front, where he had been wounded. He had been healed and thrown to the Italian front, every nerve in his body making its agonized appeal against going through certain perfectly definite horrors again. He was thankful when his knee, which was supposed to be quite cured, began once more to stiffen and swell, when in a short time quite certainly he wouldn't be able to get about and they'd have to send him home. Then before he could be demobilized he had been taken prisoner and put in that Italian camp where his feet had frozen. Such strange things to happen to one who found his pleasure as well as his daily bread in those dusty ledgers, and whose conversation was largely made up of references to 'Das Ministerium.' It was one of the first words he remembered from his childhood days, as familiar as 'guten Morgen.'

Now after all the agonies, the incredible agonies, it had been granted to him, out of so many who had been heaped in nameless graves everywhere in Europe, to be coming into his own home from that very same Ministry, greeted by that delightful odour of food, prepared by a beloved, loving and lovely wife. 'I'm certainly lucky,' he often said to himself, and asked no further grace of heaven than to grow old in the Ministry, moving slowly, as his forbears had moved, up through various rooms, indicative of various grades.

He was pale and wore eyeglasses. His face was the somewhat round-cheeked face of the average Viennese, with rather small nose and rather full lips under a brown moustache. Unmistakably a Government employee who would set no river on fire but could be depended on to go his serviceable little way, hour by hour, day by day, year by year . . . the traditional 'rond de cuir.'

There were always rumours of reducing the number of employees, but Steiner's work was so exact, his handwriting and figures so beautifully neat, that he was as safe as anybody in those unsafe days. He could, furthermore, answer any question put to him by any superior, even the strange questions of new men, who, momentarily 'protected,' came into the Ministry in the upper grades, passing in and then out. The administration was fairly snowed under by employees. It was reckoned often (not, however, by those employed, they kept such statistics as much as possible to themselves) that 750,000 out of the 2,500,000 lived on and by the different departments of government. But mostly their positions were no more secure than yellowing leaves in Autumn. A gust of zeal on the part of some one high up and they fell in showers from the governmental tree, disappearing into the dark, wet, windy streets of hiemal Vienna. The question with each and every one was how to hang on. . . .

Hydrocephalous Austria, with that terrible will to live! A mangled trunk supported its great head, Vienna. The members through which the blood should have circulated had been lopped off, the head was growing bigger, sicker.

. .

But Otto Steiner wasn't thinking of any of these things as he greeted his Aunt Ilde. He saluted her affectionately; some not very urgent realization that she 'had had it hard' put an additional cordiality into his voice. He was further melted by the odour of those fresh noodles and hot butter just as she had been.

A sizzling sound, like sweetest music, coming from the kitchen, next fell on their ears. Liesel disappeared anxiously.

'What have you got to-day?' he cried through the door, 'do I really smell noodles and butter? I'm just dying of hunger!'

A moment after, Liesel, divested of her pink apron, in the neatest one-piece dark blue dress, a red leather belt holding it snugly about her waist, appeared rosily bearing a smoking black-and-white chequered soup tureen. Little tendrils of dark hair lay softly, damply, about her brow, her dimples were very deep, her eyes very bright. She

68

was sure of that soup, cunningly made of left-over crusts of black bread, roasted crisply in the oven and then ground up with a bountiful seasoning of onions and various other more discreetly sustaining herbs. On that dark January day it put heart into them all. Their spoons clicked joyously. Then those shining noodles! Liesel had strewn over them the crispest little heaps of fried crumbs. A very, very small golden-brown veal cutlet was put closely, significantly, by Otto's plate. Generally he and Liesel halved their small bits of meat, but to-day she set the example of taking none. It was plainly fitting that the wage-earner, the master, should have it all, and more especially in those days when nourishment was the first need, the last preoccupation. Above saving one's soul for eternity was that of saving one's body for a span.

When the pale wine was poured out Liesel said sweetly:

'We must drink to Tante Ilde's health!' and Otto cried promptly, 'Prosit,' looking at her affectionately through his pince-nez, across the brim of his glass.

She began to feel herself a new woman. Food, youth, love, happiness, the taste, the sight, the feeling of it all! Paradise in some way regained. She forgot that she was there as a poor old relative, who, for decency's sake, had to have her breath kept yet awhile in her body by the efforts and sacrifices of those of her blood; no, she was again Tante Ilde of Baden who would soon say:

'Well, children, are you coming out to me for dinner on Sunday, and will you have an Apfelstrudel or an apricot tart?'

Then Otto began to tell about the hard case of his friend, Karl Schober, who though a war-cripple had been inexplicably dismissed that very day. There were four cripples in Otto's room, for that is where, – in the rooms of some Ministry, – with a little 'protection,' they mostly and justly landed. After they had called it a shame, and unbelievable, and had given a shudder (being dismissed in those times was like being condemned to death without the preliminary security of prison), insensibly they fell to talking of other days. Tante Ilde, who had forgotten nothing that had ever happened to any of the children, began to tell the most interesting things about Liesel when she was little. How she had fallen from the apple tree in the garden of the Baden house and broken her wrist, and how Tante Ilde had held her other hand when the doctor was setting the bone, and that Liesel had been so brave and hadn't cried – at which Otto leaned over and gave his wife a pat on the arm. And the time she had taken Liesel to the races so conveniently near; Liesel remembered that well: that was the day she had first put her hair up and wore the lovely wine-coloured dress with little pleated ruffles and had gone out with her Aunt Ilde as Fräulein Bruckner instead of 'die Liesel.' They had put money on a certain Herr Hafner's four-year-old and Liesel had actually won 20 Krones!

Otto listened with his somewhat full lips parted, entranced by these tales of his treasure's earliest youth, and all of a sudden they found they had eaten everything there was on the table and drunk every drop of wine, but they continued to sit for awhile longer, pleasantly engaged in picking their teeth and sucking in their tongues. Liesel always did things well and kept the two little blue glass toothpick-holders filled. They had been given by Mizzi, who went so far and no further in the matter of presents, even to some one she liked, on the occasion of Liesel's marriage. When shown to the various members of the family they had, one and all, wondered how Mizzi had had the face. . . .

Then when Otto lighted his Trabuco, Tante Ilde found herself saying just as she had planned:

'I'm going to do the dishes. You stay with Otto, but I must have an apron.'

Liesel had been very dear and had said:

'But no, Tante Ilde, you mustn't work when you come to us.'

Suddenly her aunt's eyes had filled with tears:

'It would make me so truly happy,' she entreated.

Then Otto had cried:

'But yes, little goose, let Tante Ilde do as she will!'

So Liesel stayed with Otto, and as Tante Ilde went in and out she could hear them talking as if they hadn't seen each other for a week, trying to decide if they would go, that very evening, to a cosy little cabaret in the Annagasse, a stone's throw from their house, and Liesel wear her new pink dress; or whether they would go to the Circus Busch movie in the Prater Stern, where it didn't matter what you wore and where they were giving a wonderful moral drama in six acts called

71

'Sinful Blood,' and where they would hold hands in the dark, just as if they weren't going to spend the night together.

Tante Ilde herself even began to hum that waltz tune from the Graf von Luxenburg, though she had long been nobody's 'dear little wife.'

When she was putting tenderly away in the tiny cupboard the white plates with the gold 'S' that Liesel was also 'keeping' for her, she got suddenly a quite unexpected whiff of the once familiar salami, proceeding irrepressibly from a tightly-tied up little package.

'Sausage for Otto's supper!' she murmured to herself, and then wondered if she were mistaken, though Liesel *was* equal to anything . . . but all without any envy. She'd had a good meal, flavoured with love and happiness, and suddenly a thousand other thoughts and feelings pressed in upon her that she'd forgotten existed. She was increasingly glad of Liesel's youth and love, that out of the starving, mourning city she had grasped her comfortable joy. . . .

Finally Otto saying warmly, 'auf Wiedersehen, Auntie,' had given her a sounding kiss on both cheeks, and placing several on Liesel's red lips had contentedly limped off to the Ministry.

Then Liesel had proceeded to initiate her into some of the secrets of her wonderful management, but as they were inseparable from her youth and dimples and shining eyes, they were of little practical use to her aged aunt. The fortune-teller whom Liesel had just consulted had assured her that she would have good luck in all her undertakings. One glance at Liesel's open, happy face, framed in that glossy abundance of waving dark hair, was enough to start the least gifted of seers off in the right direction. She had, further, informed her that a blonde, blue-eyed woman was to be avoided. Liesel *had* stared at that, but when she told her aunt about it they avoided each other's eyes, though Tante Ilde did murmur something about its being 'singular.' Liesel was dying to keep the conversation on lines that would inevitably have led to the enthralling and inexhaustible topic of Fanny, but there were certain matters that you just couldn't talk about with Tante Ilde, not when you could see her eyes, so Liesel only said that the fortune-teller had further told her that she had the exclusive love of a man with dark hair and eye-glasses who had been wounded in the war. Well, you had to admit that there was something in it all, when they hit so many nails on the head (even though, as Tante Ilde couldn't help thinking, those nails were positively sticking up asking to be hit).

Liesel found that having Tante Ilde for dinner wasn't at all bad. On the contrary she had thoroughly enjoyed it. At the end she gave her some macaroni and a few spoonsful of brown sugar to take home to Irma, also a couple of Otto's old shirts; he had to look a certain way at the Ministry and she had darned those till they weren't decent any more, but for the boys. . . . And Liesel had been so sweet when she kissed her good-bye, saying, 'Now, Auntie, don't forget you're to come next Monday and

I'll see about getting something extra nice for dinner. What about a Schmarrn?'

Frau Stacher had positively tripped from the Annagasse to the Hoher Markt, in unaccustomed light-heartedness. 'Happiness – it's even more contagious than misery,' she thought, grateful to have been exposed to the dear infection, and forgot that she'd been timid about going.

But the extraordinary part about it all was that that good meal, instead of making her less hungry, seemed to engender an intolerable desire for another. She was just wild for more noodles and butter when night came, ready for a whole cutlet for herself. As they sat round the supper-table, the three hungry boys with their eyes on the soup-tureen, and Irma dipping the ladle in so carefully for Tante Ilde's share that the few bubbles of life-giving fat would not slip into it, yet so shallowly that none of the thick part came up, then Tante Ilde was, for once, not faint for food, not at all. She was just wild for food. This, however, she was able to keep hidden in her breast. Indeed she was greatly ashamed of her sudden access of gluttony, and the next time she went to confession . . .

When under the stimulating effect of the pleasant meal at Liesel's, she had smilingly, but as it proved unwisely, told Irma about the noodles and butter, Irma, taking some last stiches by the waning light of her north window, had listened with that intent expression the habitually under-nourished have in their faces when food is being talked about, but her only answer had been:

'Well, with a meal like that you certainly won't be able

to eat any supper.' She had fairly snatched the sugar and macaroni from her sister-in-law's hands, then she had held the shirts, embellished with their lace-like darns, up to the light, which had no difficulty in getting through, saying:

'I should think she would send them! They're on their last legs.'

No, Irma couldn't be gracious, she'd always been that way, even when she was young and pretty and sheltered; and since the Peace. . . .

But when Frau Stacher finally dipped her spoon into that watery soup, after having broken into it the thin slice of bread pushed towards her by Irma's careful yet resolute hand, she suddenly found that she didn't really want even that, the boys ought to have every drop, every crumb. She felt old, tired, completely superfluous, and she would have loved above all things, even above food, to have had a room of her own wherein she could hide the shame of her superfluity, shut the door on it, turn the key and drop a few secret tears over it. . . .

After the meal, consumed with lightning rapidity by the hungry boys and more slowly cleared away by their mother and aunt, they all placed themselves around the table with its heavy red felt cover, and the boys began to do their lessons for the next day in the light of the swinging lamp pulled down very low. Irma took out those shirts of Otto's, holding them again up to the light and making a clicking sound with her tongue against her teeth as she did so.

Then there was silence except for the rubbing of the boys' feet on the chair rungs and floor, the turning of the pages of their theme books and the ticking of the brown cuckoo clock with its long, swinging pendulum.

Frau Stacher sat just outside the circle of light, in deep shadow; if she had put her hand out she could have touched the curtain of the alcove. She felt increasingly useless and lonely. They would be sitting there just the same if she were dead.

Irma was continually taking off her glasses and wiping them on the piece of old linen she kept by her for that purpose. She knew her eyes were getting worse and sometimes she was very frightened. The light caught her big capable hands, fell on the heap of white linen in her lap, glowed about the fringe of the little, red, three-cornered shawl crossed over her low, heavy breasts. She had brought it from Agram in those days that as the calendar ran were not so far away, but might have been, for all their resemblance to the present, of another century. Her face was left in deep shadow which did not soften something rough-hewn about it. It was broad through the forehead and her cheeks with their deep-dyed spots of colour had very prominent bones, her nose alone was the rather formless kind that escapes memory or description. Above her short, full upper lip was a dark duvet, like a thick smudge put on with a careless finger and getting darker every year. Twisted about her head were heavy coils of rather oily black hair that anxiety had neither greyed nor thinned, though her eyes, once so bright under that low,

full forehead with those two other wide, black smudges
for eyebrows, had got quite dull. It gave her a strange
expression at times, all except the eyes keeping its freshness that way. She *had* good looks, the family had to admit
it, in a bright, square, hard way, like a strongly-outlined,
heavily-coloured poster; like a poster of a peasant woman
binding sheaves that one might come across in a railway
station, meant to be looked at from a distance and to en-
courage travel. But somehow Irma hadn't worked out
comfortably in the shorter perspectives of a city. Why
Heinie had been mad about her, his sister had never
understood. But Heinie had been a marrier. She couldn't
think of Heinie not married, though why just Irma, un-
complaisant, worrying Irma strayed into that Viennese
world of theirs, familiar and dear to them as their own
breath, with its comfortable, care-free ways. There had
been so many attractive young women about with easy
smiles and pleasant habits who would have flavoured his
lengthening years. Now the family were, one and all,
horribly bored by Irma, left heavily on their hands. They
forgot that Pauli had said when his father-in-law married
that she reminded him of a late harvest, with vermilion
melons and stacks of yellow grain against black earth, and
that Heinie knew winter was near.

There in the shadow, her useless hands lying folded in
her thin lap, her colourless head bent, her pale lids dropped
close over her eyes, Frau Stacher shivered, suddenly remembering that phrase about winter being near. In the
warm haze of the protracted Indian summer of her life

she hadn't in the least understood what it meant. She fell to thinking of that and of other long past things; of present things she had no thoughts, only confused, painful sensations, which were cutting deeper wrinkles and scars in her face than all the living through of her pleasant threescore years and ten.

Ferry, the eldest boy, thin and tall for his years, with very long black lashes shadowing his blue eyes and falling upon his thin cheeks with their tiny spot of bright colour, had closed his books and taken a rattling, illy-jointed knife out of one coat pocket and a little figure in wood that he was working on out of the other. Even with that poor blade he had given it a touch of life – a woman with her arms hanging at her sides.

'I'm going to make two little buckets to put into her hands, one for apples and one for pears,' he whispered to his mother as he held it up – 'see how she's already bending under the weight,' he added with his slight but persistent cough.

He had, for all his pale adolescence, a strong resemblance to his aunt Ilde. She had always cared a lot for Ferry; he'd been a snuggling, affectionate baby, something inexpressibly dear and unexpected in her elderly life; they had, in a way, she and her brother, forgotten such things. Now she was aware of a hot yearning to give him a new knife. From somewhere that knife must come.

Gusl, the next, was formed in his mother's image: thick-set, short with a certain roughness in his ways and those same bright, hard eyes under a full brow and shaggy dark hair. . . . The peasant caught in the city, and what he would do with the city or it with him was still tightly rolled on the lap of the gods. Ferry's future was easier to foretell — he would betake himself and his talent to some garret and starve, after the immemorial way of poverty, youth and genius. Gusl hated desperately his books and he was always hungry. Any meal that his mother set out he could have eaten alone. Calories were nothing to him. He wanted lots, lots. But Ferry was always dreaming, sometimes even over his food.

Little Heinie had almost immediately fallen asleep, leaning against the table, a ring of brown curls and two big ears catching the light as it played about his bent head.

Yes, that was the way they would be sitting if she were not there, if she were dead. She felt thinly miserable, like something that had been and no longer was . . . like her own ghost. Irma was wiping her spectacles again.

'Give me the mending,' said her sister-in-law, but somewhat timidly, she never quite knew what Irma would do. 'I haven't used my eyes to-day.'

Irma passed it over to her silently and changed places with her. She felt a little less useless then; coming into the circle of light with the boys seemed to take her out of that shadowy, unpleasant world where superfluous, dependent old women were waiting uncertainly, wretchedly, to get into the cold grave. No, Irma's ways were not comfortable ways, and it was all a part of the general misfit of things that it was Irma who was the widow and had the alcove and the three sons and needed help.

When from time to time Ferry coughed, just a tiny cough, but quite regular, almost like the slow, sure tick of the clock, his mother's black brows would contract at that spectre of the 'Viennese malady' which had found its way into her home. Her sister-in-law wasn't the only ghost there.

Irma was from the Plitvicer Lakes, beyond Agram, now become Serb. There was always that something rough, even fierce about her, not at all like the easy-going Viennese, not like the fiery Hungarians, not like anything Frau Stacher was familiar with. Perhaps it was what had attracted Heinie. But she was vaguely afraid of it.

Irma had at one time tried to go back to her own country, to her people, with her sons – a woman bringing sons would be welcome. Then the extraordinary, the un-believable thing revealed itself. She found she didn't exist there any more, no more than if she were dead; less than that even, for then she would have had a grave. Austrian papers were of no use to her and Serbian papers she could not get. The little town where she was born, on the wild Milanovac Lake, was no longer a Crownland. Her people were no longer her people; even her brother was no longer her brother. The white house with the warm brown roof and the vine growing over the door that got so red in the autumn, and the chestnut tree that got so yellow, there in front with the circular seat – all that, their father's legacy to them – she no longer had any share in it. There were, it appeared, many of these spots, these veritable no man's lands, where children had no rights and strange people went over thresholds worn by parental feet and strange people slept in the beds they were born in. If only she could have gone back there with her boys and wrested her living in some way from the wild soil, . . . and Ferry in the mountain air! No wonder Irma was sombre, was fierce, and bore her sorrows heavily.

Frau Stacher kept reminding herself of all this, but what could she or anybody do about it? They were all caught in a trap . . . simple and terrible as that. As she sat measuring the tuck in a shirt sleeve, she was suddenly aware of being worn to exhaustion with the changes and excitements of the new order of her days. Such desperate exertions just to keep the breath in her body! She wanted to get her clothes off, lie down, shut her eyes, be in darkness with the effortless night before her. But she sat on silently, drawing the thread weakly in and out of the thin stuff and now and then looking up at the boys. They were pale, but they were young. They could — even Ferry — expect more brightly-coloured, fuller years. But for herself! . . . With difficulty she kept the tears from falling over her work, but only when Irma said:

'Now, boys, to bed, you've studied enough,' did she feel free to lay it aside.

Then Irma quite ostentatiously told the children to say good night, though Ferry was already leaning affectionately, after his way, against his aunt and saying that he would help make up the divan, but Irma, who suffered terribly from jealousy and could ill endure these signs of love, told him it was late and that she would help Tante

Ilde. The three then kissed her resoundingly, but sleepily. When she felt the nearness of those young bodies, their adolescent strength held in leash by that sapping under-nourishment, she realized all the more that she was useless, her sands run. She forgot that she was paying for the alcove and wondered if this was the way things would always be, as she finally laid herself down on the old brown divan, on that divan that had for years been in the sitting-room at Baden, and when all the beds were in use had offered a pleasant night's rest to the last-come child. Now she was sleeping on it herself, but as an intruder, fitfully, unquietly, from time to time hearing Ferry cough and turn in his bed, and always Irma's loud, empty snore.

III

ANNA AND PAULI

Innig, lebhaft   Du meine Seele, du mein Herz,
Du meine Wonn', O du mein Schmerz.

★

PAULI BIRBACH especially disliked the Mariahilferstrasse, an endless street. Here and there a century-old peasant house caught up in the tide of the growing city; here and there some rococo palais in a side street visible from a corner; here and there a great department store. But mostly there were little shops, little businesses connected with little lives, the lives of the middle and lower-middle classes that crowded its interminability. The true motive power of every one in that street in those post-war years, and in every one of the side streets, no matter what their condition in life, was the desire for food. Indescribable meannesses were practised, crimes even were committed, for a bit of fat, a little sugar or molasses. Those who weren't actually confronted with starvation had that terrible hunger for fats, for sweets, a hunger that touched the brain, that could arouse in the gentlest soul cruel, predatory thoughts. Now and then the rumour would get about that a certain delicatessen shop had cheese or salami. It would be stormed by those who had money to buy, and the entrance encumbered by those who could only see, or others more fortunate, who could get near enough to smell. Those who had reason to get in were few in comparison to the many who remained outside. Indeed the only peace in Vienna was that which reigned inside certain expensive provision shops.

Pauli's dislike of the Mariahilfer street was profound and temperamental. He liked things diversified and grandiose. Mariahilfer street was neither. Now it was more than ever depressing in that drab, monotonous struggle for survival. Any one of the indwellers knew how near the potter's field was, the hospital, the asylum. A little sagging of endeavour and they would find themselves in one or another of those undesirable places. Anna had stupidly, tactlessly taken that apartment during the war, when her husband was away, and before the housing problem had come to add the difficulty of shelter to that of nourishment. He had said to himself when he learned of the new address: 'Now isn't that just like Anna – the one street I hate in Vienna.'

She had crowded their furniture, but uncosily, into the restricted space. There were three sofas in the living-room and various tables besides the one they used for their meals. No books in Anna's home any more than in Liesel's. A similar glass compartment above a somewhat similar desk held an accumulation of bric-à-brac of purely family interest. Two white and gilt cups bearing the words 'dem lieben Vater,' 'der lieben Mutter' that had been Hermine's first gifts to her parents for their morning coffee; several solemn vases that on various occasions the women had presented to each other, and in whose narrow necks outraged flowers always wilted; a slab of wood with the Castle of Salzburg painted on it against a blue background; a group of carved wooden bears from Innsbruck and other souvenirs of the days when they travelled. Some

84

gay Dresden-china figures in minuet postures immediately struck the eye, that Pauli had given Anna when they were first married, now extraordinarily out of keeping with the paralysis of their conjugal life.

The sofa cushions were in dull linen, worked in dull colours and bore the usual mottoes: 'Nur ein viertel Stuendchen,' 'Traueme suess,' and the like.

The once too-bright pattern of the Brussels rug had faded into browns and greys. The various chairs carried on their backs and arms their ugly, witless, crocheted doilies.

Even over Tante Ilde's gay little brass-bound chest, containing dear but unsaleable odds and ends, Anna had thrown a brown cloth cover worked sparsely in white and yellow daisies.

There was something dead about it all, and about the two dull women the expression of whose being it was.

To Pauli, gay, sparkling, eager, passionate Pauli, it was as pleasant to visit his home as it would have been to visit the cemetery. In one corner was the table on which, wrapped in a scarlet cloth, was Pauli's zimbalon. It was the only thing in the dwelling that spoke of its master. It was the bright flower on the grave, and too, he visited his home not much oftener than he would have visited Anna had she been lying in the Central Cemetery.

One of those stupid, fatal marriages. Anna had never understood anything about it, either the making or the un-making of it. But she continued to love him with all the force of her poor being, and accepted, because she had to, his now habitual absence.

Pauli's mother had been a Hungarian and in his bright
Magyar way he had long since put the dots on the *i*'s
of the conjugal situation: 'Anna? Dead since years. She
ought to wear a bead wreath.'

That sombre flame in her eyes that from time to time
he was unpleasantly aware of was, indeed, no more attractive to him than the phosphorescence shining about something decayed.

Sometimes he felt a brief pity for Hermine, his daughter,
so young, so unattractive, so mirthless. 'The poor girl' he
would think, and then his thoughts would turn to fairer,
brighter maids who might have been called poor for quite
other reasons. To be a woman and not have beauty,
grace – more or less – was in Pauli Birbach's eyes her one
real misfortune. Women's beauty was, indeed, the central
point in his world, that artistic, pleasure-loving, pleasure-
giving world in which he was at home. He used to think
that if he had married any one of Heinrich Bruckner's
daughters save Anna he could have managed, – but just
Anna. He sometimes thought too, that if he could have
explained why he had sighed to possess Anna he could
have explained any and all of the puzzles of the Universe.
It held indeed all riddles within itself.

But for the last year it had not been any one of Herr
Bruckner's handsome daughters. Since a certain day when
he had gone with Corinne to Kaethe's . . . since that day
when the simplest yet mightiest thing had happened. . . .

They had been standing at a window waiting for the
rain to stop. They were very near as they looked out.

86

Suddenly Pauli had been aware of a profound commotion in his being . . . something hot and sweet and cruel and his own. He was seeing Corinne as he had never before seen any woman. She was deadly pale, her eyes were closed, her dark lashes lying heavily upon her cheeks. When she opened them and looked back at him the hovering magic, descending upon them, had worked its purpose.

He was done suddenly and for ever with the pluckable maids, perpetually ripe fruit, all seasons being theirs, that abound in Vienna; inaccessible too, to the sentiments that he had periodically experienced for one or another woman who had crossed his susceptible and magnetic orbit, whom he had possessed or not possessed, as the case might have been. It was different from everything else under the sun and was growing, growing. It was hope and image in his brain, greed and hurry in his body. He was mad for Corinne, Corinne earning unnaturally yet competently her daily bread in a bank when she should have been holding court under some oak at the change of the midsummer moon. Corinne placing endless, neat zeroes across broad white pages when she should have been plucking simples or brewing potions. That elfin brood that crowded her pale heart overpowered his being, held it captive. One would have said he needed something brighter, hotter. . . . Yet, Corinne . . . out of the whole world. . . . But that none of them knew as yet save Tante Ilde in her shy, sure way. Anna, who never got things straight, had a deep, dull jealousy of Fanny, a sentiment, however, that she had been familiar with since her earliest childhood, and when indirectly she learned that Pauli had seen Fanny, she was miserable for days, after her chill, slow habit, miserable unto death almost. She suspected Fanny of having made that arrangement about Tante Ilde; Fanny, though one never saw her, was always everywhere it seemed to Anna. Two dull fires had burned in Anna's eyes, two sombre red spots had darkened her cheeks, excitement never lighted up her face, when she learned not only that her aunt Ilde was to come and regularly, every Tuesday, but that Pauli himself would cast his bright shadow over his own dark threshold on that day. She and Hermine began straightway to plan as attractive a menu as lack of talent and materials permitted. . . .

When Corinne had asked Pauli if Anna couldn't take Tante Ilde once a week for her midday meal, he had responded warmly, not simply to give Corinne pleasure, but because he was made that way.

'But of course! The poor, dear Tanterl, I'll tell Anna to get the best she can, you know she's not very clever at it, and I'll try to be there myself.'

Pauli was doubtless various kinds of a sinner, but his humanity was always to be counted on. It wasn't because Corinne was looking obliquely at him, with the look that stirred him hotly, madly. . . .

Anna and Hermine talked ceaselessly of the possibilities or rather the impossibilities of the meal. Hermine even went into her mother's bed two successive nights and stayed there late. The various Hungarian dishes he was so fond of presented immense difficulties. Those that didn't

ANNA AND PAULI

need a lot of sugar, milk and eggs, needed a lot of butter,
lard or fat of some kind. Even love did not make Anna in-
ventive and people never sold her anything as they did to
Liesel because they wanted to see her smile when she got
it. They passed in review one by one those tantalizing
dishes, pulling up round at a Paprikahuhn, chicken in pap-
rika. It rose up and clucked a ghostly cluck out of happier
kitchen days. But where to get that chicken in the flesh?
It was no easier than getting a tropical bird of bright plum-
age and stripping it. He liked sweet things too, Kaiser-
schmarn with a lot of powdered sugar on it, or Palatschinken, those traditional pancakes, filled heavily with
jam.

During the earlier years of Anna's married life, when
Pauli saw how things culinary were going, a young Hungarian servant had been sent him by one of his sisters. She
was an excellent cook and had taught Anna in a way, a lot
of things, but she had been landed, like all good cooks, in
the net of marriage, and was succeeded in the Birbach
household by various maids of varying and inferior talents.
But Anna really didn't know good food from bad, and she
got careless too. Pauli was oftener and longer absent, and
then the War came and then the Peace. Pauli by no means
let them starve, but he didn't see his way to keeping those
two ghosts, who unnaturally bore his name, supplied with
the delicacies or, to be more exact, the relative delicacies
of post-war Vienna, that oftener than not they would spoil
in the cooking.

He had his two sisters, widowed on the same day of the

war, and their broods of little children to support. It had
not been so difficult to care for them at first for they had
taken their children and gone back to the house of their
mother near Groswardein, that comfortable Landhaus
that they had all three inherited with its acres bearing wine
and grain. But when they thought the war was over they
suddenly found themselves one dark night fleeing with the
rest of the inhabitants before an unexpected army. After
days they got into Budapest and when the panic had abated
and they wanted to go back, they found to their consterna-
tion that though they were still Hungarian their lands had
become Roumanian. Some dark, transmuting evil had
been worked. Suddenly they had no civil state there where
they were born and no longer possessed what their parents
had bequeathed them . . . as unbelievable as that. . . .
Pauli enabled them to eke out a reduced existence with
their many children in some rooms on the outskirts of
Pest.

The comfortable Landhaus with its pink walls, its green
shutters, its sloping roof, the grape-vine growing up over
the door, the great plane tree in the garden, became as a
lost paradise to be described to children at the knee,—with
hints of recovery when they were old enough to fight for
their own.

Though Anna suspected that Pauli supported his sisters
and in her heart was bitter about it, she had no courage
and less opportunity to reproach him with it.

Pauli loved his sisters very much, especially his sister
Mimi, and he had never told her the tale of Geza's death

brought back by his comrade. How they were to charge a certain hill in Galicia one chilly autumn dawn in the face of the enemy, waiting millions of them, it seemed, after the Russian way of lavish cannon-food. How Geza, naturally a laughing man, had been leaden-hearted as they went up side by side; even the schnapps served out to the troops had not put heart into him. He had said, 'I'm going up because I must, but it's quite useless – I'll never come down again.' . . . Geza loved life . . . and when they got up to the top immediately a great splinter of shell struck him in the chest and he looked a last reproachful look at his comrade as he fell against him. . . . The end of Geza who loved life.

No, Pauli couldn't bear to think of that. Some day he meant to tell Mimi of those cruel last moments, when Geza knew, knew that his end was near. . . . Perhaps he never would, and then again the day might come when it wouldn't hurt Mimi so much. The children would never understand. And it would be as if Geza, heavy with premonition, had never charged that hill and said those last words, – as if he had never been at all. That was the way of life, but Pauli didn't like to think of it . . . all that being no more . . . as if you had never been; his bright, strong flesh rejected it.

He was, somewhat vaguely to his wife, in business that brought with it frequent mention of the Travel Bureau in the Kaerntnerring and entailed many absences. They had grown accustomed to his travels, and anyway the thoughts of his wife and daughter ran, with that of the rest of the population, on what they were going to eat and how they were going to get it, rather than on the coming or going of any non-edible, even husband and father. So, though they were among the relatively well-to-do in the starving city, the two women talked almost entirely of what they had eaten or were going to eat and Hermine was to experience her greatest enthusiasms when scurrying home with a bit of fat or a can of jam.

. : . . . ,

The difficulty of getting to Anna's from the Hoher Markt was occupying Frau Stacher's thoughts as she lay awake in the early dawn, watching the day grow stronger, till she could see Haydn leading the young Mozart by the hand, and the gilt of the flat, white vase on the bracket underneath began to glisten faintly in the dull light coming in over the top of the curtains.

The trolley that she could take at the Opernring was itself far off and the fares had jumped up to prohibitive prices. Foreigners, workmen and Jews alone had the wherewithal. She decided finally as she proceeded, soundlessly as possible, to make the limited toilet the alcove permitted, that she would walk. The hot cup of ersatz coffee with the ersatz sugar and the thin slice of gritty bread seemed somehow quite sufficient. She had entirely lost that wild hunger of the night before, so curiously the result of the tasty meal at Liesel's. She made up her divan, put her things in order and carefully pulled back the curtains of the alcove. She had been made aware, the morning before, that Irma liked to have them drawn back early and tight, and certainly it did give a more spacious aspect to the living room, off which were the two little bed-chambers, one occupied by Irma with her youngest boy and the other by Ferry and Gusl. Except for the fading photograph, on the chest of drawers, of the long dead Commercial Advisor in its wooden frame of carved Edelweiss, got when he and his bride had gone to Switzerland, his widow was completely wiped out of that living space. She felt no more at ease there than if she were suspended in mid-air, or pressed into some shadowy yet too narrow dimension, – in a word horribly uncomfortable. . . .

The boys had had their cocoa, their thick slices of bread so carefully measured and cut, and had gone off to school. Heinie would get a midday meal at a relief station near the seat of learning, which provided for one scholar out of each needy family each day. The three boys took turns, coming home for dinner on alternate days. There was a fierceness about Irma where food for the boys was in question. When they had licked their spoons and looked about at the empty plates on the table, with their eyes a trifle too big, and Ferry with those bright spots on each cheek, Irma's jaw would set and her brow darken. Not long before she had discovered however, a way of adding to their nourishment . . . the 'Friends' in the Singerstrasse . . . you received a ticket there and then you went to the Franzensplatz to get the package. But as the endeavour of the various foreign relief societies was not to fully nourish any one family or quarter at the expense of other families and quarters, but to the best of their limited ability to keep as large a part as possible of the two and one half millions from actually dying of hunger, that relief in any one case was only palliative. . . .

When Tante Ilde set out on that tramp to Anna's, dressed again in her best things, — Pauli always noticed what women wore, even old women, — she left Irma planning the midday meal. Irma in an extraordinarily fortunate way had got hold of some chicken legs, — it would never happen again she was sure, being inclined to pessimism. She had scraped and washed them, and was going to cook them with the rice. Furthermore into the rice she was going to put a little of the evaporated milk that had come in the thrice blessed package from the Franzensplatz, it would be nearly equal to meat. Enough for three plates full, two large ones for Gusl and for little Heinie and a smaller one for herself. A box of zwieback had come in the package too, and a piece for each would be dipped into some of the milk. It was a good day and she warmly returned Tante Ilde's farewell and told her she hoped Anna would have something fit to eat. She had a feeling that she couldn't get rid of, that some day Tante Ilde would have a cold or something and wouldn't be able to get out. However, sufficient unto the day, and that morning she was almost affectionate.

When Frau Stacher got down into the street a great puff of wind caught her and slapped her dress about her legs, but she disentangled herself and stepped, not unbriskly, into the Rotenturm Street. The day was cold and overcast, but the rain had not yet begun to fall. She passed St. Stephen's, crossing herself as she did so, and got into the

Kaerntner Street. In spite of the chill dampness and the great slaps of wind doing full honour to the reputation of the windiest of cities (the Windobona of the Romans, that name on which generations of windswept inhabitants have made their jokes and puns), she felt more at home than in the alcove. After all, the pavement was free to everybody, just as much hers, when you came down to it, as anybody's. Quite unlike the alcove which in some pervasive, though not at all indefinite, way seemed not to be hers. She tried to comfort herself with the thought that she was paying for it, just as Irma decently tried to remember that fact. But Irma clearly wanted to be alone with her children. Irma's nerves, for all her seeming bodily health, were certainly in a bad way. . .

Passing down the Kaerntner Street, Frau Stacher stood a moment looking in at Zwieback's windows, such warm stuffs in such bright colours were displayed, gay knitted jerseys and scarves — a purple one that would have lain consolingly against her pale thinness. There were silk stockings, too, beribboned underwear, and in another window incredible evening dresses. Who on earth wore evening dresses — now? She remembered how she had got her grey silk dress there for Kaethe's wedding. In the old days she had shopped just like anybody else, buying things she didn't need and would soon forget she had. . . .

Then suddenly she found that her heart was beating thickly. She was passing Fanny's corner, timidly looking away from it, magnetically drawn to it; the pavement seemed somehow alive under her feet. . . . She longed yet feared to meet Fanny; Fanny wrapped to her sea-blue eyes in her scented furs, Fanny young and beautiful, Fanny who knew neither cold nor hunger, nor about being unwanted. Fanny's desirability, though it brought no images with it, sent the blood pounding up darkly to her face. . . .

But she was white again as she passed the Hotel Erzherzog Johann, remembering with a sudden stab how she had always driven there in a droshky when she came to Vienna from Baden for a day's shopping, and how pleasant that great, laughing, singing city had seemed. Now the iridescence had gone out of it. It was drab where once it had gleamed with a thousand vivid tints; beggarly where it had dispensed with a lavish unconcern.

She had been in the habit of taking her dinner at the Erzherzog Johann's, the proprietor had been a friend of her husband's. The old head waiter would always greet her warmly as a friend of the house he had served so long, and he would recommend a quarter of a roast chicken, the wing and breast, of course, and tell her how the noodles had been made fresh in the hotel that very morning, and then wind up by singing the merits of a Linzer or Sacher tart.

She'd leave her bundles there and come back at four o'clock for her coffee with whipped cream, and he'd cut her a slice of the fresh gugelhupf. Such happy days. She hadn't really had the slightest idea how happy they were; she thought how she had often worried about the stupidest things. She became conscious of an increasing sadness as she passed on down the street, realizing miserably how little human beings make of their actual blessings, whatever they may be; and she found herself sending up a prayer to be trusted with a little happiness – just once more. She thought how never, never again, should they miraculously be hers, would she take as rightful dues her three meals a day, her comfortable bed, her clothes befitting the seasons, but that always, up from her heart, would well thanks to the mysterious Giver or Withholder of these things.

She felt a little faint as she hurried past the delicatessen shop on the corner. There wasn't much in the windows; food wasn't kept in windows in those days, but inside there would doubtless be a maddening smell of cheese and sausage.

A one-legged young man, his leg gone to the thigh, in a tattered combination of military and civil coverings, stood always on that corner selling his miserable shoelaces. . . .

But there was another note, quite another, that rang lustily out from the Kaerntner Street, for there the new feudal lords of Vienna (which inevitably has lords of some kind) walked with ringing tread in the triumph of their plenty. That mushroom aristocracy come out of Israel and the war had pushed into some shadowy, scrawny underbrush of life that once great, powerful 'First Society.'

As Frau Stacher got near the 'Bristol' the flooding crowd seemed almost entirely made up of large, showily dressed women and bright, alert, stout men, whose prosperity was immediate and inescapable. Before it her seventy years of

D

gentility were swept up, a bit of dust, into her otherwise bare corner. What had she to do with that new princedom arisen from the ruins of the war, or it with her? Their ways, their gestures, their looks were alien, inimical to those of the Princes, Counts and Barons of that old world; that old world, the pride and joy even of those not of it. What the new Lords did and how they lived was a mystery to Frau Stacher that she had no desire to solve. Her fear increased. She felt but a bit of pallid wreckage in the flooding of that active, highly coloured element. It beat against her suffocatingly, frighteningly, that new blood flowing vehemently in Vienna's veins, its only blood, indeed. In the familiar street she was both stranger and outcast daughter. She couldn't even look at the 'Bristol,' whither so many of those new lords seemed bent, there where people still crumbled their bread at dinner instead of eating it. . . . It was Fanny's world. Perhaps even now Fanny would be on her way there with her light, straight, flying step, like a bird in the air. They all knew that walk of Fanny's. . . .

That first comfortable feeling of owning the pavement, of independence, had gone. She was increasingly confused by the myriad signs and symbols of money of which she had none. Everywhere 'Cambio-Valute,' 'Devisen' in gilt letters, and bank-notes laid out in patterns in the windows . . . exchange bureaux, in which unholy rites were performed by those chosen men standing fatly, firmly, on gold, while the rest of Vienna tottered and fell on paper. She was exhausted, too, by the buffeting of the everlasting wind, and she suddenly and recklessly decided to take the three hundred crowns remaining in her purse and get on the trolley. There was one at the very corner that, mercifully, would take her up the interminability of the Mariahilfer Street. After lunch the wind would perhaps have fallen and she could walk back. She tried not to think how far it would be. She was too spent for thought by her impact with that new world, that world that suddenly had too much, trampling to death the world that almost as suddenly had too little or nothing. Outcast indeed.

The crowd was thickly waiting at the stopping-place. In the rush for seats as the trolley slowed down, she was pushed frighteningly but fortunately along and up the high step, and in a second found herself sitting, breathless and hidden, between a man with a large sack of something that had, to the eager eyes of the other occupants, the interesting appearance of flour, and a pale young woman with a spindle-legged, big-eyed child of four or five in her arms. In her sympathy with the young mother and the doomed child and her relief at being seated, Frau Stacher forgot her hunger and her fatigue and delivered herself up to the delightful sensation of being borne clangingly, powerfully, along. She descended quite lightly at the crowded stopping-place, though she was jostled and jammed again by the crowd fighting to get in. Crossing over she turned into a grey little street and entering a sombre doorway went up to the apartment where Anna was awaiting her husband and her aunt.

There was an air of expectancy about the room as Frau

Stacher entered that somewhat relieved its terrible dullness. On the table was a fresh, fine linen cloth, from the days of comfort, and four places were set; a bottle of pale Tokay, like a streak of sunlight, caught the eye. There was something sadly festive about it.

'I thought it was Pauli when I heard you outside in the hall,' were Anna's words as she opened the door. But her aunt accepted the vicarious greeting without indeed noticing it. They all knew about Anna. That was the way she was.

Her heavy dark hair that Tante Ilde had once so faithfully brushed back into beauty was braided in a thick braid and twisted twice around her head; but when you had said that about Anna, that was all there was to be remarked. The rest was long, faded, shadowy. From those once noticeably broad, fine shoulders, now simply gaunt, her thin breast fell away into her flat waist above her bony hips. There was not one single thing about Anna Birbach to cause anyone to suspect that she belonged to a smiling, art-loving, easy-going, fatalistic race, with something of the West and much of the East in its make-up. Indeed, the broad highway that leads east from the city is the straight road to the Orient, is already the Orient. Something only vaguely diagnosable, but highly coloured, slips in through that Eastern Gate to tint more deeply the Viennese population, a happy enough mixture when only a tenth of them, not nine-tenths, are starving. Hunger there has always been in Vienna. Even in the days of plenty there were thousands who, palely shadowing the street corners, had nothing — the bare, spectral want of the East without its sun and leisure. . . .

Hermine was in the kitchen. She had no more knack at cooking than her mother, but the War had caught her in her earliest youth and the Peace had taught her a few lessons of culinary survival — though her omeletes would always be hard and her pancakes tough.

The smell of the onions in the potato soup had its own peculiar charm, however. Tante Ilde found that she was very hungry and she was quite ashamed of certain uncontrollable rolling sounds that proceeded from the empty region beneath her belt.

Anna began immediately to tell her that they had finally decided on a goulash — it was safer and simpler to make than anything else. Both Hermine and her mother had an uneasy knowledge that Pauli was critical in regard to food, though he wouldn't say a word if a dish hadn't turned out right; only he wouldn't be seen again for a couple of months. Instinctively desiring to flatter him they had kept as far as possible along Hungarian lines; the potato soup had been a second choice, for Hermine's imagination had played at first opaquely about a Halászle, a fish soup that he loved, but she had no fish, and she didn't know how to make it, so she slumped back on the potato soup as offering least resistance. She was hoping for great things from the Palatschinken; however, she had the batter prepared for cooking at the physiological moment, and the can of gluey apricot jam (ersatz) was already open. Both women were obviously quite excited. Anna had those dull, maroon spots on her cheeks; Hermine was paler than usual and kept running into the kitchen and coming back and changing something on the table. It was a quarter of an hour later when they heard the somewhat rusty sound of the master's key in the door. He still kept that key hanging on his chain, though for all the use he made of it the bell would have sufficed. 'The key of the cemetery,' he called it to himself, and was thankful as he went in that he would find Tante Ilde there among the graves.

He was a very handsome man of forty in a full-coloured, ample way, inclining slightly to embonpoint. His brown eyes were for ever flashing and going out as he lifted or let fall his pale, heavy lids. A rosy shade lay upon his cheeks contrasting pleasantly with the clear olive of his skin. A dark moustache did not conceal his white teeth when he laughed, which was often, and they gave an additional accent to the whole, the colour scheme becoming even blinding when he wore, as on that day, one of his favourite red neckties.

Immediately he filled the grey room, or perhaps it dissolved about him. . . . Life, life. He brought the life of his pleasant, easy-going, musical Viennese father; the life of his impetuous, fiery, musical Hungarian mother, that strong, active element which the Magyars infuse so happily into the more 'gemuetlich' qualities of the Austrians. Whenever anything happened in Vienna for good or evil in the old days, it was generally traceable to the more dynamic qualities of the Hungarians – and doubtless will be so again.

There was no hint of war or post-war days on Pauli's face, rather some astounding avoidance of their ills, some unimpaired eagerness for life. His wife and daughter were unacquainted with a pale shadow that of late often dimmed it.

The women, except Tante Ilde, were blotted out. She felt the exhilaration, the immediate electrification, of the air and sat up quite straight, her elbows elegantly pressed against her waist and began to smile her fine, sweet smile. Her presence lay about Pauli as a wreathing mist about a mountain on a sunny day. Again he was thankful to find her there.

Dutifully he gave Anna a robust but empty kiss on both cheeks, with a 'Well, how goes it?' and the same to Hermine, standing close by her mother. He thought fleetingly for the thousandth time that it was a calamity for women to be ugly.

Then he turned the full blaze of his countenance on Tante Ilde:

'Ach, the dear, lovely Auntie,' he cried, 'she must also have a Busserl,' and he proceeded to kiss each pale cheek and even to press her against his thick, warm breast.

'Not lovely, only loving,' she returned, but she smiled, suddenly quite happy, and Pauli felt his words had not been in vain. He liked to have happy faces about him and laughter and jokes, and if it were women who were being made happy all the better.

'I smell something good,' he next said amiably, sniffing in the air, 'and I'm quite ready. In the cafés,' he continued, 'it's 3,000 crowns for a piece of bread, 10,000 for a glass of beer and 5,000 for a smell of roast pork from the next table!' Again he sniffed gaily. Even when he barked his shins against a hard, low bench that stood unnaturally near the dining-table, he gave no sign of the impatience that always possessed him when with Anna. But in spite of his remarks about his hunger, he took very little of the lukewarm soup which Hermine had poured out too soon. And when she dragged her sleeve in the goulash as she put it on the table, he indulgently recounted a joke he had seen in the *Meggendorfer Blätter*. How a certain woman going into a cheesemonger's had skilfully passed her long sleeve through a dish of white cheese, in that way removing an appreciable quantity, and how the cheesemonger in a rage made her come back to pay for it, threatening to have her up for theft.

Sallow Hermine was greatly in awe of her highly coloured father, who expected from her, she uncomfortably felt, something that she could not offer, but now she was giggling girlishly, and even Anna's face seemed less formless.

Yes, Pauli was doing his best to make it pleasant for the quite accidental beings who bore his name. Dispensing smiles that, after all, were so rightly, though so strangely, theirs. Life was truly mysterious; they were human beings, too, come out of nothing, hurrying as fast as Time could take them to the same end. It produced undeniably at moments a feeling of comradeship – though Pauli intended to avoid Anna in the other world.   .

Tante Ilde was indeed making things easier, suaver; Tante Ilde was really an alabaster box of precious ointment, broken anew each time she went into one of those homes not hers, diffusing sweet odours about her. They would mostly (perhaps not Pauli) have thought: 'It's poor old Tante Ilde, and we've got to do something for her,' not dreaming that all the time it was she who was doing something priceless for them.

Now he was in a fever of longing to hear a beloved name. But she told them first about Liesel and Otto, everything she could without making Anna jealous; not, of course, about the sausage. Meat twice a day would have scandalized Anna, and anyway Tante Ilde would never have been guilty of the indelicacy of speaking about that sausage, wrapped up and put away, too. The fresh noodles in fresh butter were all that Anna and Hermine could really stand; they would talk about them for days; but she described in detail the package from the 'Friends,' at which Anna and Hermine pricked up their big ears and cried: 'You don't say!' and Hermine ran and got an inch-long pencil and a piece of newspaper and wrote the address on the margin. Then she and her mother nodded their heads significantly at each other. They were both thinking that Irma should have let them know immediately, and that some afternoon late, when it was dark and they wouldn't be seen, they'd go for one of those packages. . . .

As Tante Ilde was talking, Pauli noticed the white lace about her neck and how genteel she contrived to look in spite of age and disaster. Then his eyes travelled to his daughter, seeing her really for the first time that day. Hermine had on a chocolate-coloured dress with trimmings of an unpleasant blue. Pauli turned his eyes again to Tante Ilde's cameo face, from which the broad eyes seemed to look out more and more bluely as the dinner went on. Pleasure, even a little, was apt to put the colour back into her eyes. Then he looked again at his daughter. He was thinking that the devil could take him if he knew what colour would be becoming to his only child. Something, anything to emphasize her, to put her on the chart, so he followed out his natural taste as he said:

'I must give you a new dress, Hermine, pink or red or a good bright blue?'

Hermine was delighted at this mark of paternal affection, and Anna astonished. When a long time after he saw the hard and vapid blue she chose he was finally and for ever discouraged. No, Hermine had no flair, she always went wrong on colours, like Anna. His wife and daughter were beyond Pauli. Just those two women out of all Vienna he could rightfully go home to; Hermine was even named for his mother. 'Na, dos ist kein Leben,' it's no life, he often thought in his broadest, most expressive Viennese. Pauli, who could speak perfectly half a dozen languages, always chose that in which to clothe satisfactorily certain unsatisfactory thoughts.

At last when Hermine was out in the kitchen smearing up with her finger the bit of jam that remained on the platter from the Palatschinken, Tante Ilde spoke the name Pauli had come to hear . . . Corinne . . . and stupid Anna didn't care. It was the mention of Fanny that she could not have borne. Anna never caught the truth about anything.

'I'm going to have dinner with Corinne on Friday,' Tante Ilde said finally, a soft radiance spreading over her face, and turned her eyes, suddenly a lovely azure, full upon him. 'Corinne is an angel.'

Perhaps Tante Ilde shouldn't have said that right there before Anna, in Anna's own house, but Anna created an unendurable vacuum about herself; it made people want to throw something, anything, into it to fill the horrible void.

'She thinks you are one,' answered Pauli with a sudden deep breath, and there was a note in his voice that his wife, or at least his daughter, standing at the kitchen door, should have noticed.

Then his eye wandered to the only bit of colour in the room — the scarlet cloth covering his zimbalon.

'Shall I make a bit of music, Tante Ilde?' he suddenly cried with an indecipherable gesture, and laid his cigarette down on his plate where, wastefully in Anna's eyes, it smoked its life away. He pushed his chair back from the table and getting up uncovered the instrument without another word. He was suddenly one vast flame of love for Corinne. He knew the feeling well, — consuming, — he was really beside himself . . . in an instant . . . like that. He began to play a wild Czardas of his mother's land. The light grew brighter in his eyes, the colour deepened in his face, but it was of a moonbeam woman, shadow-thin, that he was thinking.

The music beat mercilessly upon the three listeners,

with its cruel, splendid life-throb, with its piercing intimation that even a thousand years of love would be all too short for the longing heart. From time to time he emitted a wild cry and his nostrils would dilate; his body swayed rhythmically above the instrument. He was indeed 'thirsty in the night and unslaked in the day.' . . .

Anna remembered the short love-madness Pauli had once wrapped her in and pressed her hand against her flat breast.

Tante Ilde thought, too, of things for ever gone, – not of love, that was too far off, but of her lost dignity and use, of all that would not, could not, be again; she had no time to wait upon events.

Hermine was possessed by vague, youthful expectations of what life could so easily bring her, out of its whole long length, a life wherein some one would surely love her, – for want of another the thin young man she sometimes met on the stairs, who gave violin lessons to keep a passionate soul in a delicate body. Perhaps, sensitive, artistic, he would indeed be goaded on by that lurking, tricking spirit of the will-to-live to take Hermine, dull Hermine, for wife, wrapping her for the brief moment necessary for the act in his own passion which would so perfectly conceal her essential poverty. . . .

Suddenly Pauli stopped, the blood had gone from his face, leaving him very pale, but his eyes were full of a dark fire and in his bones was a grinding pain. He was in a mad hurry to be gone from that house of ghosts where he couldn't hold his being together.

'I'm rushed this afternoon, heaps of things to attend to,' he cried as he laid down his batons and threw the scarlet cloth over the zimbalon. To his good-bye to Tante Ilde he added the reminder loudly, distinctly:

'It's understood, Tante Ilde, you're coming every Tuesday?' Then suddenly he was gone, leaving the room dim and chill.

Anna went over to the window and stood by it, though she couldn't see into the street. Hermine almost immediately began to clear off the table.

But Tante Ilde sat quite still. She was thinking, 'poor Anna, poor Anna.' There was something very tender in her leave-taking, something that Anna gratefully, dumbly accepted without knowing what it was that was offered her, and then Tante Ilde slipped away to walk those several miles back to the Hoher Markt.

She had vaguely, diffidently hoped that she might go away when Pauli did, be carried along on his momentum. But he had gone so suddenly, there hadn't been time for any little arrangement or suggestion.

It was beginning to rain. The wind blew flat cold drops against her face. She stood a moment looking at the trolleys clanging up and down the Mariahilfer Street. Why hadn't she walked in the morning?

IV

HERMANN AND MIZZI

Staccato

Hin ist hin! Ver-
loren ist verloren

*

WHEN Doctor Hermann Bruckner was suddenly called
from the security of his civil practice to take charge of a
field hospital, so great was the joy of his secret heart that
even his wife became aware of it, and in her rustiest and
most contentious tone asked him what on earth he was so
pleased about, he was going out to the 'olly' front where
he was certain to be either killed or mutilated, and walking as if on air at the idea of getting there!

Skilful in diagnosis, resourceful in treatment, compassionate concerning the imponderable ailments of his
patients as well as those visible, he had, it is true, bestowed
a brief anxiety on certain of them left to the care of
the diminishing number of proportionately overworked
physicians in Vienna; but for himself. . . . Home, where
his heart was not, where Mizzi nagged and scolded, was
icily disdainful or loudly reproachful, had long been a
place in which he was desperately uncomfortable.

The day he left for the front his aunt Ilde had come in
from Baden to say good-bye to this much-loved, and, as she
knew, much-tried nephew. Looking out of the window
she had seen him settle back into his seat in the motor,
laughing in a gay new way with the colleagues beside him
as he opened his cigarette case.

Hermann had indeed been delivered by the War from

something from which he had thought never to escape. For years, almost his only happy hours had been spent in his office, or hurrying about on his sick calls. He had a particular and personal regard for each patient, and the professional affection they awakened in him had a magnetic, communicable warmth, even the uninteresting old women, the chronic cases, received impartially, glowingly their share. His bedside manners were truly consoling and his warm handclasp, his reassuring pat on the shoulder made a visit to his office something to look forward to. In fact, just seeing Doctor Bruckner made his patients feel that with his help they were not in any immediate danger of leaving this vale of tears for a world which, though they had always been assured was a better one, they had a singular distaste to entering And then his gentle way with suffering children. Doctor Hermann Bruckner, specialist for women and children, was born to do just what he was doing.

But when he got home that flowing, busy life of his would suddenly stop, turn back chokingly upon itself, obstructing his every thought and feeling; for though Mizzi was unspeakably bored by him, she couldn't let him alone. The very sight of his pleasant face, the easy way he had of letting his six feet settle into an arm-chair, the slow smoking of his Trabuco, in some extraordinary, always unexpected way, would give rise to reproaches; never a moment when he could sit at ease after a hard day's work and talk about pleasant things, little, unimportant things. He never could tell just what would

III

unbind Mizzi's tongue or uncork her temper. He made an easy living and they could have had many pleasures, but Mizzi was always wanting the one thing that the hour had not brought. It was considered by the family that Hermann had a hard time of it, that it was unfortunate that Mizzi was as she was, and Hermann, for reasons in the beginning not at all related to his own being, was now generally called by his relations 'poor Manny.'

They didn't realize, any of them, that Mizzi was a woman of great natural energy which had no outlet, and that that was one of the reasons why the small supply of the milk of human kindness with which her Maker had provided her had early soured. She got quite stout, but in her smart Austrian way, and each year became more easily annoyed and controlled her irritation less. Even the War, which opened out activities to so many women, had helped Mizzi not at all. She hated misery, disorder in any form, and the sight of blood made her sick. She was inexpressibly bored by the whole thing and always spoke of it as 'dumm.'

When the War claimed Doctor Bruckner he was a very tall, broad-shouldered, deep-chested man. His mobile, smiling face was ennobled by his prominent but finely-formed nose, and his very black beard and moustache gave his whole person a last significant accent. When the War had no further use for him and passed him into the still more pitiless arms of the Peace, he was broken, disabled, derelict, meaningless even. He reminded himself of a train wreck he had seen near Lodz in the beginning, the telescoped cars, the messy, shapeless débris. . . . That last month at Gorizia a bomb had fallen into his field-hospital. It had solved effectually the problems of his wounded, but it had increased his own. His right arm which had been shattered and hurriedly attended to, now hung nerveless in his sleeve. Mizzi's heart and temper had been briefly softened at the sight of his misfortunes; they were so evidently complete. His helplessness, however, soon induced a new note in her voice; one of condescension and later of hard unveiled impatience.

Finally neurasthenia, on the track of so many, claimed him for its own. He developed a bad case of agoraphobia – could scarcely ever go through open spaces without a discomfort that amounted at times to agony, and Vienna seemed full of wide, open places. He would creep along walls, close to houses and doors, but when it came to crossing the street, unless, indeed, it were full of vehicles his eyes would sink and darken, his nostrils get blue and pinched. It was but one of various things, – that intolerably stupid going back and touching objects a second even a third time on his bad days, that continual putting on and taking off his coat when he was dressing, sometimes he was hours getting into his clothes, and other equally asinine matters. He still went to his office, across the hall, – but a one-armed, neurasthenic doctor! Half the patients who came needed something done that could only be done with two hands. His clientele dwindled till mostly the poor alone came. To them he was an angel of mercy. But they made another complication. Mizzie hated the poor in any form, even the new poor, who had once been rich and whom she had envied in the old days, and when the quite thin pity engendered by his futile return had evaporated, she was constantly reproaching him for having a clientele to whom he couldn't or wouldn't send bills. Hermann's life became a new kind of hell from which there seemed to be no more escape than from the final place of punishment. But for all Mizzi's unpleasant conjugal traits she was, as we have indicated, a woman of ability. She stepped out, on his return, when her practical sense showed her that the family fortunes in Hermann's hand would inevitably go from bad to worse, to retrieve them; and she did.

She boldly opened a lingerie shop, and with her good taste, her industry, her heartlessness and her voice soft as honey to customers, she soon began to do quite well. Fanny had advanced the necessary loan and sent her the first customers who brought others in their train. She developed an unsuspected talent for selling. Naturally impatient she was accommodating to the last degree in her shop. She took back things that had been paid for and returned the money with a smile. She exchanged things, she adjusted things. She could always be counted on to have extra sizes for the dark, stout, often bearded ladies who patronized her in increasing numbers. They generally had the most elemental of underwear, thick, machine-made garments, with machine-made lace and terrible pink bows; some had none at all.

Mizzi initiated them into the pleasant mysteries of

transparent 'dessous,' real lace-trimmed and beribboned in delicate shades. And they had money. 'Jesus, Marie, Joseph!' Mizzi would often exclaim, 'what money! Great wads of it!'

Mizzi had a way of loosening their thick, high corsets and pulling them down, thereby dropping those shelves of flesh from under their chins, and with her cunningly-made brassières, those famous 'Bustenhalter' that reduced the mountains of fat, or at least distributed them towards the back where the owners themselves couldn't see them, she was especially successful. 'Taktvoll kaschieren,' tactfully conceal, was what she modestly claimed to do with super-fluous fat. Being inclined to embonpoint herself, fostered by her love of the truly tempting sweet dishes of her native land, yet having that smart, pleasing figure, she could say confidently to the stoutest:

'I'm a good deal thicker than you are, and look at me!'

They looked at Mizzi in her impeccable loose black dress over her snugly-worn corset and were both delighted and convinced. Mizzi's business was inevitably destined to go from good to still better, just as Hermann's was dwindling to those so begrudged office hours for the very poor, now his only treasure. . . . His aunt Ilde thought secretly that Hermann must be greatly loved by his Creator to have been found worthy of so many misfortunes. . . . He only occasionally took money for his services and except for a few crowns spent in a certain café sitting before his beer or his coffee, reading the newspaper, talking to a chance acquaintance, or oftener just thinking, thinking, he turned what little he did make back again, a pitiful drop, into the river of black and fatal misery that flowed through his office.

Mizzi had something quite ruthless about her. Openly and cordially disliking the poor in general and poor relatives in particular, the last thing she would have thought of was having one of these latter come to her regularly for a meal. But when Fanny sent old Maria to ask if she could have Tante Ilde for dinner on Wednesday, or to choose some other day if that wasn't convenient, though she had thought it a monstrous nuisance, that day being no more convenient than any other of the days of the week, she had said 'Yes' in a voice gone quite white from lack of enthusiasm. But, Fanny, – she couldn't afford to offend Fanny.

. .

The establishment once known as 'Hermann's' was now known as 'Mizzi's.' She had suggested his giving up his office and renting out the rooms to Americans who would pay in dollars. They could make a 'heathen money' that way. But so strange, so terrifying was the look that had come into his face that Mizzi for once had quailed before it. She hadn't felt safe, and anyway Fanny probably wouldn't have stood for it.

Her dream was to have a smart shop at Carlsbad. She had awakened to a brief political interest when she found that almost overnight the Czechs had become, unaccountably, the darlings of those against whom they had so recently fought, and later she discovered that Carlsbad was filled with victorious foreigners who turned their gold joy-fully into Czechish crowns and she was for ever comparing the rising Czech currency with the descending Austrian, and was visibly impatient at the senseless fact that the war had left her, a perfectly good Czecho-Slovak, high and dry in Vienna as the wife of a crippled Austrian. There wasn't any sense in anything, and Mizzi vented mercilessly her dissatisfaction on Hermann.

She was always thinking to herself and often proclaim-ing openly that Hermann was 'dumm, but dumm,' as little of a 'Nutznieser' as anyone ever had the bad luck to be married to. With even the slightest sense of values, he ought to have got something out of the war. Privately Mizzi adored profiteers. But Hermann wasn't made that way.

In the end, he got tired of hearing what his father-in-law would have done in this, that or the other case. That canny Czech, Ottokar Maschka, had, unfortunately for Mizzi, died just as he was about to gather in the fruits of his labours, and when Mizzi married the promising young Viennese doctor the only visible goods she brought with her was the furniture with which they furnished their home; large, solid, comfortable pieces of mahogany and maple, and a lot of linen. But all that Mizzi had long since changed. Mizzi was a forward looker and liked to keep up with, when she couldn't run ahead of, the styles. She had a *flair* about novelties that was to stand her in good stead.

Hermann had ineffectually protested when she got rid,

bit by bit, of the furnishings of the parental house. The only good thing about it all was that it kept her busy. But when he found himself sleeping in a narrow grey bed with conventionalized lotus flowers in low relief, one at the head and one at the foot, he felt himself completely and for ever a stranger in that house. Then, too, the new chairs were extraordinarily uncomfortable, the tables small, while the pale mauve upholstery gave him a continual sense of being in a warehouse glancing over things he had no intention of buying. . . .

The small shop in the Plankengasse, with the tiniest but smartest of show windows, was near enough the thoroughfares to be accessible and not as expensive as the Graben, the Kärntnerstrasse or the Kohlmarkt. Little by little Mizzi was wriggling her way into that world of the new dispensation, peopled by the acquisitive wives, daughters, and 'friends' of profiteers, – that full, loud, clanking, overfed world, that world of people mad to possess at last what 'the others' had so long possessed. Theirs was the world of plenty. The promised land indeed. She was happier than she had ever been before. Her activities had full scope. She had no heart to bleed over the miseries of the starving city and she felt herself getting a really firm foothold in that 'Schieber' world of every tradesman's desire. That 'First Society' in whose uprisings and outgoings she had once delighted, in the reflection of whose splendours she, with the rest of the worthy burghers of Vienna, had once proudly shone, was gone, its glory the bare shadow of a shade. For thin, ruined countesses, for economical prin-

cesses Mizzi had no use, only inasmuch as she could say
to the wife of one of the new lords of creation:

'That's the very dressing-gown the poor Countess
Tollenberg was so enchanted with, but not a kreutzer to
bless herself with, only such taste! It made me sad not to
let her have it, but now I'm consoled, for you, dear,
gracious lady, it's just the thing.' And the 'dear, gracious
lady' would fall for it with a golden crash.

Yes, Mizzi was doing well and intended to do better.
When she wasn't selling, she was buying, like others in
Vienna, who had little or much cash in their pockets,
trying to imprison the vanishing value of money into
objects that would remain visible, buying anything in fact
that wouldn't melt before their eyes. They called all this
'Sachwerthe,' real value. For the antics of money were
extraordinary; no one realized that better than Mizzi. No
matter how carefully you guarded it, the next day it was
less, was gone. You couldn't store it up any more than
you could daylight.

. . . .

As Tante Ilde that Wednesday noon was about to cross
the Revolutionsplatz, once the Mozartplatz, overlooked
by the Jockey Club, the Archduke Friedrich's Palace,
the Opera and Sacher's Hotel (the last two alone continu-
ing to fulfil their ancient uses), she caught sight of a
tall, familiar form hesitating by a lamp post. It was her
nephew Hermann, evidently about to cross the street.
He stood so long by the post that she easily caught up
with him.

'Manny!' she cried, and touched him on the arm, but he turned towards her a face so strange that she was suddenly very frightened. Great beads of perspiration stood on his brow, about his mouth; his eyes were sunken, his nostrils blue and pinched.

'Auntie dear, you've come at the right moment. I can't,' he hesitated, a look of agony and shame on his face, 'get across alone. Give me your arm. I was waiting till some wagons came along. It's easier then. Don't say anything about it to Mizzi. She doesn't understand,' he ended entreatingly. Bending, he passed his hand through her arm and with a tightening of his body, slowly crossed the street, then kept close by the houses, as far away from the kerb as possible.

'You see,' he said with difficulty, 'I'm quite done for'; tears stood in his dark, kind eyes. 'And I'm not going to die either,' he added, 'I've seen so many others go just where I'm going.'

'Manny, Manny, you'll get better. You must get better. Think of all the good you do!' his aunt cried at last out of her grief for him. She hadn't been able to say a word at first, only pressed more closely against his side.

'All the good I do!' he laughed bitterly and stood quite still in the street and couldn't seem to stop laughing.

What was happening to Manny, dear, kind, loving Manny? He made her even sadder than Kaethe. Where could he get help? Perhaps Fanny . . . they'd been such a loving brother and sister. Perhaps if he could take a trip, somewhere, anywhere. . . .

120

They were proceeding at a snail's pace. Hermann's step had no life in it. Frau Stacher began to be afraid they would be late and tried to hurry him a little, but he continued to move mechanically with that sort of heavy dip, and didn't seem to notice her hurry.

As they reached the house he pointed to his name in black letters on the white porcelain sign, and then looked at her with a trembling of the lips just as he used to do when he was a little boy and had some childish grief.

'When I remember all the happy years . . . why, I thought I was going to heal the world,' he said slowly, 'and now' — then he added, suddenly anxious too, 'I hope we're not late.'

Tante Ilde gladly quickened her step and they almost ran in at the doorway. It would be a calamity to be late. Mizzi could generate about her a thick, cold, opaque atmosphere when she was displeased that could take away the appetite or impede the digestion of a starving person. They both knew that it wouldn't at all do to be late, and in spite of age and disabilities they made quite a dash up the stairs.

Mizzi kept a servant and kept her busy. No 'Faulenzers' in her house. Gretl instantly opened the door, then quickly resumed her occupation of setting the table, putting a pleasant, soft-looking little bread at each place.

Mizzi, sitting up very straight in a mauve arm-chair, was measuring with a tape measure lengths of pale shining French ribbons, billowing over a little grey table. She was a woman in the early thirties, with dark eyes inclining to opacity, abundant dark hair and an agreeable, smooth, rather bright complexion, pleasant enough to look at, though her features were negligible. She held herself very erect, even as she sat there was no lolling or relaxing, and when she stood that full, smart figure of hers was impressive, even commanding. Pauli, who detested her, said she ought to have been a midwife, though perhaps in that he was unjust to the profession; but it was undeniable that Mizzi had an eye that in a few years would, as he had further remarked, have no more expression than a hard boiled egg confronted with arriving mortality.

The little table was drawn up by the window with its lavender hangings striped yellow by light and years, and held back by faded ribbons. It was all quite different from the smart freshness of the shop where was Mizzi's heart. Between the windows was a picture of the Prague Gate and in rummaging about she had unearthed, for less than a song, a fine old engraving of Wallenstein conspiring at Pilsen. Where could one find a more loyal Czecho-Slovak than Mizzi Bruckner, bound hand and foot to Austria? – Till she got to that little shop in Carlsbad, over how many dead bodies she cared not – that little shop especially designed for easing foreigners of their golden loads, that she was unswervingly headed towards and would inevitably reach.

As they entered aunt and nephew gave each other an involuntary look of relief. They had made it.

'Well, Tante Ilde, how are you?' Mizzi asked amiably

enough as she looked up, but there was something steely in her tone. She had no objection to Tante Ilde, except that Tante Ilde was so definitely, and it was easy to prohesy permanently, in the class of poor relations, and to such a certain tone came spontaneously to her voice. No trace of the sugary accents that she used in speaking to the large dark women who made commerce take its only steps in the paralysed city. She was polite, but she was cold beyond the power of any thermometer to register. Of her husband, Mizzi took not the slightest notice.

Frau Stacher felt something shrink and shrivel in her. A shameful consciousness of being very poor, of being very old, of being very useless, tinted her pale cheeks.

She hadn't wanted to come to Mizzi's. She had known that she would feel just that way if she did. They all knew about Mizzi, hard as a rock, somebody for the old, the feeble, the dependent to steer clear of.

Then a thick, smoking lentil soup was put on the table. Some pleasing suggestion of having been cooked with a ham-bone came from it. In a quite definite way it changed the atmosphere. Good food in Vienna that winter could work miracles. Natural and unnatural antipathies would melt as dew before the morning sun when enemies found themselves seated together at a full table.

Mizzi herself underwent a subtle change and she was nearly smiling as they sat down. Hermann was still pale, but the blue look had gone from his nostrils, the sweat about his brow and mouth had dried. Tante Ilde was permeated by the delightful sensations of the hungry person about to be filled. . . . The nose, the eyes, then the first mouthful. . . .

The soup quite fulfilled the expectations awakened by its odour. Mizzi never had materials wasted through poor cooking in her house. She always got the best available and this last maid had a light hand. Mizzi had turned one girl after another away till she got the pearl for which she was looking.

The repast, as far as her own feelings went, proved a surprise to Mizzi, though she didn't analyse the increasingly pleasant sensation that animated her as the conversation got easier and easier. Mizzi didn't for an instant suspect that that despised poor relation was distilling about her an odour suaver than that of the lentil soup, even with its suggestion of ham-bone.

By the time the herrings, and the potatoes boiled in their skins, and actually served with butter, were put on, Mizzi was in full flood of conversation; her tongue was hung easily anyway, quite in the middle. During the soup, she had been distinctly grand with Tante Ilde, the immensely superior Lady Bountiful dispensing mercies, but Tante Ilde was so greatly and so genuinely interested in the shop and asked such tactful questions, just the sort Mizzi was delighted to answer, that things got pleasanter and pleasanter. She showed signs of irritation, however, when Hermann, not too successfully, tried with his left hand to separate the meat of his herring from its backbone, and gave an impatient click of her tongue and cried harshly, 'Give it here.' But that passed, and when the

Apfelstrudel was put on, she fell to telling amusing stories of the unbelievable ways of the various stupid geese, those wives of profiteers who had, all the same, led her, Mizzi, out of the captivity of hunger and cold. She made fun of their horrible underclothes and told how she changed all that, opening their eyes to a lot of other things to which they'd evidently been born blind. Even Hermann got less pale and from time to time looked affectionately across at his aunt. When they were having their coffee, just as they used to in the good old days, real Mocha, that one of those very 'Schieberinnen' had given her, Mizzi even said quite gently to Hermann: 'Aren't you going to smoke?' Hermann was surprised and grateful beyond measure. Very little would once have made so soft-hearted a man as Hermann unduly and permanently grateful. Mizzi, though she hadn't the slightest idea of it, was continuously responding to the pleasant harmonies struck from the gentle being of her poor old aunt by marriage, and when they had drunk the last drop of coffee and were still enjoying the pleasant memories of the Apfelstrudel, she found herself saying, somewhat to her own surprise:

'Tante Ilde, come with me, I want to show you the shop. It's time for me to get back. The girls don't take a stitch while I'm away!'

Then she stepped into the kitchen to put on a plate, for Gretl's dinner, a head of one of the herrings and two potatoes (the others were to be saved for salad that evening), and to the amazement of Gretl, she added a bit of the

Strudel, casting at the same time an appraising eye over what was left and which she certainly expected to find intact on her return.

Tante Ilde longed to stay with Hermann whose plight was more and more engaging her thought and sympathy. She had had time while Mizzi was in the kitchen to press his hand lovingly and to tell him she was going to Kaethe's to-morrow, and to try to get there too, Kaethe was worrying about Carli. He had answered listlessly.

'Yes, if I have a fairly decent day. You've seen how hard it is for me to get about.'

Instinctively she had not mentioned the Eberhardts in Mizzi's presence. It would have darkened her brow and salted unduly the repast. People that couldn't get a living somehow! Mizzi had no use at all for them. In some mysterious, but certain way, it was their own fault. Even the Peace was no excuse in Mizzi's eyes.

When she came back from the kitchen saying briskly, and they realized, without appeal:

'Well, are you ready, Tante Ilde?' Frau Stacher hastily put on her coat, that is as hastily as possible. It had tight sleeves and they always stuck on the little white shawl she wore underneath for warmth. Mizzi came to the rescue, gave it a poke down the back, a pull about the shoulders and crossed it over the frail chest with a final energetic punch that left Frau Stacher breathless. Then she slipped easily into her own ample coat and turned up its large beaver collar. But after all Mizzi pleased, Mizzi on the

road to success, was not so terrifying. She was safely
diverted out of family discontent by the pleasantly exciting
difficulties and triumphs of her business. Then, too,
those thin, pale girls who sat by the window at the
back of the shop, and worked without looking up when
Mizzi was there, were continual escape-valves.

Even little Tilly with fingers like a fairy, got her share.
No one could tie a bow like Tilly, not even Mizzi herself,
and then those diaphanous garments that she turned out,
delicate bits of nothing, the very stitches themselves were
like trimming. Mizzi knew first-class work when she saw
it, and she further saw that she got the greatest amount
possible done in the day.

Tilly's mother was dying in a back room, reached by
a third stairway in the court of an old house, and Tilly
never answered Mizzi back, was never 'fresh' and it was
quite evident that she never dreamed of giving notice but
only of giving satisfaction.

In face of Mizzi's pleasant, flowing briskness that could,
however, so easily curdle into thick displeasure, Tante
Ilde, though she longed to stay, could but say good-bye
to Hermann, with a secret pressure of his hand. For a
moment she felt the encircling warmth of his great chest
and shoulders as he bent down to kiss her. Then he sank
heavily back into his chair. She turned at the door for a
last sight of him, but already he was plunged in his
thoughts and did not look up again. She could have wept
for Hermann then and there.

As she followed Mizzi down the stairs, they met two

young-old women with pale, head-heavy babies in their arms.

'Manny's patients,' said Mizzi, who was really a terrible woman, an abysmal contempt in her voice, 'I don't know how I put up with it.'

'Manny is very ill,' answered Tante Ilde gently.

'Nerves,' returned Mizzi promptly, finally. 'We'd starve if I hadn't started in.'

'You are a wonder,' said Tante Ilde, and quite honestly she thought it was little short of a miracle, how Mizzi in that dreadful city had not only wooed but won fortune.

Of course, they all knew that Fanny had started her, but even so she was a wonder, making money that way. She would survive. It was beings like Hermann who went under – gentle, loving, wise, once-strong Hermann.

Her thoughts clung tenaciously to Hermann, slumped down into his chair, Hermann who hadn't looked back at her. She couldn't know that he had, for quite a while, been conscious of her loving touch on his arm, and that he was thinking, 'Some time I'll tell Tante Ilde about Marie.' Yes, while he was still able to talk clearly of precious things. It was one of his worst days. Often on such days he didn't keep his office hours . . . the uselessness of the terrible struggle. In that city of misery, let a few more die in those black hours before dawn, without warmth or food or even a match to strike a light that those who loved them could see them go. He was losing, and was conscious of its slipping from him, that strong professional feeling of saving life, any life, just to save it, fulfilling a deep

128

instinct, working according to habit that was as natural to him as breathing. Sometimes nothing mattered, not even Mizzi's lash-like tongue on his bare nerves. On other days, difficult as it was to get over the open places, he would leave the house quite early in the morning, trying to shake off its devitalizing atmosphere. There was a café off the Opernring, he didn't have to cross the Ring itself to get to it, where they knew him and his little ways; sometimes he would sit for hours at a certain table watching the coming and going.

But that morning he'd got there too early; it was still deserted and he had been witness to certain dismal preparations for the day. A pale woman in damp, thin garments was washing up the floor, ends of burnt-out matches and cigarettes were piled in a corner, in a little heap on a chair were a few carefully collected cigar ends. The pikkolo under the emphatic direction of a waiter was brushing off the billiard table, the Tarok games were being laid out, the newspapers put into their holders. The pikkolo, who put one in upside down, had forthwith received a box on the ear from the waiter, supplemented by a kick on that part of his undersized person where, however, it would be least injurious; but his reaction was not against the donor of these morning favours, but rather induced the consoling thought that if he ever got to be head waiter he would return it with interest to whatever pikkolo was then about.

The arrival, a bit late, of the buffet Fräulein, with her blonde hair too tightly crimped, too thickly puffed, started

things at a more lively gait. A pale lavender tint lay over
her face – the hair bleach, the rice powder, the long hours
in the crowded room. Energetically she proceeded to count
out a few lumps of sugar, unlocked noisily from behind
the counter; then she looked scrutinizingly at the liqueur
and fruit-juice bottles, holding them up to the light,
her pale eye appraising the exact condition of their
contents.

One by one frequenters of the café began to come in,
dissipating more and more the forlornness of the place,
wiping their feet on the wire mat, putting their bulging
umbrellas into the stand, hanging up their dull hats, sitting
down in their overcoats, taking packages of paper money
from their pockets and putting them on the table just as
if it weren't money. Finally the café was quite full and
Hermann sitting before his empty cup, smoking and
watching apathetically the familiar sights, became conscious of the passage of time. He remembered that Tante
Ilde was coming to dinner that day, and he wondered
what Fanny could have said to make the arrangement
possible, it was so unlike Mizzi. Then he looked at his
watch and saw with immense relief that he still had a
little time, . . . a calamity to be even that short distance
from home, . . . he hoped he'd get back, . . . some
time probably he wouldn't. He had been thinking all
that morning with an obsessing, nightmarish horror of
something that had happened to him in his own office
the day before. . . . Because a pale, uncertain-yeared
woman had had nose-bleed, he had been overcome by a

horrible nausea, an intolerable, hitherto unknown feeling in the pit of his stomach. Why, he had seen blood, felt blood, smelt blood, worked swiftly, calmly in blood against time and death – and now a pale woman with a nose-bleed. . . . He'd had to go into the inner office. . . . It was unbelievable that just *that* could happen to him. Then after she had gone, after they all had gone, he sat thinking about it and he had laughed terribly, loudly, and then trembled and wept and Mizzi on the other side of the landing knew nothing about it, no one knew, no one must ever know just *that*. Yes, he was going very fast. He knew it himself; knew that he was headed for the mad-house, as straight even as towards death. Some day he'd do something of a sort that nobody had any right to do. Often he would awake, icy cold, at the fear of what he might do. He couldn't imagine at all what it would be, but something that people who were dwelling freely among their fellow-men were not allowed to do – and rightly. . . .

Sometimes his thoughts would turn with nostalgic longing to the gay, full years of his student-life; those busy years as intern at the Allgemeine Krankenhaus. The luck he'd had when old Professor Schulrath but a year before his death, had taken him as assistant. . . . The eager beginnings of his own private practice; that unforgettable thrill the first time he had seen his plate hanging outside his own door. . . . Pride, bound up with a hot intention to conquer, misery, pain, death even. Soon he had found himself fully launched on the tide of an ever-swelling general practice. Then one Sunday at Pauli's he had met Mizzi – full-bosomed, soft-voiced Mizzi, underneath as hard as a rock, as cruel as the grave, crueller than the grave. . . .

That whole first year of the war he had been among those detailed for general duty in the great city. Afterwards, the civilian population was left to be born or die as best it could. Every available physician was rushed to the front. The mortality among the wounded had become too great. Poor fellows sent back from one or the other fronts would sometimes have been two or three weeks in their uniforms, still in their first-aid bandages, or not bandaged at all; and when they got to Vienna after the torture of their transport in springless luggage-vans, there was often little to be done for them except bury them in those great mounds that grew and grew as the hospitals eased themselves of their dead. It had to be managed less wastefully. Lives were to be saved that they might be thrown again into the struggle. . . .

He had partaken of the tragic, senseless exaltation that able-bodied men everywhere were experiencing on starting for the front. . . . Then deliverance from the carping tongue of Mizzi; the simplest things more and more caused her to fly unexpectedly up in the air like a rocket; there would be a sputtering and something would darken and go out. These were among the reasons why Hermann had settled back in the motor that day and with a laugh set out for the front. But there was something else that none of them had known about, that then, that now, was

always in his mind, in his heart, in every fibre of his being.
Even when he was watching the most indifferent things,
such as the buffet Fräulein that very morning – he didn't
need to be alone – suddenly *she* would be with him and
fling her lost radiance around him once again, and wrap
him up into that magnetic world of longing for the might
have been. He wouldn't hear the 'wer giebt,' 'Pagat,' 'an'
dreier' of the Tarok players, or the rustling of newspapers
being turned on their sticks, or the 'Sie, Ober,' or the
'Pikkolo, du dummer,' – *she* was always more real than
anything else, . . . even at the café, when he would be
holding the *Neue Freie Presse* and pretending to read.
She was everywhere and all. Even as he dropped back in
that chair, with Tante Ilde's touch still warm upon his
arm and his eyes apparently fixed on the quite uninteresting
enlarged and coloured photograph of Mizzi's dead father
(Mizzi year by year was getting to be his very image,
with that hint of moustache), he was thinking only of
her – Marie.

. . . .

That January of 1915, one windy, icy twilight, he had
had a hurry call from the Elizabethspital and had put off
many patients still waiting and closed his office.

Before he got to the gate of the hospital grounds, out in
the street even, he found row upon row of stretchers laid
down low upon the earth, bearing shattered forms whose
silence was more terrible than groans; their grey cloaks
were wrapped about them, their poor boots, in which they
had marched to destruction at the word of command,

were mostly tied to the handles. . . . Pale faces, bandaged heads, arms crossed on their breasts or inert by their sides, under their capes. . . . Raised but a foot from the ground where the stretcher bearers had deposited them they looked already like their own graves, as grey, as voiceless. Yet the biting cold of that windy twilight was heavily charged with their unuttered groans.

Within the hospital it was still the same. The corridors were blocked. Outside the douche rooms they waited for their turn. At last clean, sheet-covered, they waited again at the door of the operating room.

He had met Marie von Sternberg that very evening . . . so quiet, so deft, her pale blue eyes so compassionate under her heavy, dark brows and lashes, her jaw so nobly strong, her hands so beautiful in spite of the discoloration of acids and disinfectants. He had suddenly noticed her hands as she was passing him a probe.

But he hadn't looked at her face then; it was only some hours after — not even in a pause, for still the men were being brought in — when a young, yellow-haired Tyrolese had been put on the table. As Doctor Bruckner bent over him, he had cried out in a loud voice 'Mother' and had suddenly given up his youthful ghost. Then Doctor Bruckner found that he was looking full into the blue eyes, so heavily lashed, so darkly circled, of the woman at his side. He saw there a spark of the same everlasting pity that flamed in his own. They hadn't said anything even then, for quickly the youth had been carried away and his place had been filled by a swarthy family man from one of the Slavic Crownlands, his wedding ring still hanging about the finger of his mangled hand. Hermann had never forgotten either of those two men, for in between them was set, like a jewel in death and pain, that look that he and Marie von Sternberg had exchanged.

All that winter, that winter of his content, of his happiness, they breathed the same air, did the same work, to the same end. Those afternoon hours had been, quite strangely, enough for happiness. In the early summer she had been sent to the Russian front. When he was mobilized she was still there, and that was the true reason why he was laughing the day he left Vienna. A thousand miles of battlefield and ruined towns might lie between them; then again she, like himself, might be sent where the need was greatest, their roads could easily converge. He hoped blindly, confidently from the war; all his hope was in its vicissitudes.

Then one evening, after the fiery setting of a hard, red sun over a scorched, interminable plain, the dim air thick with odours of blood and death, cut now and then feebly by disinfectants used not too generously, as he stood outside that hospital tent, thinking of her, longing desperately for her, a quick, light step approached, he heard her voice:

'Hermann, it is I.'

And all the dust and fatigue, the blood and agony that covered his body and his spirit fell away and turning he had cried out her name in straining passion.

They had embraced in such deep longing that they

seemed to be lost out of time and space . . . to be together, even for that minute . . . even in that way. . . .

The battle-field with its dreadful débris had seemed to Hermann Bruckner like some paradisaical garden. . . . And those glorified days of September, October, that followed, the unit keeping up as best it could with the great army throwing its roads and bridges across the Pripet marshes. . . .

Then one day she had had fever; two degrees only, but suddenly she had sickened terribly, sickened hopelessly, and died immediately of typhus. . . . Hermann who had hung over her hadn't taken it, but he hadn't been able to live or die since. He'd just gone from bad to worse; he'd done his work, yes, that was what was left; she would have been doing hers if he had died. . . .

But after Gorizia, he had known it was all over with him, as a man that is; as a poor hulk of flesh and blood and bones and nerves, oh, there were perhaps many years waiting for him. Sometimes when he looked at his nerveless arm he remembered how warm and firm his clasp had been in hers, hers in his. . . . There were so many things to think of before he ceased to remember. . . . Rarely her spirit visited him in that house of Mizzi's. . . . But in his office continually he found her, sometimes in each ailing, miserable body he seemed to find her, beautiful and of an endless pity. Oh, he needed her. Even without his arm, *that* way it would have been all right. Something could always be done if the will is there. . . . But without her he no longer willed anything.

Yes, he was very ill, but not in a way to die. Death might not come to him till he had forgotten everything, even Marie. . . .

Mizzi was like a sharp point in his being. She had worn sore spots all over him, and strangely from Mizzi he must receive that which would keep his will-less breath in his useless body. . . .

But Mizzi really knew nothing about her husband, indeed never had known anything about him, beyond his name and age and personal appearance and a few of his habits. Now he weighed a thousand tons upon her life.

When with her aunt in tow she turned into the Plankengasse, she was in the usual pleasingly expectant state with which she was wont to approach her shop. As they neared it they saw a dark, stout, ponderous female dressed in a thick, brown cloth suit, a heavy black hat with waving ostrich plumes, a long sable scarf hung inelegantly about her heavy shoulders, projecting herself cumbersomely from a much bebrassed auto.

'That's one of them,' said Mizzi, eagerly, greedily, 'it's Frau Fuchs. You'll die laughing, she doesn't know beans about anything, but that big bag of hers is full of banknotes.'

In a moment, Mizzi in velvety accents was greeting Frau Fuchs as if she were a queen. She touched appreciatively the sable scarf, lauded its beauty, saying, 'You certainly get the best of everything.' Then she turned and presented her aunt, Frau Kommerzienrath Stacher, born von Berg. Mizzi laid it on thick, resting some of her 75 kilos on the Kommerzienrath, adding the full weight of the others to the 'von.' Then she proceeded to show Frau Fuchs a certain red velvet jacket with a little gold border, and Frau Fuchs had gone into raptures over it, and had said she must have it, and then her eye had lighted on a leather handbag ornamented with Irma's medallion of 'petit point.' Though Frau Stacher recognized it, she was somehow not surprised to hear Mizzi, as she drew attention to its workmanship, say that it had been made by a certain Archduchess, positively starving, and Frau Fuchs sniffing up the subtle perfume of royalty that Mizzi's words caused to rise from the bag, had taken it eagerly. 'No, is it true?' she had cried in ecstasy, and had drawn her glove from her thick beringed hand and opened her humpy alligator skin bag with its loud green and gilt clasp and counted out a sheaf of bank-notes. Mizzi herself had wrapped the bag and the dressing sack up in her finest paper and sent one of the girls (the one who did the least good work) out to put the parcels into Frau Fuchs' Mercedes.

'Isn't she awful?' said Mizzi when they were alone, 'but without her and a lot more like her, we'd starve. Her husband is stone-rich, has an Exchange Bureau in the Kärntnerring. How she used to hate to pay out the money! But I changed that, she's a bit afraid of me.'

There was indeed something awe-inspiring at moments about Mizzi, something that she could invoke to decide wavering purchasers. Then still under the charm of Tante Ilde's gentle but quiet appreciation, also under that of good business dispatched, Mizzi gave her a little handkerchief. It had a yellow stain on it that they hadn't been able to get out, still it was a handkerchief and a gift, and Tante Ilde gratefully receiving the attention for much more than it was worth, thought perhaps she had misjudged Mizzi.

It hadn't been at all bad going to her for dinner, except for that terrible depression when she thought of Hermann. No, it hadn't been at all bad that first time, and she repulsed certain lurking suspicions that every week might prove too much for Mizzi's longanimity.

Then, too, she had good news to take back to Irma; the bag had been sold, Mizzi had counted out the money that she had promised Irma for the medallion, and though it didn't in the slightest correspond to the price Mizzi had received for the bag, Tante Ilde could be trusted to keep that hidden in her breast. Indeed, Mizzi said it had cost her a monstrous amount of money to get the bag mounted, that she didn't know how she could afford to take anything else from Irma, she hadn't made a kreutzer on that bag, she only did it to help Irma, etc. etc. No, Tante Ilde didn't repeat from one to the other. Those little households that day by day were spilling their secrets before her whom they received in charity, – out of their goodness, out of their pity, – were sacred to her.

That night, as she lay awake hearing Ferry's hacking little cough, she was thinking almost entirely of the plight of Manny. Nothing had ever been too much for Manny, when it came to doing something for some one else, and now. . . . If the time did come for Manny to be put somewhere, Mizzi would have money to pay for him, and what she didn't do, why Fanny, there was always Fanny. Down whichever miserable road of their misfortunes they looked, Fanny glitteringly stood, Fanny dispensing benefits generously, easily, not always wisely, after her own special way. Tante Ilde suddenly felt she didn't understand the first thing about life, and she had filled the threescore and ten of the allotted span. When did one begin to understand?

V

THE EBERHARDTS

Rallentando   'Süsses Leben! Schöne, freundliche
                Gewohnheit des Daseins und Wirkens!
                von dir soll ich scheiden!'

★

FRAU STACHER had folded up the light brown camel's-hair
blanket with the dark brown Greek border that she had
slept under for years, and the sheets with the von B-S
monogram, and put them, together with the equally
familiar pillow on which her head now so uneasily lay,
into the divan and shut it down. Then she stood up on it
and dusted the flat white-and-gilt vase under the picture of
Haydn leading the young Mozart by the hand. Finally
she pulled back the curtains of the alcove, which last
gesture always seemed to wipe her completely from the
room, somewhat as if she had been carried out in the final
box. Her movements were brisk, with a business-like
dispatch about them. She looked years younger than
when she had stood that afternoon gazing at the trolleys
clanging down Mariahilfer Street, and which, striking
out their noisy, powerful flashes of light, had seemed like
heavenly chariots, conveying certain fortunate ones,
strongly, swiftly over immeasurable cobbly and asphalt
stretches to their homes, to their alcoves even, out of sight
and touch of the damp, cold misery of the streets.

She had put on her oldest suit, with the black and white
stripes without once thinking that it had always been a
failure. Business – pleasant business – was engaging her

attention. But she stood at the door a moment too long, holding in one hand her umbrella, in the other a large, brown, string bag. In her worn pocket-book was money to buy wherewith to fill it. Her eyes were bright; in her cheeks was the faintest pink. Irma was irritated in spite of herself at the sight of that brisk fervour. She knew perfectly well the chronically desperate situation of the Eberhardts, yet to see her sister-in-law stepping lightly over the threshold with that bag in her hand, going out to buy food that she, Irma, could well have used for her own children, provoked an unreasoning envy. Frau Stacher had not dallied in face of that sombre look, that terrible look, born of the brooding solicitude about food, food, that seemed to hold but slightly in leash unnameable things. She fled hastily before it. Only Irma's nerves. But she had come to know a lot about Irma's nerves in those few days. Irma was a beast of prey for her children. No one and nothing that came into conflict with their interests had the slightest chance with her. Ferry's cough seemed suddenly from one day to the other to get worse. She had taken him to his Uncle Hermann, and his Uncle Hermann had said to Irma in the back office, while Ferry turned over a sport journal of eight years before in the front room:

'What's the use, Irma, he needs milk, eggs, high air.'

Had he said pearls, diamonds, rubies, it would have been the same to Irma. How not to sink to irrecoverable depths with that sinking population of which they were a part, was Irma's one thought. The rent was a small matter. For a long time she hadn't paid anything. At least

the 'crazy Government' prohibited turning families into the
streets, even if they didn't pay. All the Government really
wanted to know was that every room of every apartment
was filled to overflowing with samples of the Viennese
populace.

In that back office Hermann had further said, ten-
tatively:

'Perhaps . . . Fanny would send him away for awhile.'
Irma had tartly answered: 'Fanny, it's always Fanny.'

But all the same the suggestion, though annoying, had
fallen on fertile soil. She had been turning over certain
possibilities, or rather methods of approach, for twenty-four
hours, and she was terribly jumpy . . . if that slender,
ageing figure had stood a moment longer on the threshold
with that string bag, sign and symbol of marketing . . .
Nerves, nerves. After a moment Irma had gone on with
her 'petit point.' She was putting the pale brown background around the delicate moss-roses – really quite lovely.
Mizzi, for all she'd hum and haw, would take it, but at her
own price, Irma was reflecting bitterly. She pulled the red
shawl closer about her and bit off absent-mindedly a piece
of silk on a tooth that needed filling, then miserably, with
a groan, she continued her work. Tante Ilde had said
something about her own teeth that morning – she had a
loose front one that was beginning to hurt unmercifully
every time she took anything hot. But at *that* age, Irma
had thought disdainfully, what did it matter if they all
fell out? Money for a dentist at that age, in such times!
Now she was full of Ferry's need, of plans for him. She

hadn't yet decided how to go about the matter which presented certain undeniably delicate points. Even Irma, obsessed by mother-love and mother-fear, was aware of their delicacy.

．　　．　　　．　　　．　　　．　　　．　　　．

The Eberhardts still lived in the apartment they had taken when they married, on a street in the Alsergrund, near the University. It had once seemed very big, magnificent even for two people; now their handsome, hungry children overflowed it.

The family had been very proud of Kaethe's distinguished young husband; 'a genius,' they would always say impressively to less fortunate friends when speaking of him, and dwell delightedly on Kaethe's relations with the University and with certain distinguished people who visited Vienna when the Kaiserstadt was a font of wisdom. Her husband was indeed well embarked on a brilliant career, any and all honours were possible; Privy Councillor certainly, and later perhaps a 'von' to his name. When scientific Congresses met in Vienna, he was always called on to read papers, and colleagues from other cities were eager to confer with him. He often used to bring one or the other home with him for coffee, proud of his smiling, soft-eyed, bright-cheeked wife, of his lovely babies, his comfortable house. When things began to get bad, Kaethe would tell the children what she used to have for the 'Jause,' that extraordinary, incredible meal that came in the afternoon, *between* other meals – coffee and chocolate, with thick whipped cream (the now quite legendary 'Schlagobers'), apple tarts with butter dough, the fresh coffee cake, and certain little crescents that would fairly melt in the mouth. The children were in the habit of asking their exact colour, shape and taste; they seemed quite unrelated to the War and Peace bread that alone they were acquainted with, and certainly they never could have sprung from the same harvest field. The real difference between milk and cream, too, was an absorbing topic, and they all loved Resl's joke that if it rained milk instead of water she would be out all the time looking up with her mouth open, though Maxy invariably reminded her that it would be better to take a pail and bring a lot home and then everybody could have some. When Lilli learned at school about the Milky Way, she taught them a game called living at number 1 Milk Street. But lately they hadn't talked much of the 'Jause' of the old days, nor made so many little jokes. They were tired when they got home from school, and only errands connected with food had any interest.

Though all of Herr Bruckner's family were musical in their easy way, Kaethe had a real talent; she could not only play through by ear the latest operetta, but Beethoven, Schumann, Brahms, with a sure yet fiery touch. Eberhardt had played the 'cello since his boyhood. Sometimes Kaethe, her fingers tapping out a measure on the table after the piano went, would think with hot longing of certain quartettes to which those walls of hers had once resounded. Poor Amsel who led them . . . his songs, written during a protracted period of starvation in a garret, were now being sung everywhere; but he had been killed on the Eastern front that very first month of the war, — he'd scarcely had time to send back a post card — and had been buried with his talent and a half a hundred luckless fellows in a huge mound, that had been promptly flattened and all trace of it obliterated by a retreating army. And Koellner, with his Amati violin. Kaethe often hummed a motif of that Mozart trio and thought of herself at the piano, Koellner swaying slimly, his eyes closed and the long black lock falling over his forehead — they hadn't seen him after the signing of the Peace. As for Rosetti from Trieste, who played the viola, he hadn't been heard of since the day before the mobilization, certain rumours got around about him. . . .

But all these things were really as distant to the Eberhardts as the Tertiary Period; they themselves had been thrown up by the convulsions of War and Peace into strangely diversified, completely unrelated strata.

For a long time, however, those bright days had left the glow of their setting on the sombre war period. And then wars didn't last for ever, and when over, except for mourning mothers, things would doubtless be as they had been. No one foresaw the Peace. . . .

It had lasted four years, that first full, happy life, during which time Kaethe had had three children — Lilli a pansy-eyed, pale-haired little girl, now grown too beautiful for safe adolescence ; another clever, dark child, Resl ; and Maxy who had been a 'sugar baby,' something to eat up, as he lay gurgling and cooing in his mother's arms.

The pendulum of Eberhardt's life had swung unvary-
ingly between that beloved home and the equally beloved
laboratory, where daily he pursued hotly, closely, certain
secrets of nature, always enchantingly about to be caught;
or with a warm note in his vibrant voice and a light in his
grey, speculative eye, communicated to eager students
those he had already seized. . . .

On the 28th of June came the news of the assassinations
at Sarajevo. Unbelievable news; the Dual Monarchy
shaken to its foundations. Its heir, its keystone gone like
that, in a foul moment. Still everybody talked of the
Emperor's grief, not dreaming that each, in one way or
another, would partake of that grief. They counted his
many sorrows, scarce one save poverty was missing; the
Emperor's sorrows had always been an absorbing theme;
it had got so that there weren't enough fingers on both
hands to record them. This, and this, and this and still
this had he suffered. Had not his son miserably perished
by his own hand — or another's? Had not his lovely
Empress been assassinated? Had not his brother been put
to death in far-off Mexico? Had not his sister-in-law been
burned to death in a charity bazaar? Had he not been
obliged to exile another brother from his court for nameless sins? Had not another heir died of a dread disease?
And other, other griefs. Now this last, this fatal blow in
his old age, personal, dynastic. Those catastrophic griefs,
heaped high with the years, in a way had become a matter
of pride to happy Austrians; and the unhappy ones, because
of them, had a feeling of kinship with their beloved

'Franzerl.' Who could have foretold that in five years they would seem remoter, less interesting, than those of some Roman Emperor? . . .

For a few weeks things seemingly went on just the same. Suddenly Europe was in flames, and from the conflagration no one could flee. . . .

The first two years hadn't been so bad for the Eberhardts. The Professor had been detailed for laboratory work in Vienna, and things went on somewhat as they had been going. Two more children were born. Then, unexpectedly, through some tragedy of errors, Eberhardt found himself in a delousing station on the Eastern front. By that time, everybody was talking about hygiene as well as victory. But he was only gone a few months, returning gaunt and white, a startled look in his once thoughtful eye, and evidently quite unfit for further service. He had been side-tracked for days with a dozen others, suffering from dysentery, heaped together in a luggage-van. No food, and worst of all, no water. The whole first week after he had tottered in over the threshold of his home he had said nothing, except repeat the word 'schrechlich' – terrible. Then, strangely, he got better, even well, and went to the nearly empty University every day, trying to knot the torn threads of learning. Then the terrible Peace broke out. The War had been bad enough, but it was war, and unless one was killed one knew how to take it. The peace was quite another matter, a starving, freezing matter for women and children in city streets. The civilian population was suddenly plunged into it, up

to the neck in it. . . . That collapse of the winter of
1919 . . . that terrible food-blockade over half Europe.
. . . There was nothing to hope for, nothing to fight for,
except bread, bread, bread, in ever-diminishing quantities.
More were going down in that battle in the windy city
than before machine-guns. Each street was a battle-
field, heaped mostly with children's bodies or the bodies
of the very old.

.   .   .   .

The Eberhardts' apartment was far, too, from the
Hoher Markt, but not far like the Mariahilfer Street,
Frau Stacher kept reminding herself as she trudged along,
her string bag full and her purse empty, and at the end of
the walk there would be darling Kaethe and the lovely,
hungry children.

It had not been easy, buying the most usual things, and
the thin soup of the night before, and the ersatz coffee of
the early breakfast had prepared her but illy for the
venture. She had gone into various shops where unholy
prices or empty shelves confronted her, for Vienna had
mostly done its buying for the day when she started forth.
It was late when at last she found herself, quite worn out,
hesitating in a certain provision shop, between rice and
lentils. One got a lot more of the latter, but what were
they unless cooked with a bit of bacon or fat of some kind?
And she was further confused by the sudden memory of a
certain smoking dish of lentils, with shining bits of pork
laid around the edge of the platter, that she had often
served in the old Baden days.

There were a good many people in the shop and not much time for hesitating old ladies to make a final choice. Suddenly, tremblingly, she decided to take the rice, while it was there to take, for quite close to her, overtopping her, stood a large, hook-nosed, hard-eyed befurred woman who was evidently ready to swoop down upon it all. Indeed, she was looking about her with an unmistakable look that could only come from money, a lot of it, in her pocket, as if, indeed, she could buy everybody as well as everything. No eggs, no butter, no fats of any kind were in that shop, but as Frau Stacher was paying for the rice, she suddenly saw on a lower shelf behind the counter an object that, had it been set in gold, could not have been more attractive: a tin of Nestlé's milk. She stammeringly asked for it, but as the man, placing his hand almost affectionately on it, named the exorbitant price, and as trembling with excitement she was about to take it, the large, befurred female cried out harshly:

'I'll give you double what the old woman is paying!'

The man – what decency could be left in that fight for food, for existence? – took it out of Frau Stacher's un-resisting hand. A murmur went up from those watching the unseemly operation. But the shopkeeper only shrugged his shoulders, muttered something about the 'pig' war, the still piggier peace, and the stout woman, hastily paying for it, departed to unmistakable allusions to 'pig profiteers.' That was the kind of world gentle Frau Stacher was living in. It would have been a frightening experience for her, but she, too, was armoured in that

grim determination to get food. The great city's fight
was for food, not against the enemy at the gates, but for
the food that was at the gates, and shoulder to shoulder in
serried lines, they fought for it against each other. She,
Frau Stacher, once 'rentier' in Baden, was fighting for it.
She was lucky to have got even the rice. Leaving the
shop she espied on the street corner a small fruit-stand.
Some shrivelled apples, so evidently grown in the four
winds, were being offered in little piles of five, by a raw-
boned pleasant woman, whose hands were wrapped under
her small, three-cornered grey shawl, while she stamped
from foot to foot.

Frau Stacher remembered longingly the beautiful Tyrolese fruit that had filled the Vienna markets in the days of
plenty. Corinne had lately had a letter from the adopted
daughter Jella, married to her tall, blue-eyed, yellow-
haired, square-headed Tyroler, now Italian, saying that
the fruit that autumn had lain rotting on the ground.
There was no way of getting it over the frontiers, those
invisible but none-the-less impregnable walls that had been
suddenly built up around Vienna, north, south, east and
west. Fruit and grain, sugar and fats could not pass over
them nor get through them.

Now those little apples, even on that raw day, had a
strange fascination for Frau Stacher, out of all proportion
to their merits. They certainly resembled in no way the
full, rosy-cheeked specimens she had been wont to pass
out to visiting nieces and nephews and into which white
teeth would promptly, juicily, crunch, but they were a

reminder, a symbol of them. She longed foolishly once more to see white teeth dig into apples. She bought, hesitatingly, a little pile; obviously she had lost her nerve about shopping for food since it had become a matter of life or death; in the old days she had been a lavish provider. . . . Not much more than a mouthful in each apple, and certainly they wouldn't be nourishing, but Frau Stacher was of a sentimental nature, and the pale, innocent eye she turned upon the fruit grew bluer, softer in expression. The woman, saving her crumpled bits of newspaper, dropped the apples into the string bag and quickly put her hands, swollen with chilblains, again under her shawl.

Then Frau Stacher began to think anxiously of little Carli, the next to the last of Kaethe's children, beautiful, smiling little Carli who had no strength in his legs and whose face was alabaster. Fanny did send condensed milk for Carli, but there was always an urgent reason why one or the other of the children, with a cold or a sore throat or a stomach-ache, should have some of it. She wanted, above all things, to get a can of milk for Carli. Thinking desperately 'Saint Anthony *must* help me,' she found herself outside a small grocery shop. Few of the usual articles for sale in such shops were visible in the dusty window – varnish, boot-blacking, washing-soda and other inedibles safely showed themselves behind the grimy panes. Somewhat dizzily she went in and asked for the milk. She wanted that can of milk more than she had ever wanted anything – wanted it enough, it seemed, to create it out of empty air. The man, to her relief rather than her surprise, reluctantly reached down under the counter and passed it silently out to her, doubtless thinking of his own under-nourished children.

'I knew it,' said Tante Ilde under her breath, and she suddenly found herself delightfully warm as she exercised a truly á propos gratitude to the Heavenly Powers. She was emboldened, too, and almost loftily asked him if he had a can of green peas, she wanted them to put into the rice to make the 'risi-bisi' that the children so loved. Of course he didn't have it and scarcely answered her foolish question. But she espied a very small piece of hard cheese under a very large glass – it was extraordinary how many things there were in the world that you couldn't eat, and how much of them! Then she saw a small package of 'feinste Keks,' with its picture in blue and red of a child eating one in rapture. She took recklessly both cheese and cakes. She knew she had lost her head, and besides, she was feeling quite faint. Buying food in those days, even when one of the Saints visibly stood by, was an exhausting matter. She brightened up, however, as she went out of the shop at the thought that another twenty minutes of putting one foot before the other would inevitably bring her to Kaethe's door, and the heavier the bag the better. . . .

Frau Stacher's ring brought a scurry of young feet to the door; she heard welcoming shouts, 'Tante Ilde's come! Tante Ilde's come!' even before it was opened with a rush. She was smiling a breathless smile, after the stairs and the blessedly heavy bag, as she went in. It was known that she was coming with the dinner, but *what* had she brought? They surrounded her, they embraced her, they overwhelmed her. They were all there save Maxy, whose turn it was to eat his midday meal at the Bellevue Palace, and Lilli not yet back from fetching a few briquettes.

Kaethe was nursing that youngest, rosiest of her children who knew, as yet, only the sweet fullness of her mother's breast. Carli was sitting at her feet, his head hanging listlessly against her knee. He hadn't run with the others to meet Tante Ilde because he couldn't even stand. He would laugh, a sweet, somewhat surprised little laugh when he tried to pull himself up by a chair and would fall down; but his mother always wanted to weep when she heard the soft little thud as he slipped to the floor. Carli was an angel. Carli, quite evidently to any but a mother's eye, was not to pass another winter on earth. Even in the week since Tante Ilde had seen him he had become more and more like something made of crystal, so smooth, so shining, so transparent was his little face. But she concealed the sudden fear that came over her as she looked from him to his mother.

'I'm nursing the baby earlier so I can be ready to help with the dinner,' Kaethe said, as her aunt bent over to kiss her and Anny, – one fat little hand spread out over her mother's breast, and making soft, contented noises, – little Anny, the last, she must be the last of Kaethe's children, Tante Ilde was thinking. . . .

Kaethe wore a frayed, but evidently once expensive, wadded blue silk wrapper. It struck an unexpected note in that denuded room, whose immediate air of indigence was inescapable. Not only was the piano gone, and long since Eberhardt's 'cello, but gone one after the other the pleasant, superfluous tables and the little objects once set out upon them. Even the bookcases. . . . What remained of the books was piled in a corner and received many a careless kick from romping children.

Whenever Frau Stacher entered that room she was confronted by a quite flashy portrait of her mother in the Winterhalter style. It had been sent to Kaethe's for safe-keeping and now hung frameless on the wall. A dealer at the time she sold her furniture had offered her a surprising and unrefusable price for the frame. The young face that looked out at the ageing daughter, though like her in many ways, had a point of competent malice in the wide blue eyes that was neither in her daughter's eyes nor in her heart. Sometimes, too, from under that broad, floppy, rose-trimmed hat with the long pink streamers she seemed to look reproachfully, severely, at her daughter – leaving her elegant prettiness thus unset in so cold a world. Frau Stacher had never felt easy about selling that frame, and she cometimes had useless little night thoughts, or equally useless morning thoughts, of getting another. But it had been hanging just like that since she gave up the house in Baden, near an enlarged photograph (whose pressed wood frame picked out with gilt no one had wanted) of the departed Commercial Advisor. She would gladly have been unfaithful to the memory of her husband, now become exceedingly hazy, anyway, and replaced his image by that of her mother. But her mother's portrait was square, and his photograph unprophetically had been taken in oblong form. Things were like that now. Nothing fitted. . . .

Kaethe got up a moment after her aunt had greeted her and laid the sleeping baby in a battered crib in the next room, filled with beds of all sizes and sorts. *That* child was nourished. She would have felt quite exhausted herself, but for the thought of the dinner Tante Ilde had brought. She was still a handsome woman, in the early thirties – even treading up that Calvary to which every road she knew now led her, those seven roads of anguish for her seven children and for Leo whom she adored. Once, not indeed so long before, she had been softly, sweetly alight with a kindly inner warmth, that flamed easily, attractively, in her face, in those sparkling eyes, in those bright cheeks, hanging about that wide, red-lipped mouth with its irregular white teeth. And then those quick, generous, outward gestures! Now that soft fire was banked and her movements were often listless. But as she stood by the kitchen table, she became animated, even gay, because of that natural gift which neither time, nor wars, nor miseries could quite destroy, and clapped her hands, as her aunt had known she would, and talked about the great feast they were going to have. The water was boiling and bubbling, forecasting near delicious moments, and Tante Ilde had begun to grate the cheese which was sending up its sharp, appetizing odour.

Carli had been put on the table in the very beginning, that he might be nearer than anybody else to the goodies, as Tante Ilde took one package after the other out of the string bag and made them guess what was in it. Kaethe opened the can of milk to prepare a drink for him.

'Hungry,' he said, turning his blue eyes somewhat languidly towards her and shaking his shining curls about his crystal face. They all cried lovingly in one or another way:

'Yes, gold child, yes, angel, yes, little lamb, you'll have some soon!'

'I bought a whole half-kilo of rice,' said Tante Ilde grandly, 'suppose,' she went on dashingly, 'we cook it all at once? We're seven to eat it and we'll put the cheese on thick!'

Kaethe gave a gasp. But she, too, was no saver.

'Magnificent,' she cried. She was faint with hunger herself. Yes, for once . . . then she turned to Carli.

'Carli must drink his mimi,' she said, as she held the cup tenderly to his lips.

The other children looked on absorbed in the spectacle. Resl cried, drawing her breath in:

'Carli's having such a wonderful drink!' And Hansi, with his eyes very big, asked:

'Carli, does it taste good?' and they all hung close about him as he drank in tiny not very hungry sips.

'I'd show Carli how to drink if I had the chance!' continued Hansi, moving his feet up and down in famished impatience.

'I do wish Leo were here to see the children,' said Kaethe to her aunt, 'but he won't be back till past one o'clock, though he goes as early as he can to the Stephansplatz. It's just wonderful to think they're going to have enough. It's seeing them after they've had their dinner that is sometimes the worst.'

A long, impatient ring was heard at the door. Resl ran to open it and Lilli came in with a dash in spite of the broken handle of her basket of briquettes. She threw off the disfiguring coat she wore and revealed herself in a very worn, sea-blue dress of some smooth, silky material. It lay beautifully about the white column of her young neck, it repeated the blue of her wide eyes, it heightened the fine pallor of her cheeks, it burnished the pale gold of her hair. There were gleaming bits of embroidery in places meant to accent the curves of a more mature figure. Quite evidently made-over, too, was the elaborate, dark blue cloth dress that Resl wore. Indeed, they all wore garments or parts of garments quite patently not fulfilling their original *raison d'être* that struck a note of gay luxury in the large shabby room.

Lilli's objective was the kitchen. She was greeted with shouts. The rice was boiling briskly, the odour of the cheese was in the air. The package of 'feinste Keks,' made of a combination of ersatz substances meant to deceive the palate and annoy the stomach, looked gaily, impudently at them beside the little pile of apples. As Lilli took it all in, a tiny line that sometimes showed itself between those lovely eyes was quite smoothed out.

Then Hansi made a diversion by being discovered with the thin rind of the cheese that his mother had put aside for the seasoning of another day's dish.

'What are you doing, Hansi?' she cried and took it from his chubby six-year-old hand.

'But, Mamma, I'm so hungry, I can't wait for the rice,' and tears rose to his eyes, 'I didn't mean anything bad!'

'I know, I know,' his mother answered, those stupid tears that were always ready springing to her own eyes, 'mother didn't mean anything bad either, but whatever we have is for all of us.'

Hansi had dark curls and soft eyes and seemed like the merest baby as he stood looking at her, great round tears rolling down his cheeks. But there was something sturdy about his thinness and pallor, something resistant; Hansi, like Resl, was one who would survive.

Lilli and Resl followed about by Else had put the plates and forks and spoons on the table and drawn up the motley collection of chairs.

'Is everything laid on nice and straight? Tante Ilde has brought us such a good dinner!' their mother called out as she came in with the great smoking platter of rice sending up its maddening odour and placed it heavily on the table. But she turned and kissed her aunt before she began to serve it.

Frau Stacher was conscious of the softest, warmest pleasure. One moment like this and hard things were forgotten. Kaethe's very expansiveness, that could so easily be released, communicated joy. And Kaethe never minded how much noise the children made, so others were undisturbed. Kaethe never fussed, though she sometimes wept and often silently despaired. But now that full platter, those clattering spoons! Though mortals were certainly composed of spirit as well as flesh, hot food, even one meal of it, could change everything. Yes, everything. The children got uproariously gay, and Tante Ilde and Kaethe began to feel sure something would soon happen to make things all right again. . . .

Then Tante Ilde heard how Lilli, instead of her mother, now went out early every morning, too early for her thirteen years, and stood in the bread-line at the bakery (her father had tried it but had proved singularly inept at holding his place), and how you just had to keep your wits about you or you would find that some one had sneaked in ahead and it was such a trouble getting back your place.

There was a certain protocol observed even at those bread-lines. No one with impunity was caught taking another's place, that is unless there was a stampede by those behind if the news got out that there was very little left. Then what a pushing and hustling. Something terrible, hard, relentless would suddenly come up out of the crowd that had seemed composed of pale exhausted men and women and underfed listless children. That precious loaf that Lilli generally managed to bring home, would, with some of the equally precious cocoa that was in the heavenly package they got from the 'Friends' in the Franzensplatz, be the backbone, somewhat weak it is true, of their day. The package and the wonders it contained – the little tin of lard, the little box of sugar, the little bag of flour, the coffee, though it could not fatten a family of nine people, dulled noticeably the sharpest edge of their hunger and helped to get them through the week. It was really equal to several meals if you counted that way. Then sometimes a raven in the shape of old Maria, tapping, flew in at the door. As for the other meals, the Eberhardts went without them.

It was a mystery to the Professor, surpassing any he had ever before tried to solve, that he could no longer make a living out of his grey matter. Being a 'genius' was plainly a misfortune. It was the working classes, fortunate possessors of muscle, that frequented butcher and delicatessen shops, while the intellectuals and their families starved. It made science look like something seen through the big end of a telescope. Biology? Eberhardt got so that he hated the very word. The only science of life that was of any use was knowing how to get something to put into your family's stomach and your own. Naturally mild as summer dew, Eberhardt had been getting bitter.

Those radiant years lay far behind, when a word, a thought would set his brain on fire, startling into instant action those secret springs of his talent; when the imponderable why and whence of man's being was the paramount interest of life. The ponderable things necessary to sustain that life came naturally, undisturbingly in the train of work. Now his gifts were useless; the world in which they had once functioned so easily, so shiningly, was in some chill, shadowy abeyance. Again and again came from his lips nostalgically: 'Süsses Leben! Schöne, freundliche Gewohnheit des Daseins und Wirkens! von dir soll ich scheiden!' Sweet life, sweet, pleasant habit of being and activity! Must I part from thee?'

He went to his classes, but with the laboratory completely run down, sometimes even the electric light didn't work, and that listless, stupid look on the faces of a handful of hungry students, or that wild look, and everywhere the word 'revolution,' there was certainly little incentive and less chance for successful inquiry into those whys and whences, the indulgence in which was gone with other luxuries. The great thing was to keep out of the cemetery or the streets or worse places of last despair, where the broken but undying went. It all seemed a nightmare from which he must awake, some tight and vicious circle out of which he must soon break. Yet this was the seventh year and all that he was, all that he had, those once sweet furnishings of his mind, those pleasant uses of his faculties, were as worthless to himself and his family as diamonds to a man on the rack.

The children got taller and thinner. Lilli was obviously too pretty to be out alone, unwatched. A terrible beast had lately followed her from the Singerstrasse to the Franzensplatz and then all the way home. Lilli hadn't quite known what he meant or wanted, but she had been desperately frightened and had trembled and wept in her mother's arms.

162

There were, truly, devils prowling about, seeking whom they might devour, and Lilli, bright and beautiful like a taper in the dull grey streets, was one to catch their greedy eyes.

Dark tales were whispered too, of hunger-mad mothers who sent their girl-children into the streets where such devils awaited them. Hunger — dying of it — made even mothers mad.

Doctor Steier had told him unbelievable things of children in his clinic, things that the bare mention of had enveloped him in a thick, hot, pricking misery. Doctor Steier was not yet forty, but his eyes were deeply sunken and his hair gone white. They had once been colleagues at the University. . . . Lilli's beauty — it made her father's heart both sad and glad. . . .

But nobody was thinking of any of these things as Tante Ilde opened the package of 'finest cakes.' Stripped of its saucy coloured paper, it proved to contain twelve tiny, oblong, dry, sweetish biscuits. She gaily apportioned out two to each child. They were seized upon covetously, the very thought of sweets could awaken, in old and young, mad, selfish, exclusive longings.

But Carli didn't want his and leaned his head heavily against his mother's breast.

'Carli not hungry any more,' he whispered. He hadn't eaten his rice either, though his mother had taken him on her knees and tried to coax him with little tricks and stories; the girls and Hansi had finally divided it into the most even portions possible

His mother made another cup of milk for him and soaked one of his 'Keks' in it; he had taken a tiny mouthful, then again leaned his head heavily against her breast and seemed to go to sleep. She got up gently and bearing him into the other room laid him on a cot near the rosebud Anny's crib. So dear he was to her as she laid him down, that her heart seemed to come out of her breast in a great beat of love. The only colour in his face was those violet eyes, which now were veiled so thinly by his transparent lids, that standing back from his bed, she thought for an instant they had opened, and that he was looking at her. But he lay so still that in anguish she bent over him to see if the breath were really fluttering from his waxy lips. . . .

When she got back into the living-room that look, mask-like, antique, of mother-fear still lay upon her face.

Tante Ilde softly rose from the table and stood by her without a word. 'It will be all right in a moment,' Kaethe said looking up at her gratefully. 'It is silly, of course, to be so frightened,' and she kissed the thin hand that hung over her shoulder.

A moment later there was heard the well-loved sound of the latch key, but somewhat slow, uncertain even. Lilli ran quickly to open the door.

Her father was not, as she expected, alone. A miserable little girl of five or six was clinging to his hand, a pale, anxious child that the wintry monster Life had been grimacing at and frightening terribly.

Professor Eberhardt gave his wife one look, but he knew his Kaethe, and it was a look of confidence rather than anxiety that he bent upon her as he stood in the doorway — a tall, once very handsome man, who had been mangled by the War, then stamped on by the Peace till he had lost all semblance to his former imposing self. His grey eyes were sunken into deep pits on either side of his thin, pinched nose. The blond beard and moustache had had the yellow taken out of them by the early grey of his griefs and anxieties. But as he stood there, his shabby overcoat buttoned up to his chin, some brightness lay about his face; it seemed for the moment quite filled out.

'I met Koellner coming back,' he said to his wife, and then he bent gently over the child, 'This is his dear, good little girl come to make the children a visit.'

Something rose up in Kaethe, admonishing her to defend her own. Another child! no, no, no. . . . But turn that frightened, shivering mite away? It was equally impossible to the elastic kindness of her heart.

It was a situation that in the end beings like the Eberhardts meet in but one way. When that which they have not has been taken from them, they find that they have still something left that they must give.

There was no doubt about its all being a shock to Kaethe, rather than a surprise. She couldn't be surprised by another sight of misery, even though brought up round before it. . . . Her eyes filled with those weak, ever-ready tears, then she smiled quiveringly. At that smile for

which he had waited, entirely trustful, Eberhardt turned
to Lilli:

'Take Marichi into the kitchen, darling, and find her
a bite of something.'

The children suddenly quite still, had been looking at
the little girl. Resl thought she wasn't too dirty, and
Hansi that she was of a convenient age to order about.
Else didn't understand.

Lilli's thoughts were confused, only out of that confusion seemed to come some sudden, new understanding.
In that moment, indeed, Lilli grew from childhood into
adolescence. She silently reached out her hand and
received the little girl from her father. She gave him a
long look as she did so. Something quite beyond the scope
even of her new understanding, though within reach of
her new feelings, was happening. Something hard to do,
yet in another way fluidly, hotly easy. As she was turning away, the child's hand in hers, she hesitated, then went
back and threw her arms about her father's neck. Eberhardt had a moment almost of ecstasy as he pressed his
lovely daughter close to him in some suddenly opened
heaven on earth. Then she withdrew herself from his
embrace and took the child out of the room.

'It's a desperate case,' Eberhardt said to his wife after
a moment's silence, 'her mother has just died – consumption – and he's starving himself. He knows a waiter at
the Hotel Imperial who gives him some bread every day
. . . poor fellow, I was all broken up, so talented too;
his clothes, only hanging on him, no overcoat, just buttons

his jacket up to his neck. I told him about the Stephans-platz. He had a look on his face I didn't like. He was so worried for his little girl. They've lost their rooms; I didn't quite understand how. Anyway they've nowhere to go. Kaethe, I couldn't but say to him, "Let us take the little one for awhile," we *have* a home,' he ended.

Kaethe met his gaze quite clearly now. Those stupid, weak tears were gone. She was thinking, and he knew it as if she had spoken the words: 'Every crumb that child eats will be taken from our own children.' But Kaethe, inflammable herself, had caught from her husband some of that light that shone about his face and after a second she was saying, and warmly:

'But naturally, she can stay here till things get better.'

Both Eberhardt and his wife were very beautiful in that moment wrapped in the bright flame of their charity.

Just why he had met his old friend Koellner in the street that noontide was quite clear. It wasn't for anything that he, in his own great need was to get out of it, but rather for what the child whose Father in Heaven knew that she had 'need of all these things' was to get – in that hour and in that way.

Then Tante Ilde, who had been both entranced and troubled at the scene, spoke for the first time and very gently:

'She'll bring a blessing into the house, Leo.'

At that Eberhardt turned and greeted her affectionately.

'Ah, Tante Ilde, pardon, it's good to see you.' And as he embraced her his act of compassion was still so warm about him that she was conscious of some gentle heat, almost corporeal, emanating from him.

Though his now constant preoccupation as to ways and means was added to those temperamental fits of abstraction, suddenly in that moment he saw distinctly the shape and substance of Tante Ilde's hard destiny. That frail figure, in that worn striped gown, Eberhardt who never knew what women wore, was suddenly conscious of its old-fashioned cut, its threadbareness, perhaps it was its symbolic sense working on his imagination that saw at times both more and less than the run of men. He perceived, as under a microscope, in all its magnified significance, not alone that sagging face, that furrowed brow, that thinning hair, those broad, pale, colourless eyes reflecting something immeasurably patient under the double burden of old age and penury, but it was old age itself, in all its component parts that separated, as if under his glass, on his table, resolving themselves sharply into their elements. He was aghast at what he saw – those diminutions, those with-drawals – more horrified than at the accidental tragedy of the Privatdozent Koellner. This was integral, final. She could hope for nothing more from time, that was clear – time that brings so surely both good and evil, that very time that was his hope had nothing more for her. He repressed a cry. . . .

Then suddenly, or so it seemed, they all got very gay again, with an infectious gaiety. The children were tumbling about noisily after their good meal. The little stranger kept looking from one to the other. That desperate apprehension was wiped from her face. This that was happening was clearly good. She hadn't seen anyone smile for a long time, except so sadly that they might as well have wept. She had entirely forgotten about laughing. But all this was good, good, that she knew out of her six years.

Then Hansi climbed up on his father's lap and asked him what he had had for dinner.

'A fine cup of cocoa, so hot it burnt my tongue, and a heaping plate of very good beans, only I didn't feel hungry to-day,' he paused on the familiar phrase, and from his pocket he produced two pieces of zwieback.

Kaethe had been watching him, suspecting his next gesture.

'Eat it yourself, Leo,' she interposed quickly, almost sternly, 'we've had all we can possibly eat. Tante Ilde brought *so* much.'

But Eberhardt, with no hesitation in his hand or heart, or at least none that one could have noticed, said to the strange child, the child of whose existence he had been unaware an hour before:

'Come, dear child, come, Marichi,' and handed her the zwieback. That grimy, claw-like little hand closed over it. In spite of her hunger she was too dazed to eat. She looked from her hand up to her protector with the mysterious glance of childhood.

'It's good, eat it,' he said. She put it in her mouth, one piece and then, very quickly, the other. Hunger, she knew about it, all about it. This was something different and she was getting warm.

The silence that fell somewhat heavily upon the room, was broken by Hansi recounting to his father, boastfully, stoutly, what they had had for dinner, and smacking his lips and showing him the coloured picture from the package of 'feinste Keks'; then how Carli hadn't wanted his rice and how they had had that too.

'Carli isn't well to-day,' said Kaethe, 'he seems so languid, but he's asleep now. He dropped off as soon as he had had his milk.'

'I'm coming every Thursday,' put in Tante Ilde comfortably at this point. She was feeling quite happy, almost joyous. 'Fanny,' she added in an aside, 'sent word by Maria that I was always to get enough for everybody!'

Eberhardt flushed slightly but made no answer. Lilli and Resl were getting on their coats. As Lilli again put on her mother's old black cloak over her blue dress it was as if a snuffer had been put over a light – a white, blue and gold light. Her father was content that it was so. About Resl they didn't worry. There was something strong, inevitable about her, even in those young years. She was clearly one who would get through. She was very like her mother, but behind that soft, dark resemblance was something steely that Kaethe had never had.

Things were always happening to Resl – pleasant things. Those bright-dark eyes of hers, that round, smiling face that somehow kept its roundness through all those terrible winters, had something compelling about it. An American woman on one of the relief committees had seen Resl on a windy day looking into a delicatessen shop, and had taken a fancy to her. She had given her a meal a day for two months, and shoes and other things, often something to take home, then she had passed out of Resl's orbit into new circles of want. Another time coming home from school, Resl had stopped to swell the crowd around a smashed taxicab, and some one had cried, 'Do look at that bright-eyed little girl!' and had given her a ten-shilling note — just like that! She hadn't understood what they said, but their smiles that she promptly returned and the money that she dashed home with were perfectly intelligible. Once she had found a gold piece in the street, when she and Lilli were going along together: of course she had been the one to find it. Lilli, when she saw Resl pick it up, had hoped that it had been dropped by some very rich person, instead of by some one who hadn't anything else. To Resl, however, such fears were unknown, she would always take unquestioningly whatever goods the gods provided.

Tante Ilde was telling them about the woman who had grabbed the milk out of her very hand, and Hansi was saying with his chest out and his eyes ablaze:

'I'd have beaten her well, Tante Ilde,' when they heard a scream from the next room — a terrible scream, despair and supplication were in it.

Eberhardt and Tante Ilde rushed in, followed by the children, Marichi stayed behind, cowering again. That scream had something frighteningly familiar about it.

Kaethe was holding Carli up to the window, where the light shone full on his baby face . . . quite gently, quite easily, Carli had slipped from them leaving only his little waxen image.

.   .   .   .

Throughout that long night Tante Ilde kept miserably repeating to herself: 'A child came in, a child went out,' finding herself in a confusion of faith and doubt dark as the night that lay about her.

Irma was confirmed in her opinion that charity was dangerous.

VI

CORINNE

A la Sourdine   Das Herz ist
                                   ein weites Land.

*

BUT towards morning Frau Stacher's heart threw off its
sorrow; she had suddenly felt its weight leaving her breast,
why or how she did not know, for there in that distant
house whence Carli had for ever gone one she loved was
still weeping. Perhaps she was done with grief – long
grief.

She was strangely all love that morning after the night
of tears. Love emanated from her with a gentle radiance
and played about her warmly. She loved even Irma. Even
Irma who on account of her nerves couldn't bear to see that
fine, soft light in her sister-in-law's eyes. An unreasonable,
unseasonable light given the fact that one child had been
reft away and another might as easily be taken. She should
properly have been creeping about with her spirit quenched,
instead of looking almost happy. It struck Irma, who was
inaccessible to metaphysical changes, even as unseemly,
and she proceeded to extinguish it, somewhat as a wet
finger on the flame of a candle.

'Corinne to-day, but who's taking you to-morrow?' she
asked flatly, meanly. Irma had a way, well tabulated in
the family, of getting over pleasant spots at the quickest
pace possible.

'To-morrow,' Tante Ilde answered, the light in her
eye indeed put out, but her face quite pink as she stepped

into the kitchen to put the broom, worn down to its wooden handle, back in its dingy corner, 'To-morrow,' she continued resolutely as she reappeared, 'I'm going to Fanny's.'

'To Fanny's!' echoed Irma blankly, and started to cry 'I find it disgraceful!' But she stopped quite short as a thought came to her. . . . The easy way to do a hard thing. A little more of *that* money! What did she care? She wanted Ferry to live.

'Won't you tell Fanny about Ferry?' she began again, but gently, almost imploringly.

There was a long pause, in which the thick-boned figure of the woman her brother had loved loomed up before her in an imperative, almost menacing attitude as she waited for the answer. She had been bending closely over the hemstitching she was to finish that day for Mizzi. She had large, square-shaped hands, but she held deftly and delicately the diaphanous trifle that Mizzi would sell to some thick lady. Now she laid it down and took off her glasses, showing her eyes very strained. Her face seemed to broaden, her cheek bones to get higher, the spot of colour on her cheeks was dyed deeper, harder. Everything was accented about Irma in that minute. Even the red of the little, fringed, three-cornered shawl was like life-blood spilled over her shoulders as she waited for her sister-in-law to answer, and there was something increasingly minatory about her.

Strange, Frau Stacher was thinking, that Heinie should have desired her, Heinie almost an old man. But she couldn't really reason about such things, certainly not in that pause. Her thoughts had wandered because she was feeling quite dizzy and then, of course, she would do it. Irma might have known that. Those three boys had to be helped somehow into manhood, according to their needs. A generation lay between the two women, yet for a moment Irma, with that ancient mother-fierceness in her face, seemed the elder. She continued staccato:

'Ferry's got to go to the mountains. Fanny can send him if she will. Fanny's rich. Fanny's in the only good business for women in Vienna.'

Frau Stacher felt the blood rush to her face. But it was pity for Irma that suddenly reddened her cheeks rather than shame for Fanny. All the pity of her heart for a moment spent itself lavishly on that unloved sister-in-law.

'It's one of the reasons I'm going — for Ferry. I'd thought of it too, and to-morrow you know it is Fanny who is taking us all — with Carli, to the cemetery,' she answered finally with an immense gentleness. In her heart she handed that business of Fanny's to God, and she hoped He wouldn't take His price for it.

Irma suddenly broke into wild weeping.

'Don't speak to me about Carli again. I can't bear it. *My* Ferry, *my* son, *my* first born, *he* must live.'

Then she tried to stop weeping. Those hot, salty tears that were scalding and dimming her eyes were an indulgence she could ill afford.

'Tell Fanny everything about Ferry, help him not to go where Carli has gone,' and she stepped quite close to her sister-in-law, her hands clasped. 'You are truly good,' she found herself unexpectedly, even softly, ending.

Then Frau Stacher, warm with a love that was not for Irma, but whose warmth spread infinitely, embraced her, saying:

'Don't weep, Irma, we'll surely arrange about our Ferry.'

The two women spoke no more. Irma's sobs turned into long, quivering sighs and her sister-in-law soon after slipped out.

Somewhat reproachfully the thought came to Irma that Tante Ilde did, perhaps, bring a blessing into the house and that she, Irma, had needlessly wiped away the look of happiness on her face. They all knew that she adored Corinne. Why couldn't she have let her have her pleasure, which was certainly not costing her, Irma, anything? And she remembered how broken her look and voice had been as she told about Carli the day before. Then repentantly almost, she thought that, after all, Tante Ilde couldn't be comfortable in that little alcove, though as she didn't know about the need of being alone, she couldn't understand just how uncomfortable. Then she thought that she would not ask her to draw back the curtains. She even fell to planning how when Ferry went away she would put Gusl to sleep in the alcove and give the little room to his aunt. Hermann had terrified her by saying that Gusl ought not to sleep any longer with Ferry – was it really as bad as that? That was one of the things that made it a further nuisance having Tante Ilde. Then

176

suddenly with the whole wild strength of her being, the strength of untamed generations living by the wild Plitvicer Lakes, she thrust her arms out and would have burst the too-narrow walls of that dwelling, made room, room, the way one had room there where she was born – out of the terrible city.

.   .   .   .

Frau Stacher got out to find the sun shining on the slippery streets, still covered, from the cold rain of the night, with a thin, glass-like substance. She went cautiously, slowly along. From St. Stephen's half-past eleven was sounding. She had plenty of time. Then she became aware again of a new and evil discomfort that had made itself felt from time to time that morning; not at all the usual undernourished, discouraged feeling, but as if something inimical, foreign to her body, had got into her circulation; unpleasant little shivers kept running up and down her back. She was relieved, however, for the moment of the weight of her penury. Corinne truly loved her. Corinne truly wanted her to live. She knew *that*, knew it as she knew that she existed. Corinne, lovely, loving Corinne. She could have sung a hymn to her. She crossed the Revolutionsplatz. It was still a little too early to go to the restaurant Zur Stadt Brunn where she was to meet Corinne at noon – and perhaps find herself alone in the restaurant with her empty purse, if anything happened to prevent Corinne from coming. No, she couldn't have borne any such 'blamage.' She was timid about so many of the most usual things. She then crossed the Lobkowitz

Place, looking, for an unrelated instant, up at the Lobkowitz Palace – long the French Embassy. She had once
been used to read eagerly about Royalty and the 'First
Society' going to receptions there, their titles, their
decorations, their gowns, and how their jewels shone in
the great marble ballroom; – now past, all past – both for
them to do and for her to enjoy. She slipped falteringly
down the street to go into the Augustinian church. She
wanted to pray for Corinne – that Corinne might have
her happiness. But Corinne's happiness was a tangled
affair. Corinne's happiness could only come through
Anna's death, and how wish the death of any being? As
she knelt down she found that she had to put from her the
thought that human destinies resemble hot peas jumping
about in a pan – no more meaning than that. Then her
heart repented the wickedness of her thought and she
was able to put it from her, and to pray that, as it was
quite evident that she, Ildefonse Stacher, could not be
trusted with a little happiness, the Lord might in some
way trust Corinne with it. Then she prayed for Carli,
though Carli, bright among the angels, needed no prayers
. . for Kaethe, Leo, Hermann, Ferry – Fanny.

Her knees were trembling as she knelt, and she felt a
deathly cold, a grey cold, it seemed to her, like that of the
stones of the high-vaulted church. She got up stiffly.
Noon was sounding from the tower as she passed the
marble tomb of one of Maria Theresa's daughters, so
beloved by her sorrowing husband. She herself might well
have taken position among the carved, grey, mourning

figures that stood before the entrance to the tomb, so drooping, so shade-like was she.

As she went out the terrible, mumbling old man with sore eyes held open the door for her; the pale, young cripple who stood by him didn't move when he saw that spectre of genteel poverty. So many just like that went in and out of the church. They had no more to give than he himself. . .

The sun for a moment was fairly flooding the winter streets; they shone in bright splashes of wetness. She stepped across the road into the doorway of the restaurant. To enter a restaurant again! Such a simple thing, she'd been doing it all her life. She felt like a fish suddenly thrown back into its own waters.

Corinne was crossing the street. The light was very white and dazzlingly enveloped her slender swaying figure. How sweetly, softly her blue eyes shone as she approached.

'My little Dresden-china auntie!' she cried, and kissed her right there in the doorway. Then they passed in, and made their way to a table.

'For three,' said Corinne, 'a gentleman is coming. Shall we wait a moment, Auntie dear, before ordering?' she asked as they sat down.

Now the smell of the small, fresh rolls that the waiter was counting out, somewhat as he would once have counted gold, and three of which he had put on their table, made Frau Stacher suddenly quite faint, but the feeling was so familiar and she was so happy to be there with Corinne that she only said:

'But naturally,' knowing, too, for whom they waited, and her eyes looked more deeply into Corinne's than she herself was aware of.

Corinne glanced away with that oblique glance that could veil her thoughts more completely than fallen lids. She flushed slightly.

When Tante Ilde spoke again it was to say:

'I just missed you last night. I was again at Kaethe's, only a few minutes after you had gone. . . . Fanny was there.' She leaned heavily against the table and continued, 'I couldn't bear not to go back. We mustn't weep for Carli,' but all the same tears filled her eyes and Corinne's own were wet.

No, truly she knew one needn't weep for Carli, but she felt so stupidly weak, there in that warm room with an abundant repast about to be served to her; she leaned more heavily against the table, she wanted terribly her soup, but after her way she said nothing and was able to continue, as she broke off a piece of her roll and began to eat it:

'Kaethe's grieving for Carli just as if he were her only child,' and both childless women, soft as their hearts were, looked at each other, not quite understanding.

'You ought to see the wreath of white roses that Fanny brought and coffee and cake. She was so sweet. She kissed Kaethe, in that way of hers . . . you know, and when she knelt by Carli she wept as if her heart was going to break. She was always so fond of children when she was a girl. She would kneel awhile by Carli and then she

180

would come back to Kaethe. She kept saying she should have done more, that she was a wretch, a monster, you know how she is, and it ended by Kaethe's comforting *her*. I made coffee for them all.'

'I thought she'd go when she knew,' began Corinne slowly, to add suddenly as a child, with a wondering look: 'Tante Ilde, I don't understand anything about anything.'

Though her aunt returned her gaze, there was no answer in it. She didn't understand the least beginning of anything either.

'I'm going to Fanny's for dinner to-morrow,' she said at last picking up the thought at its only concrete point. And this time there was no blush in her face. Why always blush about Fanny?

'To Fanny's to-morrow?' Corinne echoed quickly and turned a deep scarlet, the colour flooding her face to disappear under the low brim of her hat. Tante Ilde at Fanny's! It was the ultimate disorder in their upset world, the rest of them, yes, any, all of them if need be, but not Tante Ilde. There was something snow-white about Tante Ilde. Threescore years and ten in a grimy world had left on her no slightest smirch, and even now in the process of her despoilment she was at times blindingly white. That whiteness was the one ornament she still wore and it became her exceedingly.

'You can't, you mustn't,' said Corinne slowly after a moment.

'I can, I must,' answered Tante Ilde firmly, finding herself suddenly in a new position, for the other side of both good and evil. 'She didn't want me to – at first – but I begged her so. She brought me back from Kaethe's in a taxi last night. Corinne, I *knew* when I went there again that I was going to be brought back, that I wouldn't have to walk, though I couldn't know it would be Fanny. . . . She threw her arms around me and wept and said she was miserable herself, that she would be better off dead.'

Neither of the two women let themselves wonder what her griefs were . . . Fanny's griefs. . . .

'I thought to-morrow you would go to some nice little café or just buy something for yourself and eat it at Irma's,' continued Corinne, lamely for one so generally adequate.

'Perhaps another time,' answered her aunt with an involuntary gesture of putting the chalice from her as Corinne spoke of Irma. It was her nearest approach to complaint, but Corinne quite knew what it meant.

'Except for Carli it hasn't *all* been too bad?' she questioned entreatingly.

'No, no, indeed, truly. Only I've seen so much, Inny,' she answered, saying the baby name for Corinne, so long unused, 'so much of – of human beings,' she ended quite detachedly, and her eyes got very wide and wandered a little.

'Irma is hard, I know,' and Corinne put her hand out to find her aunt's, to hold her attention, 'but she has that alcove and I thought, too, it would be a way to help the boys. I'm always worrying about the boys, and

182

then it's almost impossible to find a place to lay one's head.'

'The foxes of the earth,' began Tante Ilde with a still stranger look on her face, and then stopped.

Corinne was overcome by a quick anguish. Something was hurting her terribly, though she couldn't have said which one of many things, and her aunt was suddenly as some one she had never known.

Tante Ilde had always had her little phrases and mottoes – but not like that. 'Time brings roses,' she would say consolingly to any child who was unhappy in the old days. 'Hard work in youth is sweet rest in old age,' when the boys wouldn't study; and she often reminded the girls that 'Beauty goes, but virtue stays.'

'You're looking so pale, darling, you're not ill, are you?' Corinne asked, after a moment breaking anxiously into that new, disturbing silence.

'No, just a little cold, my shoulders ache a bit – then all the tears,' she answered, 'nothing more.'

'Are you warmly enough dressed?' pursued Corinne, after another pause during which her eyes had wandered again to the door.

'Oh yes, I have on two waists,' and she smiled weakly.

'I believe you're faint for food,' said Corinne at last, with a strange, burning look on her face, 'we won't wait for Pauli, we'll have our soup right now,' and she called the waiter.

It was still early and few people were in the restaurant, the waiters mostly standing idly around, smoothing their hair or flicking their serving-napkins about as they talked, but it seemed to Frau Stacher an eternity before the order was taken and another endless period till the soup was brought and the waiter poured it hotly, appetizingly, from the smoking metal cup into her plate. The first spoonful did its blessed work and the palest shade of pink came into her face. It seemed more delicious than anything she had ever tasted, and she pitied all poor creatures who felt as she had been feeling and were not, like her, sitting before a steaming plate of bean soup.

'It's the tears and the fatigue, and perhaps a bit of a cold coming on,' thought Corinne as she, too, partook gratefully of her soup, quite ready for it after her three hours at the bank, working at those interminable billions that threatened to run into trillions. Life at the bank was now composed of seemingly countless zeroes, orgies of zeroes, and often a fine headache after.

As they took their soup, with what remained of their rolls, they ceased to mourn for Carli . . . something bright and beautiful that had been and was no more. . . . They didn't try, either, to look into the wherefores and whys of Fanny's existence, neither its splendours nor its miseries, though as Tante Ilde was taking her last spoonful of soup she leaned across the table and said, a confidential note in her voice, something deprecatory, too:

'Last night the boys didn't wake up, but Lilli and Resl kept peeping in at the door while Fanny was there. They followed me into the kitchen when I was making coffee and asked about "Tante Fanny"; if I'd noticed how sweet her furs smelt and if I'd heard how her bracelets tinkled, she wears a lot of bracelets, broad bands of jewels that jingle and glitter. Lilli wanted to know who her husband was and Resl said, "Ssh, she hasn't any," ' ended Tante Ilde with a sigh. But Corinne had ceased to listen, inherently fascinating as the theme of Fanny's bracelets was, for behind that pale waiting she was in a turmoil. Suddenly she flushed and then as suddenly grew white.

Pauli was standing at the door looking about. In a moment he was beside them and as he sat down in that eager way of his, life seemed to stream from him, more than he needed for himself, something overflowing, always something to give.

He was just as kind to Tante Ilde as to Corinne. She didn't feel a bit in the way . . . for once . . . like that. She was again in a world where, given enough to eat and a warm place to eat it in, human beings still loved and longed for each other, not simply for food and shelter. A whole cityful of human beings with hearts and brains as well as stomachs thinking solely about what they were going to eat! It suddenly seemed a terrible waste to her . . . in a world where there was love, beauty, wisdom, hidden, lost though they might be.

The waiter was standing by them with his pad in his hand waiting for the ladies to decide or for the gentleman to decide for them. Nothing like that had happened to Frau Stacher since the winter before she lost her income. The soup had put new life into her, and if it hadn't been for that vaguely evil thing she felt in her veins, she would have been almost her own gentle, pleasing, easy self again.

'Don't look only at the prices, Tanterl,' Pauli was saying with his smile that so easily became a laugh. 'How about half a young chicken with rice for each?' he suggested lavishly, surprised to find it there on the otherwise meagre list.

'Oh, Pauli, how reckless! If we're going to have *meat*, boiled beef would be nice.' Indeed, to Frau Stacher, desperately needing the stimulus of meat — any kind would have done, though the boiled beef she humbly suggested didn't inhabit the Paradise where young chickens abided, eternally cut in two waiting to be cooked and eaten.

'But not at all!' he cried, 'we're going to have a feast,' and he gave the order for the chicken and asked for the wine-card, selecting an Arleberger, that a friend in Budapest made a specialty of

Tante Ilde felt vaguely, pleasantly like a woman in a romance, interesting but unreal. It wasn't only the food, but that looking at the menu and ordering right out of the heart of it, without other guide than what was the best. It conjured up the agreeable ghosts of those far-off comfortable years; and then to be carried along on that stream of love and immediate affection. She blessedly forgot the dark depths of those waters that surged about Pauli and Corinne. .

'Next week, if you insist, we can be less grand,' Pauli was saying, 'boiled beef then, and the week after no meat at all. That's the way it goes in Vienna now,' he continued cheerfully. And then Corinne in her pleasant way of alluding to pleasant things said:

'Auntie, you remember the "marinierter" carp you used to give us at Baden on Friday?'

Frau Stacher flushed at this, that was like a blow on memory, but she only said with a retrospective look:

'Yes, Frieda did do it well – and the Fogosch, too,' she added. In those days the beautiful blue Danube had seemed to fill one of its natural uses in supplying her table with that, her favourite fish. But it all seemed strangely uninteresting to her. She was trying vainly to keep her thoughts, so unaccountably, so uncomfortably wandering, close within her body, within that pleasant room from which all three of them must too soon depart.

Pauli's love was almost visibly enfolding Corinne, just as his affection was flowing about Tante Ilde. So different the two, as different and distinct as two primary colours, yet blending. She felt wrapped in something warm and many-coloured, and what its pattern was she no longer tried to see. Then suddenly and anxiously she was aware that there was still the transparency about Corinne that, as she watched her approach that morning, she thought had come up from the wet shining streets, but there in the warm dark restaurant it was the same. . . .

Her likeness to Fanny, too, was very apparent, there were but two years in time between them . . . though so many other things. . . . She had never noticed it so clearly, not even when they were children. The same blue eyes, with their sudden oblique look; in Corinne it was disturbing, in Fanny devastating. The same pale shining hair, the same fine nose; only in Fanny all was more accented, more complete. Her eyes were bigger and bluer, her hair yellower and thicker, her complexion more dazzling, the oval of her face more perfect. Yet Corinne. . . . her face had not indeed the glitter of Fanny's blinding noonday beauty, but its moonbeam charm was for ever working its own pale magic. . . .

Then the half chicken for each with its little round mound of rice was brought on, and though Pauli took out his glass to look at his, and speculated on the evidently not distant hour of its hatching, still it was quite delicious, and that shining gravy over the rice!

'I'm speculating in everything,' he continued vigorously, 'I've joined the Black Bourse Brigade, it's where you pick up trillions,' and with an airy gesture he pulled out a wallet and showed Tante Ilde some magic-working dollars and some potent English pounds, but which last in a subtle way gave place to the noisier charm of the dollars.

'Everybody speculates,' he went on, 'the lift-boys in the hotels, the porters at the stations, the old women selling newspapers. Everybody. It's in the air.'

Then, as they were finishing the last of the rice and gravy, with little crumbs of bread added so that not a bit should be lost, Corinne gave voice slowly to what she had in mind, looking narrowly, slantingly, at Pauli:

'Tante Ilde is going to Fanny's to-morrow for her dinner.'

'To Fanny's to-morrow?' he questioned in an astonishment that caused Tante Ilde's face to flush a deep rose. To Pauli's way of thinking, though a good many things were done, certain others weren't. Tante Ilde's going to Fanny's clearly fell under the latter head. Saints and sinners were mostly all the same to him. One could rarely tell which was which, anyway, but somehow this . . .

'Fanny is so good to us – I don't think she always has it – as easy as it seems,' she faltered, feeling quite uncomfortable, not because she was going, but because of Pauli's strange look.

'Fanny *is* a good fellow,' he answered slowly, reflectively, but he looked at neither of the women as he spoke. The fact was that for all his experience of men and matters Pauli himself had come to a point where he didn't understand anything any more than they did. Life was for him, as for them, one great confusion. Except his terrible need for Corinne, clear, urgent, urgent beyond any words. . . . But now this picture of Tante Ilde at Fanny's! Tante Ilde shining white, Tante Ilde who thought that all wolves were lambs inside and even in process of being devoured scarcely perceived their true nature. Life was, indeed, presenting itself in its most unreasonable and confounding aspect. 'Much will be forgiven her because she has loved much,' was all right for everything except just this . . . or if a daughter had been in question. Then he tried honestly to think, not according to that feeling that had leapt up in him at Corinne's words, but according to his usual way of easy judgment.

'Fanny has a gold heart, I can't tell you not to go,' he

hesitated, 'she deserves it,' he finished at last, but evidently against the grain. Pauli was really very ill at ease at that special manifestation of the disorder of their world. *Where* were your feet and where your head? Tante Ilde at Fanny's! What, after all, did it mean? All kinds of saints in the world, he knew. Still it was a pity, among a thousand other pities. Indeed, Pauli was shocked in a way that neither of the women were. Pauli, to whom nothing human was foreign, was shocked at a little thing like Tante Ilde's going to Fanny's, when everybody, everywhere, was up against real death and destruction – a detail like that and he who had seen everything was not only shocked but horrified. Riddle. Riddle. Then suddenly he changed the conversation and pulled out his wallet again, crying, without any noticeable preamble:

'Tante Ilde must have a presentli!'

Uncomfortably he felt that the special problem confronting them had grown out of material ruin; lack of security was, after all, regulating that situation. In a word, when you didn't have money you did a lot of things that you didn't do when you had it. It was as plain and as stupid as that. . . . It put decency on an indecent footing or vice versa. And morality – why, morality positively had its legs in the air.

What little he could do for Tante Ilde wouldn't be enough to give her existence a basis. He knew what he could do for her and what not. Life was now a small sheet on a big bed and whichever end was pulled, somebody was left bare.

Corinne gave Pauli one of her palely flashing looks that always left him blinded as he laid those bank-notes by Tante Ilde's plate, almost in among the bare bones of the chicken. He had a strange expression on his face, something final that made Tante Ilde suddenly and terribly anxious, as he returned it.

'Oh, Pauli dear, you spoil me,' she only said tremulously, glancing from him to Corinne, whose look like some slow-turning beacon was now shining upon her. But still she was anxious with a grim, new anxiety. Corinne's danger was so clearly imminent.

Then that fear, too, passed; her existence seemed but a long street, with figures appearing and disappearing, signs and symbols were quickly flashed before her and too quickly gone for understanding. It was the processional of life that she was aware of for the first time. Then again things shifted and passed, and she found she was happy, not because of the money, though that was pleasant enough, but quite simply because she was warm and nourished and loved. She couldn't, in that moment, accept further calamities, nor even look at the shadows they cast before them. . . .

Then with that money on the table, they turned quite inevitably to the everlasting subject of Exchange, which was plunging to unfathomable depths, and the whole population headlong after it.

But Frau Stacher for the moment continued to feel pleasantly distant from the abyss, and as the sounds of those once almost unreckonable sums flowed over her ears, she caught again the agreeable 'rentier' feeling of happier days. Corinne could talk in figures, too, from the vantage-ground of the Depositen Bank. She was doing well; next year she expected to be doing better. 'Then,' she looked lovingly at her aunt, 'I will hunt for that tiny, tiny apartment.'

'Next year!' interrupted Pauli, not included in the heaven Corinne's words evoked, and so deep was the longing in his voice, in his words, that Frau Stacher bent her eyes quickly upon her plate.

He put his hand out over Corinne's. She was flushing and paling under his touch; his dark, unexpectedly small hand had, on the little finger, a thick gold ring in which was sunk a turquoise turned very green. That ring was somehow like Pauli. Colour, Pauli loved it – and yet in moonbeam Corinne with no more colour than the palest opal, than a pearl, lay all his desire.

Frau Stacher had long since forgotten what being in love was like, the love of man for woman, perhaps she had never known, but suddenly it seemed clear, the pulsing mystery of such love, and she was very frightened. Just Pauli's hand over Corinne's made it clear, much clearer than his words, than his tone even, as he cried:

'Oh, Corinne, if everything were different, save you and I – and Tante Ilde! If I could only take you and care for you, never let you go to an office again – and always dress you in silver, Corinne, Corinne!'

'Next year,' Corinne was repeating slowly. Her look was very oblique and distant, and her face was suddenly pale, though quite bright – as if consumed to pale, hot ashes in the look Pauli bent upon her, consumed to last resistance.

Between these two looks Frau Stacher was suddenly crushed; she could scarcely breathe, another intolerable distress came to join that pain in her chest.

Would they hold out, those two who loved each other so, hold out in the dark grim city that now took heed of little save food? Would they build themselves a house without foundations, in a nameless street, above ruins? Or would Corinne wander alone till her sunset, homeless as a cloud? . . .

Then Frau Stacher became aware of a great exhaustion. The life-force had done with her, was slipping from her body, she could feel it retreating, something finally, inexorably destructive taking its place. . . . But those two in whom it surged so high, so hot? . . .

It was over. And how is anyone to know that something has happened for the last time until the irrecoverable afterwards? Corinne had, indeed, sweetly said good-bye to her aunt, brightly, warmly, visibly leaving her, as always, the gift of her love. But every fibre was straining towards Pauli as she slipped away, a shadow palely gold about the head, attenuated to last expression in the black sheath of her coat. Pauli (how pale, too, as he watched her disappear) was going back to the Travel Bureau he so ably managed, seeing to it that 'Protection' and favouritism were practised to their fullest extent for those travellers who could pay for them. . . . Pauli who spoke all known languages; Pauli who could conjure up special trains from the void; Pauli who smoothed the way incredibly for foreign millionaires come to see for themselves how things really were in Vienna, or for indigenous exchange lords who knew the time had come to travel; Pauli, to whom almost everything seemed easy. . . . 'Get Birbach to attend to it' was the peace phrase that replaced the references to his luck during the war. Nothing was too good – or too bad – for those that could pay for it. On the other hand, Pauli was often impelled to do something for those who couldn't pay. Lately, too, he had been drawn into politics, trying to help leash those dogs of destruction let loose upon his country. He was found to have something hotly convincing in his talk, or he could pierce an adversary with a thin point of ridicule that would make his listeners laugh till their sides ached. It wasn't a meal, but it certainly warmed them, and Pauli was always sure of a full house. But now that love for Corinne had begun to waste him, to crumble his other interests and activities. His strength, his time were mostly spent madly, hotly hoping for something, anything, out of the void whence events come – the void known to every longing heart. Pauli was temperamentally aware of the fluidity of life – for all except the very old, *they* were caught like fragile shells in the hard stratum of age. It was one of the reasons for his tenderness towards Tante Ilde, and his farewell had in it much of the love of a son, and the pity of the very strong for the very weak. So many out of her little world, in their several ways, had been saying their farewells to her. Of them all, Pauli's alone, had it been knowingly the last, could scarcely have been more tender.

.   .   .   .

Then she found herself once more alone in the Augustinerstrasse. You were always, when you were old, finding yourself alone like that. She went on, suddenly forlorn to desperation. The sun had long since disappeared behind some leaden clouds hanging over the Capuchin church, the rain was coldly falling and the streets were getting slippery again. The warmth in her veins was gone, the colour departed from her face. Those unpleasant sick shivers were passing quickly up and down her back, and that point of pain stuck between her shoulders. She pressed her umbrella, needing a stitch at one of the points, the cloth had slipped quite far up – when it happened she couldn't think – close down about her head. The damp hurrying crowds were jostling her unbearably, carelessly poking their umbrellas into hers. She finally turned in at one of the less frequented streets to get back to the Hoher Markt, a little longer, but out of the relentless pressure of the crowd. She kept thinking about Pauli's hand over Corinne's, on the table; the crumpled paper napkins, the few tiny breadcrumbs, the wine-glasses with their deep red lees, Pauli's dark hand with the gold and turquoise ring over the slim, unringed whiteness of Corinne's. . . . She wanted suddenly there in the cold streets to weep for Corinne, for Pauli. She was conscious of some faint wordless prayer that went up out of her weakness, just frightened supplication rather than thinking, and 'Oh, my little, *little* Inny!' . . .

Then her eyes were caught and held by the fatal, antique symbol of ultimate, entire misery that was inescapably presenting itself.

There, creeping along the walls of the houses, under their eaves, was a very tall, pale, heavy-eyed woman with a child in her arms covered by an end of her tattered colourless shawl. She was soon, very soon, perhaps that very night, to bring another into that wintry world. At her skirts dragged a rachitic little boy of four or five. . . . Das Elend. . . . Misery.

Suddenly Frau Stacher's heart grew so big, so big with a desolate pity that she thought it would burst the thin walls of her aching chest. It was indeed the symbol, the living, cruel symbol of the misery of that wintry, starving city. It was all caught up into that wretched group, to which so soon that other, unwanted and unwanting, would be added, that child still safe in the womb. . . . She caught her breath stickingly, sharply.

Where did charity begin? She no longer knew. She had meant to take Irma the money Pauli had given her, that she might use it for those children of their own blood. But no, it was for this, so clearly for this, for beings whom she had never seen until that very instant and never would again. She was saying to herself – aloud though she did not know it – 'Let them eat once.' Then she accosted the woman who turned dull, unexpectant eyes upon her, while the little boy who knew only hard,

cold, empty things, clung tighter to his mother's damp
skirts.

'Take this. Eat. Get warm for once before your time
comes. Feed the children,' she cried hoarsely, her voice
still thick with her anguish.

The woman's claw-like hand closed over the money.
Some stammered words of thanks, some muttered 'Ver-
gelt's Gott' fell on Frau Stacher's ears. She turned hastily
away. She couldn't bear to look even for a moment longer
into that hopeless face.

But she turned back after a few steps. The woman
was walking almost quickly away in the direction whence
she had come. She knew, doubtless, the miserable entrance
to some very relative heaven where if she had money she
could get food, and if she had money she could get warm
and sit or perhaps even lie flat on something however
hard – out of the icy drizzle of the streets. . . .

Then suddenly Frau Stacher became tremblingly afraid
that there, so near the house, Irma, out on some little
errand might have seen her. And never, never could she
have made Irma understand. She didn't understand herself, only that it was something, however ill-considered,
that she had had to do, out of that sudden feeling of the
oneness of life. . . .

But as she entered, there in the fading light Irma was
unsuspectingly taking some last stitches, standing with her
work held up close to the window. She turned, not
unexpectantly, as her sister-in-law entered; blessings often
flowed in through Corinne. She carried no parcel, but it

might so easily be that she would open her old black bag with its uncertain clasp and say:

'See what Corinne has sent!'

But Frau Stacher, quite pale and spent, said not a single word even of greeting. She seemed to Irma very old and broken, quite different from the smiling woman who had gone out a few hours before. She wondered again in alarm if she were going to fall ill on her hands and need taking care of. But for once she didn't say all this, nor do more than frown when her sister-in-law dropped her wet umbrella on the floor. When she did speak it was only to ask:

'Well, what did Corinne give you to eat to-day?'

VII

FANNY

Allegro con fuoco   The Viennese Waltz.

*

FANNY had a cosy little apartment just off the Kaerntnerstrasse, a pleasant corner apartment only up one flight of
stairs, easy to drop into. Her sitting-room had windows
looking down two ways, a south window and a west
window. Superfluity was its especial note. It had been
done up in varying styles at varying times – French,
English, Italian, according to the vagaries of its mistress.
The spring of 1915 had found it Italian, but when on that
soft, May day the Italians declared war, Fanny had cried:
'Out with it!' and had got rid of all her transalpine furnishings. The room had then settled down permanently to
its more logical expression of Viennese 'Gemuethlichkeit,'
that was accented by the miseries of the once gay city that
surged blackly about it. On the walls were reproductions
of pictures of various well-known beauties, Helleu's etch-
ings of the Duchess of Marlborough and of Madame
Letellier, a copy of the Marchesa Casati in pastel by some
one else. Fanny being quite sure that they, and various
others hanging on her walls, had no more than she herself
to do with the war, had left them there. Between the two
first-mentioned ladies was Ingres' 'Source' which Fanny
was thought to resemble.

The ill-fated Empress-queen hung over the door leading
into Fanny's bedroom – the picture of her in profile with
her heavy coronet of black hair high above her imperial

and beautiful brow, while the rest fell, a dark cascade, down her slender back. The Emperor, blue-uniformed, his breast a mass of decorations, smiled pleasantly and paternally from above the entrance door opposite.

The Archduke Franz Ferdinand and the Duchess of Hohenburg, head against head in a medallion, hung between the windows. Above them was a gilt laurel branch tied with crape.

On one of the tables was the Empress Zita, sitting with four of her children, the Emperor Karl standing behind her. Fanny was through and through monarchical. The new princelings, not of the blood, had their uses, but in her heart she despised them . . . what they were, that is, not what they had.

Fanny's own portrait by a certain renowned Hungarian painter of lovely women, on an easel, showed her in one of the blue gowns for which she was so famous. Her sea-blue eyes looked beautifully, innocently, from under her plainly parted, pale yellow hair; one long curl, falling from the simple knot behind, lay on her white shoulder. Fanny's hair was stranger to hot tongs or curl papers.

The room was full to overflowing with bibelots of every description – cigarette- and cigar-boxes, smoking-sets, leather and enamel objects from the smart shops in the Graben and the Kohlmarkt.

On the table on which stood the photograph of the Empress Zita was a collection of elephants in every imaginable precious or semi-precious stone. For a time Fanny let it be known that the elephant brought her luck, and it rained elephants; but those animals, mostly with their trunks in the air, had been superseded as mascots by rabbits, and on another table was an array of these rodents, also in every possible stone: jade, crystal, lapis lazuli, cornelian, amber, with jewelled eyes of varying sizes according to the pocket and the mood of the donor. The collection of rabbits being nearly completed, Fanny had begun one of birds. Two little jade love-birds pecking at each other on a coral branch had lately flown in to join a pale amber canary with diamond eyes.

Fanny was an expert in the matter of getting gifts. There was a pleasant, compelling air of expectancy about her, and a pleasant child-like rejoicing when a gift was offered that induced giving. And then when she was out of temper those animals were an unfailing and resourceful subject of conversation, playing often useful as well as ornamental rôles.

There were deep leather chairs, and between the windows a pale blue silk divan, that symbol of Fanny herself, piled with every conceivable sort of blue cushion, cushions with ribbon motifs, with silver flowers, with lace flouncings, painted, embroidered, of every shape and style. The carpet was blue and thick and soft and covered the floor entirely. In one corner was a large, cream-coloured porcelain stove that once lighted in the morning gave throughout the day its soft and genial heat. A comfortable room, indeed. No books but some piles of fashion journals on a little table by some piles of the inevitable *Salon Blatt*. Fanny did like to know what the 'Aristokraten' were about, dimmed and attenuated as their doings now were. She quite frankly said that she never read; indeed, the book of life took all her time, and she had turned some pages that she didn't care to remember.

An old servant from her father's house had followed her along that flowery path that had proved to have its own peculiar and very sharp thorns. She'd been witness to Fanny's wounds and bleedings as well as to her successes. She scolded, flattered and adored. Those watchful eyes were worth their weight in the legendary gold to her mistress. It was old Maria who gathered up the remains when Fanny gave her suppers and took them the next day to the Herr Professor's; it was she who brushed and took stitches in garments before they were given to Kaethe. It was she who said to herself, 'Kaethe can do so and so with this or that.' Nothing was lost really in that seemingly wasteful house. Then, too, Maria had her own relatives, who nearly or quite starved in dark distant streets. The chain of misery was endless; here and there a little place of plenty, like Fanny's house off the Kaertner Street.

Fanny's post-war principle was simple: 'der Tag bringt's, der Tag nimmt's,' the day brings it, the day takes it. Who would be such a donkey as to save money that a week after would have halved or quartered, even if it did not quite lose, its value? No, spend and make others spend. Those were wonderful days for succeeding in a profession like Fanny's. Paper money? Easy. Vienna lived to spend, not only spent to live. That paper money went stale, dead on their hands, if they didn't spend it. Jew and Christian alike knew that. Wonderful days, indeed, for Fanny and her kind.

Fanny always went to the Hotel Bristol for her midday meal, sitting at a little table not far from the door. Everybody that came in saw her and she saw everybody. She was one of the hotel's brightest treasures, above Princesses of blood, who now so often had a way of looking like their own maids. She was always smartly, beautifully dressed in her somewhat quiet style. She gave a light, bright touch to the dark, too heavily decorated room, shone in it gleamingly, reposefully, like a crystal vase.

Foreigners generally beckoned to the head-waiter and asked who the lady was sitting alone at the table near the door. And according to the questioner so was the answer. The head-waiter, profoundly versed in human nature, made no mistakes.

Fanny's manners, like her clothes, were impeccable. She spoke to no one and no one spoke to her, and she certainly didn't look about her the way the green Americans or the ripe Jews did. She went in and out like a queen, haughtily, gracefully, her round hips swaying gently, her head erect, her beautiful blue eyes impersonal. But then Fanny was always careful, not only in mien and gesture but in words. She was not accustomed to tell, even at her suppers, the sort of stories which, she heard quite authentically, ladies of the whole world told. It would have taken the distinction from her situation in the half-world.

That luncheon at the 'Bristol' was her regular public

appearance. She occasionally nodded to a slender, dis-
tinguished-looking, dark woman, without her beauty but
very *chic*. She was the friend of a Persian prince who,
in pre-war days had ruined himself for her, but was now
fast remaking a fortune in rugs. Extraordinary how many
people there were in Vienna who wanted to buy expensive
rugs! People who had mostly never seen a rug before –
suddenly Vienna was full of them. They came easily to
the surface of the dark, troubled waters of the Kaiserstadt,
like rats swimming strongly, surely against the current of
disaster; and they wanted quickly, all the things that 'the
others' had always had. These two women sometimes
joined each other in the antechamber and went out together. The dark woman had once been somebody's wife;
but Fanny had stood at no altar save the one she served.
She would take a couple of hours for her toilet for those
luncheons, for her seemingly simple toilet that no woman
of the world with less exclusive and wider demands upon
her time could hope to rival. She dressed sometimes for the
weather, sometimes according to her mood, sometimes in
consonance with the national misfortunes. After the
Treaty of St. Germain she dressed for two months in black,
fine, shining, smooth, silky black, and then because of the
Count she dressed again in black after the signing of the
Treaty of Trianon. Her face, in those dark days and dark
deeds, shone out of her sombre raiment like a rift from
black storm heavens. But, after all, in her blue gowns, blue
of every shade, from nearly green to nearly purple, lay her
greatest successes. That is why Kaethe and her children

were almost entirely robed in blue – and Maria's relatives, too.

Fanny's own expenses, as will be guessed, were large. She had to spend money – a lot of it – to make money, to keep steady her situation, somewhat inverted, in the social body. Seven years of it and though she was handsomer she was older. She had an extraordinary canniness, for all the sweet innocence of her blue eyes and pouting red lips.

Her ways were irregularly regular. In the evening unless she went to the theatre she was always at home. And there had never been any falling off in those evenings. Good business was often done then, other than by the châtelaine. Princes of the old style had there the desired opportunity to meet the new lords of Austria – men that they would scarcely have saluted on the street in the old days, men that then they only knew in their money-lending capacity, having their habitat in small inner offices: beings with money in safes behind their desks, who gave it out at usurious rates to temporarily or permanently embarrassed scions of noble houses. Then these 'Aristo-kraten' had had the fine steel of birth with which to defend themselves, a shining sword that had made such dealings profitable and pleasant on both sides. Now that sword was gone dull in their hands, or broken at the hilt. Life was a different kind of tilting-ground. Gloves were thrown down in counting-houses and then promptly picked up and pocketed. Those whose only occupation had once been to lend money now had further pretensions.

It was known that at Fanny's almost anyone might be met. The men who came were expected to have an entrance ticket of some kind – money, wit or birth. They didn't get a chance to sit around in those deep chairs, smoking those delicate cigarettes, just because it was so pleasant. Many a poor devil whose birth or wit was his only asset was mercifully splashed by the plenty that surged about Fanny. Though each Schieber really felt, according to the expressive Viennese phrase, that each prince could 'ihm gestohlen sein,' the aureole, though thin, still hung about the heads of the titled gentlemen who frequented the little flat off the Kaerntner Street.

Fanny was both hard- and soft-hearted. In her bargains she was merciless. Her beauty and her arrogance were worth wagonloads of that paper money, and she knew it· But then how lavishly she could give! For her family she was as a horn of abundance. Indeed, Fanny was a sort of clearing-house for the relief of their miseries. When you came right down to it she supported in some sort of a way a good half of the less resourceful and more virtuous relatives with whom Providence had so richly endowed her. Without Fanny they would have succumbed to their miseries. Instead of half-starving they would have entirely starved. Fanny, who hadn't held out, sometimes wondered what on earth would have happened to the others if she had – Kaethe and the children, Irma's boys, Tante Ilde and a lot more. She wasn't always thinking of them, it is true. But when she was lonely she did it passionately, extravagantly, and would send expensive, ribbon-tied boxes of sweets to Kaethe's children or to the boys. When Maria would find it out she would scold dreadfully and say that what they needed was flour and a lot of it, and that Fanny herself was headed for the poor-house, and Fanny would go off in a huff leaving a hard word behind her for Maria. But then Fanny was like that. All or nothing. Too much or not enough; beyond the goal or short of it. In her avoidance of the middle course lay Fanny's successes and her mishaps. Maria was more reasonable and more constant; but 'We can't do everything, too many of them,' she would reflect, and 'Weiss der kuckuk,' the cuckoo knows, her favourite expression when in doubt, where they would have got what they did get, if Fanny hadn't been Fanny.

The reactions of the various members of the family to her methods had been at first purely temperamental, but according as their misfortunes increased, her spasmodic though continuous generosity had modified their sentiments as well as their miseries. Indeed, they were, all of them, in one way or another, continually running beneficently into Fanny, though as she was mostly invisible in the flesh, the 'bumps' they got were apt to be of the soft and pleasant order.

Fanny, who couldn't bear Irma, a 'sour stick,' sent the boys their winter boots, their woollen stockings and jerseys. Irma eagerly yet acidly received these reminders of relationship while in her heart condemnatory of the relative. Mizzi, on the contrary, admired Fanny extravagantly, and if she had had the necessary 'talent,' and what she also called 'Fanny's luck,' would have asked nothing better than to work out her problems along Fanny's lines. She mostly kept her admiration locked in her breast, however, and generally so harsh in her judgments she never uttered a word of reproach where Fanny was concerned. Then, too, it might have got back to her and that wouldn't have done at all. Fanny was too useful. She knew that Hermann sometimes went to see his sister, and she thought it a good thing. He might pick up something there, – which he never did, – but she considered it one of his least useless acts.

As for Liesel, Otto had grandly and early signified that it was no place for an honest woman like his Liesel. But then they didn't need Fanny and could indulge in their virtuous segregation, though the reports Liesel heard of Fanny's clothes were tantalizing in the extreme and she was truly sorry that things 'were as they were.'

As for Anna, she hated Fanny with a cold, terrible hatred, too cold and terrible for the light of day. A sombre jealousy was its chief ingredient, back from their childhood days, but Anna had forgotten that and thought it was detestation of Fanny's ways. She and Hermine could get along without her too. And then, deadliest of sins, she was convinced, though she had no definite way of finding out, that Pauli had a soft place in his heart for her. Fanny here, Fanny there, she was sick of it. Fanny doing what was done for the Eberhardts, Fanny doing what was done for Irma and the three little step-brothers,

Fanny paying, she could bet, for Tante Ilde's alcove. Ah! Bah!

Kaethe loved her sister very much, and Eberhardt, from the clouds, was apt to fall as a dew of mercy alike on the just and the unjust. Pauli and Hermann never mentioned her, though 'twas true that Pauli frequented the flat assiduously and Hermann would have gone oftener but for the terror of those open places.

'Virtue, what is virtue?' Fanny had once cried to Pauli when some thorn or other had pressed deeply into her white flesh. And what *was* virtue in that starving city? Generous giving in the end assumed the supreme mien of virtue, had, indeed, usurped the place of all virtues, theological and human. It was all, to the family, which-ever way they looked, confusingly the triumph of Fanny's sins over their own virtues. Fanny was inclined, too, to be pious – in her way and at her time. She was apt to enter any church she was passing; what the prayers she offered up, who shall say? Not entirely of thanksgiving that in the starving city she had plenty. Perhaps she begged not to reach old age – to have time on her death-bed. That was what she hated to think of. Old age! Alone! Death! Judgment! Whom the gods love of Fanny's kind they certainly snatch young.

Yet, how gay she could be! What life was in her! Even above her beauty was that sense of flooding life in her veins. 'Tis true her temper easily ran high. Maria knew well the signs of rising choler; blasts of that temper blew about impartially. Indeed she was more apt to administer a box on the ear than to bestow a kiss. It was often said by the recipients of the first mentioned gift that never was she so handsome as when lightnings were flashing from her deep eyes. It was all part and parcel of poor Fanny. It was extraordinary how the family got used to her in their hearts, though sometimes in words they still condemned her – and ah, if Fanny hadn't been *their* Fanny!

However, there she was and apparently as bright as one of those American dollars to be gazed upon in the windows of exchange bureaux, shedding their radiance over the dull waste of paper money.

Obviously they couldn't be seen with her, nor she with them – in the end no one could have said just which way it was. However, from her all blessings flowed. Pauli called her the family Doxology, and once when he had run into her coming out of St. Stephen's, he had said, with his wide, flashing smile:

'Na, Fanny, thanking the Lord God for his manifold blessings, that you will later pass on to the rest of us?'

And Fanny had called him a 'stupid ox,' and smiled and blushed and flicked him ever so lightly with the tail of her silver fox.

It was one of Fanny's many gifts, that way of blushing that she still had, would perhaps always have. It was indeed a confusing situation. The yard-sticks of the old days were broken or mislaid, and anyway few had the energy to use them.

When Fanny had been very ill with influenza in November, Corinne and Kaethe, summoned by Maria, had gone to see her for the first time; they had let it be known afterwards that it was just like any other place, only much nicer, and that Fanny had been saying her rosary. Nothing hung together somehow.

Tante Ilde, whose judgments were innately of the order abounding in mercy, had had at first only the most uncomfortably confused sensations at the mention of Fanny – sensations rather than thoughts. A flush would, at such moments, mantle her cheek. It was when she still lived at Baden and Anna and Irma would come out and tell her of certain things that to them, Anna and Irma, were nothing short of shameful, an honest family, etc. Her father would have turned in his grave, etc., and they, especially Irma, would soon have to think of the boys, etc., etc. Tante Ilde had been wont to listen in a sort of confused silence. She didn't understand things 'like that' anyway, was the general opinion. She would think glimmeringly of what happened in the end in novels and on the stage to women of Fanny's ways, and she would feel alarmed for Fanny rather than condemnatory.

But when the races began again at Baden and they heard, necessarily indirectly, that Fanny, in two shades of blue, had been the sensation of the day, they were increasingly puzzled, but a touch of pride crept in to give a new tone to their feelings. So Fanny's scarlet sins, if not washed whiter than snow in the miseries of War and Peace, had undeniably been getting paler and paler in the family eye.

Now poor Tante Ilde shared with the others a certain

miscellaneous satisfaction, all sorts of things composed the secret mixture, that came inevitably from the knowledge that Fanny was doing very well. Indeed what would they do if Fanny didn't do well? It was the world upside down. But they were all living in that same upside-down world and the relativity of their misfortunes was so dependent on the absolute of Fanny's fortunes that certain chalky lines and demarcations were fast disappearing. Though none of the women went to Fanny's, they all saw Maria, that messenger of hopes and fulfilments, that faithful *officier de liaison* between two worlds.

. . . .

When, after her habit of recounting everything to Maria, Fanny had told her all about Carli and meeting Tante Ilde at Kaethe's, they had first wept over Carli, mingling their tears as they embraced. Then they had a conversation concerning the proprieties, concerning Tante Ilde's coming to Fanny for dinner on the very next Saturday – before the funeral. At first the thing had seemed impossible, just couldn't be. Certain things weren't done, and Tante Ilde – so devoted, so genteel, so innocent. Of Tante Ilde's indestructible innocence there were no two opinions. Something to be cherished. It wouldn't be 'anstaendig,' decent, a word used with more shades of meaning in Viennese than in English. Equally Fanny couldn't take Tante Ilde to the Hotel Bristol. Yet Fanny was suddenly very lonely for Tante Ilde, she had a hunger for her and Fanny generally gave herself the things she wanted. . . . Tante Ilde, so loving, so unfortunate, the only one left of the older generation. Why if Tante Ilde died, Fanny herself, all of them, would be, dreadful thought, the older generation! She positively boo-hooed, wiping her handsome nose noisily on her filmy handker-chief. But for once Fanny didn't see her way quite clear to gratifying her desire. There were things, a lot of them, that weren't done, and this seemed quite definitely one of them.

She had her code and it was rigorous. But Maria had been saying that she noticed, too, how white and thin Tante Ilde looked when she had gone to take Irma the woollen stockings, just as if her life were being pressed out of her, though not a word of complaint, only a smile and just faint and tired, as if she didn't have a place to rest her feet or to lay her head, 'and I'll bet she has it hard with Frau Irma,' finished Maria shrewdly.

'About like sitting on pins,' answered Fanny with conviction, 'but Pauli told me Corinne hoped it would do for awhile, on account of the boys, too.'

'I could make her comfortable here for once,' pursued Maria insinuatingly, 'a little table drawn up by the stove and a good oatmeal soup.'

Maria, too, had her doubts as to the propriety of the proceeding. She was quite feeling around in the dark where you might run into all sorts of things. In ordinary times there would have been no question of such an arrangement or even during the War, but the Peace had levelled the ranks of the Viennese with the same efficiency as death – what, indeed, was virtue?

'I feel so sorry for the poor, dear old lady,' said Maria meditatively, repeating, 'I could make her comfortable for once.'

'Well, you'll probably have your way, but I'm against it, it just isn't suitable,' answered Fanny flatly. Her aunt's life was broken into bits, but there was a whiteness about the remaining pieces that they all, according to their natures, felt must not be diminished.

'But, Lord God!' at last cried Maria, whose voice could rise too, 'they all take the money!'

'They can't starve, the poor things!' answered Fanny immediately up in arms for the family, her voice rising above Maria's.

Maria, familiar with the signs of trouble, lowered her own.

'It's different her coming here,' Fanny began after a pause, with an unexpected quiver of the lips.

Maria melted instantaneously, this was so painfully, undeniably the fact, and pressed Fanny's head against her ample bosom.

'It's different,' Fanny repeated, and wished it wasn't different. Suddenly the hunger for Tante Ilde became very insistent, rising up from far out of those happy days when she had been the prettiest girl that anyone had ever seen, and had picked daisies in Tante Ilde's garden at Baden and pulled off the petals: 'He loves me – loves me not – not.' . . . And *this* was what Life was. . . . Maria could do any blessed thing she pleased about Tante Ilde. She, Fanny, washed her hands of the matter.

And even the next morning things weren't any better, and she made her toilet snapping crossly at Maria, with the corners of her mouth drawn down, looking fully her age, which though it wasn't great, she couldn't afford to do . . . considering. . . . And then she had gone out to the Bristol to the tinkle of her bracelets, and the slightest rustle of silk (just enough to let one know somebody was passing), her eyes stormily sombre under the drooping plume of her hat, her furs enveloping her softly, odorously — all in a not unfamiliar, black sea of depression. That black sea, with no slightest light, that sometimes threatened to flood up above her red full mouth, above her small flat ears, above her wide blue eyes, till she was drowned, till she was dead. . . . What was the matter that Tante Ilde couldn't walk right in to her own niece's home? And then, it must be confessed, as she walked slowly along, she used some expressions in regard to life and living that she hadn't learned in her father's house.

.   .   .   .

Fanny had been likened by a foreign friend to one of her own waltzes — beautiful and hot, gay and sad, for beneath the passion and beauty they embody is that ever-recurrent note of melancholy, woven through each sparkling melody, to be caught up swiftly into the inevitable coda that for so many of Fanny's kind is the end indeed.

Vienna laughs and weeps to her waltz music, loves and dies to its measures, to a continual 'allegro con fuoco.' Weber thus annotated one of the glowing movements of

'Blumen der Liebe': 'Breast against breast he confesses his love and receives from her the sweet avowal of love returned.' . . . Breast against breast indeed, giving and receiving, myriads of maidens in each generation embody the brief and tragic triumph of passion and beauty over the lengthier security of duty. In that very heart of Europe is a perpetual, warm, fermenting desire for love, an instant sensibility to the arts – to all beauty in its visible forms; but 'swiftly with fire' these are for ever consuming themselves, for they have little to do with material success or personal continuity.

The Turks left other things there than coffee and ruins. They dropped some seed of Eastern magic into this only half-Western soil, and a dark flower, like no other dark flower of the earth, sprang up abundantly. Its colour for a time has been washed out in the sombre waters of War and Peace; it has been trampled by the slow tread of cripples, its growth suspended in starvation. But another generation that has not seen these things and died of pity or hunger will arise, other 'Flowers of Love' will blossom. The sagging portico of that stately pleasure-palace, Vienna, will be again upheld by Caryatides with glowing eyes, with bright cheeks, with thick, shining coils of dark hair, with full, soft figures and tireless, round, white arms. And in through the portico, coming from their dark side streets, will pass 'allegro con fuoco,' passionate, gifted young men, worshippers of the arts and devotees of the graces, with their Frauenlieb and their Frauenlob apostrophes, their lovely, tragic hymns to Spring and Hope and Love – till the sun and the moon and the stars shall have done with them.

. . . .

When Frau Stacher got up that Saturday morning she found that her legs were trembling weakly and that only with the greatest effort could she stand. Her chest seemed bound in iron, too, and she was breathing quite noisily.

'I've got a terrible cold after all,' she thought, appalled at the idea of being ill at Irma's – in the alcove. 'It just can't be,' she thought desperately. Up and out was the word, though down and all in was what she felt. She was momentarily comforted by the cup of ersatz coffee that Irma always served very hot, but she had a vast repugnance to the piece of hard bread. Gusl, with his sharp eyes out had been watching it as it lay untouched at her plate.

'Tante Ilde, you're not eating your bread,' he observed finally.

'No, I don't want it. I'm not hungry,' and she pushed it towards him.

'Not hungry!' he exclaimed, and his voice was hopeful.

At that Ferry, who always noticed things, said: 'You're not ill, Tante?'

Irma glanced up quickly. But her sister-in-law always looked that way in the morning, pale and spent and a hundred years old, so she turned to the more agreeable consideration of the slice of bread. Being impartial was one of Irma's many virtues and that slice was cut into three bits, the thin end larger than the two thicker pieces. It was a pleasant sight, though no more durable than a

217

flash of lightning, to see the boys eat it, in an instant, one chew, one swallow. Then they began to get ready for school and Irma lingeringly wrapped Ferry's knitted scarf about his neck, she was strangely tender with her sons, and they all clattered down the bare steps.

Frau Stacher always rather dreaded that moment of being alone with Irma, but this morning she was glad of the sudden quiet in the apartment. She would have lain down again but for Irma's inevitable question if she did so. Clearly Irma's wasn't a house to relax in. You got up and went on. So instead of lying down, as usual she helped to wash the cups and saucers and put the room in order.

Then when Irma sat down to her work by the window, she went back to her alcove and in its semi-obscurity, leaned heavily on the yet unmade divan, trying not to cough. She could hear Irma drawing the stitches of her embroidery in and out, and the little click when she picked up or laid down her scissors. She was no more alone than that. It suddenly seemed to her that the most intolerable of all her misfortunes was never, never to be alone. She started up uncomfortably as Irma called out, speaking more gently, however, than was her wont:

'You're going surely to Fanny's to-day?' and then she heard Irma lay down her work and cross the room. As she pulled the curtain aside Frau Stacher stood up guiltily. Irma even in her preoccupation could not but see that her sister-in-law was ailing. There was no mistaking it. But Irma was determined, more determined than she had ever been about anything, that she should go to Fanny's that day, that very day. Virtue or vice, 'twas all the same in Irma's eyes, all run together. Ferry had to be saved, saved that day and not another.

'Hermann says that if Ferry gets over this coming year, he'll be all right.'

Something familiarly, sombrely fierce lay in her eyes as impatiently she looked at the frail messenger of her desire.

'Yes, I'm going, Irma, you can count on me, I won't forget,' she answered almost humbly. 'Don't worry, we'll arrange it,' and then her eyes fell on the little figure of the woman bending over waiting to have the two buckets, one filled with apples and the other with pears, put into her hands.

'I'll just take it with me – to show Fanny,' she continued.

Irma's eyes filled with tears as she took the little carving from the table and started to wrap it in a piece of newspaper.

'No, give it to me just as it is. I'll carry it in my bag,' and she put it into her worn reticule that never stayed clasped and now promptly fell open as she laid it on the divan.

'You won't lose it,' questioned Irma anxiously, seeing her put it into the precarious keeping of the bag, but her sister-in-law didn't answer, only pulled the curtains together again. Irma went slowly back to her embroidery, but after a moment or two not hearing any sounds of moving about, she asked in a tone whose irritation was but half-suppressed:

'Don't you think you had better begin to get ready?'

This having to push her sister-in-law up and along, out of the house, filled her with a sickening impatience.

'Yes, perhaps I had better,' Frau Stacher answered obediently, 'though it isn't far.'

And then Irma, hearing those soft, slow movements of dressing behind the curtain said no more. She was really only thinking of the moment of her sister-in-law's return, with the money in her purse or perhaps enough to be prudently pinned into her dress.

Frau Stacher was thinking of nothing. All the forces of her being were employed in that act of clothing her body. After she was dressed she noticed that she had on the wrong skirt, but she felt she couldn't change – and then she *had* put the velvet around her neck. One thing she didn't do that morning, she only remembered it when she got out into the street – she hadn't pulled back the curtains.

But Irma, as she saw her ready to depart, though she noticed that the curtains weren't drawn, only said again:

'You won't lose the little figure?' and Frau Stacher, with that formidable submission in her eyes, even Irma got it, answered again:

'No, I'll be very careful.' Then she turned and inexplicably to herself embraced Irma and said 'Farewell,' just as if she didn't expect to be back in a few hours. Irma heard her steps getting fainter and fainter, as she went down the resounding stairway, until they were lost for ever.

. . . .

Frau Stacher felt very weak, and her feet seemed made of lead, as she turned into the Rotenthurm Street, then

that pain between her shoulders. But she was thankful
that she had been able to get out, and Fanny, mercifully,
lived near. A pale, uncertain sun that gave no warmth,
lay momentarily over the city.

There was an undeniable excitement about going to
Fanny's, something adventurous, like going into exotic
lands, that stimulated her momentarily and in that sick
confusion of her being she did not try to analyse her varied
and commingled sentiments. Bashfulness, timidity, the
gentlest curiosity, gratitude, affection, she was conscious
of – together with that increasing pain between her
shoulders. . . .

She was admitted by Maria, whose small black eyes were
snapping pleasantly, whose wide mouth wore the most
affectionate of smiles; Maria, part of their lives since
twenty-five years, Maria, who had always opened to her
ring when she went to see her brother.

'Ach, dear, gracious lady, how good of you to come to
us!' she cried warmly, and bending kissed Frau Stacher's
hand with all the old-time reverence and affection.

She felt like a storm-tossed little craft that has at last
made port. She hadn't thought it would be that way.
It was, indeed, 'just like any other place, only much
nicer.'

'Fanny is making her toilet, I'm just getting her into
her things,' Maria continued easily.

'I'll be there in a minute, Tante Ilde, dear,' called
another welcoming voice from the next room, then in
quite a different tone:

'You old hag, you've forgotten to take that stitch in my sleeve.'

'Coming, coming,' called back Maria cheerfully and winked at Frau Stacher: 'She doesn't mean a thing. Just her little way,' she whispered admiringly; then aloud:

'If the dear lady will lay her things aside,' and as Maria spoke she proceeded to help her remove the old coat, peeling off the narrow sleeves and pulling down the little woollen shawl that Frau Stacher wore underneath; she then put her into a comfortable chair, a cushion at her back and with solicitous inquiries about her health (Frau Stacher's looks didn't please Maria), 'now you just rest while I finish getting Fanny ready,' she ended with a pat of her fat hand on the thin shoulder.

'What are you talking about?' called her mistress. 'Perhaps I'm not going out.'

Maria disappeared through the door and Frau Stacher heard her say something about 'stupid caprices.'

Before the fine, even warmth of the porcelain stove Frau Stacher forgot how chilly she had been in the street; and the deep arm-chair with its soft cushion, how it engulfed yet sustained her! She was quite happy and almost comfortable. She felt more at ease, more at home than at any time since leaving Baden.

Over a card table was spread a white cloth and on it a service for one. She felt unreasonably disappointed – if Fanny could have stayed. Once in, it certainly was like any other place and truly it was nicer.

Her heart had beat a little thickly as she dragged herself

up the stairs with those leaden feet. Certain mysterious things you didn't do the first time without a feeling . . . but she saw herself often in future coming quietly up those very steps. She would always let Maria know first, though why she would let Maria know first, instead of just ringing at the door, she didn't try to explain.

Plenty lay again about her, the dear, familiar forms of Fanny and Maria were ready to minister to her. She breathed in, as deeply as the constriction in her chest permitted, the warm comfort of it all, plenty, affection, in a starving world of old unwanted women in garrets – in alcoves.

From above the door Franz Joseph continued to smile paternally down upon her, opposite him his beautiful and luckless Empress. The banished Zita and her children struck a further absolving note of innocence and misfortune. Frau Stacher returned gratefully the benevolent look her Emperor was bending upon her, remembering that he too, had 'had it hard.' As she slipped deeper into that comfortable chair she was conscious of being so tired, so spent that she feared she could never again get up. Yet it was almost delicious, the sense of languor – in that deep chair – in that warm room.

An immense gilt basket in which was planted a young fruit tree in full blossom stood near one of the windows. It was tied with bright blue ribbons, but its flowers were very pale in the hard January light. What was it doing there in mid-winter? She breathed in the faint scent of the forced blossoms hovering about the warm air. Ah, how indeed could she move out of that chair, how close that door behind her on that atmosphere of welcoming abundance?

She was sitting near the little table on which stood Fanny's collection of elephants. One in pink jade with ruby eyes seemed to be looking compassionately at her. Then she wondered, but without impatience, why Fanny didn't come.

Fanny *was* taking longer than necessary, but suddenly she had found that she could not bear to meet her aunt's eyes. Oh, those eyes! They would gaze at her as children's eyes gaze and she dreaded the feeling she knew she would have when she met them, right out, in daylight, in her own house. Behind that closed door Fanny was in a blue funk, Fanny who would have faced armies without turning a hair, and she fussed nervously with the objects on her dressing-table and kept looking quite unnecessarily at her shining, softly-rolled back hair with her hand-glass. . . .

'Why doesn't Fanny come?' her aunt began to ask herself again somewhat anxiously, and in her humility feared it was something connected with herself. Just then the front door bell rang, and she jumped in her chair, a flush mounting to her face. She couldn't at all have said what it was she feared might be impending, but whatever it was, that ring made a genteel old lady start up when she was too tired really to move, and blush the bright blush of her long lost youth. Maria ran out of Fanny's room, in what seemed to her an anxious way, to open the door. But she only took in a box, a large, flat, pleasant-looking box, the sort of box Frau Stacher remembered from her own shopping days. She saw the name Zwieback on it as Maria took it in to the other room. Another long wait ensued. She could hear whispers and the rustling of tissue paper.

Then all of a sudden the bedroom door was flung open and Fanny appeared, holding high up, so that it hid her face, a long black coat. In a flash, before a word could be said, Tante Ilde knew that coat was for her. . . .

Fragrantly, warmly, Fanny was bending over her, embracing her; a sudden, flaming colour that had come out of no box was in her cheeks.

'Stand up, Auntie,' she was saying in her silver voice, more embarrassed than she had ever been in any other of the seemingly more formidable moments of her life.

Tante Ilde turned her wide soft glance upon her. In a pale silken wrapper Fanny was looking as fresh as lilies who have neither sewed nor spun. It was the same bright, dawnlike face that Tante Ilde knew so well, there in the cold grey light of the January day, it recalled somehow early morning clouds in summer. . . .

She got up as her niece spoke, and in another minute that warm, soft wool, that smooth, satiny lining were enfolding her. It must have cost a monstrous sum.

'Oh, Fanny,' she protested weakly, 'to spend all that money on me!'

'Money, what is money?' returned Fanny blithely, her *aplomb* completely restored. 'You can't keep it nowadays. It just rots if you try. No more old stocking!' And then she proceeded to throw that practised eye of hers over the coat. . . . Any niece with a beloved aunt.

'Come here,' she next cried to Maria, and pointed out a button that needed changing – Tante Ilde was even thinner than they thought, 'bring some pins.'

Down on her silken knees she went and put the pin where the button was to be sewed on again.

Tante Ilde quite forgot that the family instinctively lowered their voices when speaking of Fanny. She was her brother's child again, her own little Fannerl, the sweet, soft, laughing, incredibly, brightly, beautiful maiden of those far-away days. Ah, she should have married a prince!

'You are an angel,' she said tremulously, keeping back with difficulty some tears that lay heavily just behind her eyes.

' "Angel" is going a bit far,' answered Fanny modestly, though really delighted in her heart; and she wondered for the thousandth time what on earth they would have done without her.

'I'm not going out,' she said crisply to Maria, 'the devil can take the "Bristol." I'm going to stay with Tante Ilde. Bring another cover, and quick, I'm sure she's hungry – I'm nearly starved.' This last wasn't quite true, for not so very long before Maria had taken in Fanny's tray with coffee and cream and a glossy, buttery gipfel, got Maria and the cuckoo alone knew from where.

'You look so tired, Auntie dear,' said Fanny next.

Her aunt's face was, indeed, quite pinched and very pale in spite of the fresh glow of her heart, near which, between her shoulders, was that increasingly unpleasant, stabbing sort of pain. But she was a game old lady. She hadn't yet complained about anything, so she only answered:

'A bit of a cold coming on, that's all.'

'I don't think you ought to go to the cemetery with us this afternoon,' Fanny pursued somewhat anxiously.

'But going in a carriage, and if I wear my warm, new coat?' she questioned eagerly.

The new coat made the effort seem possible. Not, oh, not at all through vanity, but a new coat, her own – she enjoyed, too, in anticipation, showing it to Irma, though Irma would be sure to say something about it designed to dim its glory.

Maria was bringing in the oatmeal soup that she had fully intended since the evening before to make for Frau Stacher . . . she knew Fanny. It was steaming up pleasantly from its little blue-and-white tureen and Fanny proceeded to ladle it out generously. She had pushed the card-table close to her Tante Ilde's chair and drawn up a little stool for herself on the other side. Frau Stacher took a few mouthfuls – delicious, there was certainly some milk in it. Tired as she was she couldn't be mistaken about there being milk in it, but all the same she found she wasn't hungry. She forced it down, however, to the last drop; Fanny mustn't think she didn't like it.

Fanny had jumped up restlessly, after watching her take the first spoonful, and lighted a cigarette and then sat down again, bending forward, her elbows on her knees, and her white hand, with its immense sapphire ring, just one big square stone, putting the cigarette up to her red mouth, her rosily manicured finger-tips flicking the ash from it on to the floor. The pale silken sleeves would ripple back and show Fanny's dimpled elbows. She took a little soup herself, but, like her aunt, showed no enthusiasm when Maria brought in a cutlet and some fried potatoes.

Frau Stacher knew well Maria's fine kitchen hand. So many years she had sat at her brother's table and seen Maria put just such cutlets on with those unrivalled fried potatoes. Frau Stacher was pierced cruelly for a moment by the memories these familiar things evoked: the children sitting around the table, talking and laughing, and her brother Heinie, who had loved them all impartially, looking indulgently from one to another. Indeed, it seemed the most natural of things to each of the three women; a thing they'd done a thousand times together.

But after her first mouthful of the cutlet Frau Stacher knew she wasn't going to be able to eat it. Its odour was delicious, the edges of the tender veal were goldly brown, and towards the middle of the piece it could easily be seen how white the meat was.

'I believe you're ill, Tanterl,' said Fanny, again looking sharply at her. 'You rest here while I take Kaethe and Leo.'

'But I want to go with you,' she returned imploringly, 'I don't want to leave you.'

Tante Ilde couldn't have told why she was so deter-

228

mined to go with Fanny, but the longing took her out of her usual gently acquiescent ways. . . . As if Fanny was to do something solemn, important for her, and she mustn't be separated from her. As if she had been warned that by keeping close to Fanny she would avoid some last, some ultimate horror. It was suddenly as clear as that.

'It's only a little cold I've got,' she repeated beseechingly, like a child imploring some permission.

'As you will,' said Fanny sweetly. 'I'm only afraid you'll take more cold at the cemetery.'

But Frau Stacher felt again that sudden, almost fierce cleaving to Fanny, to Kaethe . . . to little Carli. Where they went, there she wanted to go. It seemed to her, too, that she wasn't feeling quite so ill, but rather afraid to be left alone, even with Maria, nice as that would be; Maria who would come in and talk about the old, the happy days, and show her Fanny's things – Fanny's jewels and gowns. But even so, she wanted to be with her own, her very own. She forced down a morsel of the cutlet and took a bit of the fried potatoes on her fork, but it was evident to Fanny, and Maria, watching from the door, that she was eating with difficulty. She had an unbelievable, astonishing repugnance to the meat, to the fatty smell; then, too, she was worrying about Ferry, thinking all the time that now she must speak of him. It seemed a mountainous exertion, one she was quite unequal to. But she could never go back to Irma's unless she did, and then, too, she wanted to help Ferry. But it seemed beyond her strength. Anything except sitting still and being ministered to was beyond it. Then suddenly, as she sat there toying with her cutlet, she knew that her work was done; though whence the assurance had come she could not have told. It came, a sort of glimmering presence, bringing its dim, sweet promise that effort was ended. Her attention was quite engaged by that lovely, unexpected presence, and it was as if from a long distance that she heard Fanny say:

'I think a good strong cup of coffee, right now, would be the best thing for you,' and then she called to Maria to make it quickly and make it strong.

The very suggestion acted as a stimulant on Frau Stacher, and she was able to pull herself together sufficiently to look gratefully at her niece. Then her eyes wandered again and were caught by that flowering tree, so springlike to her age. Its thin fragrance foretold a true spring that she too old, and it too young, would never see. It was palely, tenderly confused in her mind with that gleaming presence. She felt that she must recognize its beauty by some word – perhaps afterwards she would get around to Ferry. She experienced a slight timidity at mentioning that plant, however, though why it should awaken timidity, with that other sentiment of reverence for its beauty, she could not have told.

'What lovely things grow on the earth!' she ventured finally, indicating it with the slightest of gestures.

'Yes,' answered Fanny indifferently, she was thinking how changed her aunt was, 'but you should see the donkey that sent it.'

Frau Stacher thought no more of the plant.

Fanny herself was only toying with the veal cutlet and potatoes. If the truth be told she was aware of a slight excitement, following on her first embarrassment, just enough to cut her appetite . . . having Tante Ilde there . . . that way.

A pause ensued. They could hear Maria in the kitchen. On an important occasion like that Maria didn't intend to be alone, behind a closed door, and miss what they were saying. Maria herself was quite worked up. She hoped it would be decided for Frau Stacher not to go to the cemetery and then she would relieve her bosom of a lot of things pleasant and unpleasant, that really Fanny's aunt, when you had a fine aunt like that, should know; and besides, she longed to show her Fanny's things. Then she carried in the coffee, an immense cup: its aroma filled the room, drowning the thin sweet scent of the forced flowers.

'Just what I needed, Fanny,' Tante Ilde said in what seemed to be a loud tone, with that hammering in her ears; it was really not much more than a whisper. From the very first swallow she felt herself being renewed, and as she continued to sip it, a delightful feeling of actual strength regained came to her. Not go with her dear ones to lay Carli away? The thought was foolish . . . and being driven there and back and wearing her new coat? She was beginning to feel equal to anything.

'It's *so* good,' she murmured between her genteel little sips, and when Fanny dropped an extra lump of sugar in without asking her, it was still more sustaining to both body and soul, and she drank in longer swallows the sweet, dark strength.

Then Maria replaced the cutlet by two pieces of Sacher tart, one for her and one for Fanny. And that, too, was dark and sweet and she was able to eat it. A bite, a sip of coffee and then another bite, another sip. She got on really well with it, though for all its pleasing taste each bite had a way of stopping for awhile in her chest.

Then suddenly she knew it was time to speak about Ferry, quite time, before she took the last swallows.

She reached down by her chair where lay her poor bag and picking it up she took out the little wooden statue of the woman bent over waiting for Ferry to put the full pails in her hands.

'Ferry has a lot of talent,' she began musingly rather than informingly, as she passed it across the table to Fanny, 'and such an old knife, too, that he did it with. I'd like to give him a new one.'

'But naturally, we'll get him the best, with six or eight blades!' cried Fanny very pleased. Anything they needed except that eternal food and raiment and fuel was a welcome suggestion. Fanny did love to give people things they *could* live without, not just bread and coal and shoes. It got monotonous to one of her temperament. Even such a little thing as a knife for a boy struck an agreeable releasing note. She kept looking at the delicate figure. It imparted a pleasant sensation to her fingers as she touched it. It was quite evident that Ferry had talent. All was coming around as Tante Ilde had hoped.

'But Ferry is ill,' she continued with her gentlest look. 'He has night-sweats sometimes, and always a little cough.'

'Ach, the poor Buberl!' cried Fanny warmly.

'How easy Fanny makes things,' her aunt was thinking, yet somehow she still hesitated.

Fanny was passing her hand again over the little figure which kept inviting the caress of her long white fingers, of her soft, rosy palm.

'Hermann says he must go to the country, – a bit high, – if he is to be saved, and at his age one can't delay.'

So it was done – as easy as that after all. That little wooden peasant woman cried out not alone of young talent but of fresh air, the fruits of the field, you couldn't get away from it, not that Fanny was trying to; further more, the familiar story of family needs, now one thing now another, chased away the last trace of embarrassment. She was on the firmest of grounds *there*, only she was thinking again how old and ill her aunt was looking and did not answer immediately. When she did it was to exclaim warmly again:

'But naturally! Of course we must send him to the country. Manny will tell us where.' Then Fanny, who was, indeed, as Pauli said, 'a good fellow,' and no fool either, added, 'Don't you want to take the money to Irma yourself?'

So that was all it was – that stone-heavy act! Light as thistledown really – because Fanny was Fanny.

Then suddenly as she sat there looking at her, for she knew not how long, with still unspent treasures of love in her look, she saw that Fanny's eyes were wet, not because of Ferry either – he could be helped – but because of other things, things that she, her poor aunt, didn't know about. She saw that for all Fanny's gaiety there were rings around her lovely eyes and that she was pale under that merest touch of rouge. The merest touch was all she ever used. She was too wise as well as too lovely to be the painted woman. Fanny hung out no signs.

Then Frau Stacher found herself saying to her niece who lived just off the Kaerntner Street:

'Fanny, precious one, you too, have some grief.'

Frau Stacher was seeing all things from a great but clear distance. Things stood out very sharply now that that feverish blur seemed suddenly to have been wiped from her eyes. It was as if she, Ildefonse Stacher, stood on a mountain and saw the world, a valleyed plain, spread out before her. Mortals dwelt in it, doing their little best or their little worst. Sharp as their figures were it was still too far to see what exactly was their best and what their worst. Legions of them. Hosts of them. She saw Fanny fighting under deep-dyed colours, in an innumerable army of women, drawn up in array against the sons of other women. The look she bent upon her niece as she turned from the contemplation of the armies in the plain became more tender, more grave.

Fanny's eyes flooded with tears under that look; hanging crystal a moment about her dark lashes, they fell slowly, leaving smooth, shining, white little roads down her cheeks with just that touch of rouge. Such a little thing as that Frau Stacher could focus her eyes on – even after the immensity of the plain.

Fanny went over and knelt by her aunt who had always loved her – who loved her now – and put her shining head against that thin breast and wept. Fanny hadn't wept, except in rage, for a long time, and there were many tears to fall.

'I can't bear it, I can't bear it,' she whispered, but she didn't say what she couldn't bear, and Tante Ilde didn't ask her, only pressed that gleaming head more closely to her. And Fanny should have noticed how strangely her aunt was breathing when she had her head there against her breast. But suddenly she got up and said something about her nerves being 'total kaput' and went into her bedroom and closed the door.

Maria crept in from the kitchen.

'It's the Count,' she whispered. 'I'm afraid we're going to lose him. Fanny adores the ground he walks on. A fine gentleman, a cavalier' (Maria pronounced it 'cawlier' in her soft, thick Viennese), 'but not a kreutzer to bless himself with, and a South American girl, whose Papa has more head of cattle than in all Europe, is crazy about him and wants to marry him. Whatever we'll do, I don't know. She's that jumpy when the bell rings, she's afraid it's bad news coming in at the door. His family is ruined by the Peace and his father commanding and his mother praying him to save them, and four unmarried sisters, too. A bad mess we're in and what will be the end? I went to the fortune-teller a week ago, – a wonder, – and she saw cattle, cattle everywhere, and told me I was to beware of them, but how can I beware of stupid cattle stamping about in South America?' asked Maria helplessly, resentfully. 'I knew all the time what she meant – and saying, too, that she saw a letter coming. Oh, I've been that worried! Naturally, I haven't told Fanny, but I've been waiting for that letter ever since. You don't know Fanny' – Maria's eyes filled with tears – 'one day she says she will kill herself and another that she's going into a convent,' she whispered dismally, after a cautious look at the closed door; 'and if Fanny ever gets started *that* way, she'll make Mary Magdalene look about like this'; and she proceeded to measure a negligible quantity of the surrounding atmosphere between her thumb and forefinger. There was, however, pride in her voice.

Frau Stacher was listening vaguely. For all her deep interest in Fanny, she was finding it difficult to focus her thoughts. Things were getting blurred again.

Maria kept on, a warning note in her voice, 'I'll feel sorry for the family if Fanny doesn't hold out.' (Maria, it will be seen, was at the other side of 'holding out' – the far side.) 'She bought the villa at Moedling last year and we put a lot of money in England through a Jew' – here Maria was quite contemptuous . . . 'but,' she added in another and fondly indulgent tone, 'we had to let the Count, his people were starving, have a lot of that. We still get some income from it, but there are so many of us, and if Fanny should lose her nerve –' Maria broke off; only she didn't use the ordinary word for 'nerve' but the famous Vienna expression 'Hamur,' which means, beside nerve, a lot of things that are both more and less.

Tears overflowed her small, dark, friendly eyes. There was no nonsense about Maria. She adored Fanny, she was proud of Fanny, and to have the revered aunt sitting there made a priceless occasion on which to relieve her feelings. Crossing her arms over her ample bosom, she went on:

'She gives everything away, not only to the family and naturally to the Count, but yesterday, – will you believe it? – to a shameless hussy, no better than she should be, she gave a heap of money to keep her out of the hospital, where she truly belongs. I told Fanny where I thought she'd end herself if she didn't look out, but Fanny' . . . she broke off suddenly as the bedroom door opened.

'What are you gossiping about?' Fanny cried sharply to her, 'Didn't you hear the door-bell ring?' Then as it rang again a contraction passed over her face and she started to the door herself.

But Maria, in spite of her avoirdupois, was out like lightning. After a moment's parleying in the hall she was back.

'Nothing,' she said looking fondly, relievedly, at Fanny. 'It's only to say the carriage is there.'

Fanny went slowly back into her room followed by Maria, who shut the door. Frau Stacher, left alone, almost immediately fell into a doze; her eyes closed heavily and she slipped deeply into the big chair. But she couldn't quite lose herself, for she had a feeling that it would soon be time to go, and kept trying to keep herself awake.

She sat up sharply, with a start, when Fanny reappeared, how long after she could not have told, in a black costume whose long, fur-trimmed cape fell smartly about her form. A tiny black velvet hat from which she had just torn the cunningly, expensively placed blue aigrette, put her eyes in a becoming, melancholy shadow. She had an extra pair of black gloves in her hand and a fine dark leather bag that she had done with, to replace the 'horror,' as she called it to herself, that her aunt was using.

'You've got such dear little hands,' she was saying as she held out the gloves. 'These aren't big enough for me. I paid a heathen price for them, and this bag's a bit handier than yours.' But in spite of her pleasant words, her pallor was so extreme as she held out the gloves and bag, that her aunt whose eyes were again very bright and not alone with fever, noted it anxiously.

'Oh, my little, little Fanny,' she cried in quite a strong voice, and even held out her arms. She shared, in a way she could not have expressed, Fanny's grief, whatever it was. She didn't want Fanny, dear, gold Fanny to suffer. Fanny *mustn't* suffer. Fanny *mustn't* weep. She wanted to live a long, long time, even uncomfortably, denudedly, so that out of the whole careless world, Fanny might always have some one who truly loved her.

Then she became aware, for the first time, of something that intimately concerned herself. The shape and colour of her own life. . . . Loving the children of three other women had been *her* life. Her middle-class life, undisturbing and for so long undisturbed. One day, one year, like another, always loving the children of three other women . . . looking through the same windows at the same things. And suddenly now Fanny's world, Fanny's strange world . . . It had other horizons, red horizons behind dark mountains with their secrets. But of these secrets her aunt was not thinking. She only knew, as she stood close to Fanny, that it was her own flesh and blood that was suffering – beautiful and suffering.

How Fanny's beauty threw a bright, blinding cloud about everything that concerned her! She said again:

'My darling child, my beautiful child, don't weep,' as Fanny pressed against her, and she comforted her as she might have done in the far-off years for girlish griefs. Had she reflected she might have changed her old motto into 'Beauty stays, Virtue goes.'

She was breaking in Fanny's house for a last time her alabaster box of precious spikenard. From it, in the blue room, a strong fragrance came, overpowering the scent of lily of the valley from an expensive shop in the Graben that hung about Fanny's clothes, and the thin perfume of the too-early blossomed plant. She was thinking only of Fanny's generosity and why she could indulge those many generous impulses she thought not at all – just as if the family didn't lower their voices when speaking of Fanny and look around to see that the children weren't there. She felt, too, intimately joined to Fanny. Deeply beneath consciousness was that feeling that Fanny was yet to give her something essential, had some ultimate gift for her, that she must be there to receive. . . . That it was to be her deathbed she didn't know. She only felt that something final and priceless would come through Fanny.

And truly 'tis a great thing to give anyone. For mostly each one, no matter how he wanders or is denuded, has, in some strange way, his own.

. . . .

They were driving slowly up over the noisy cobble-stones of the Jacquingasse on their way to the cemetery, Kaethe and Fanny and Tante Ilde on the back seat of the big, black mourning-coach. Kaethe, wedged between them, was holding on her lap the white wreath. Opposite sat the Professor. On his knees for a last time was Carli; Carli in his little white box; Carli on his first and only journey.

The sable horses struck the cobble-stones with their slow, accustomed beat. It seemed to Frau Stacher the loudest sound she had ever heard, and 'some day for you, some day for you' seemed cadenced unmistakably. . . .

In the dark Minorite church Fanny had been a model of piety and recollection. She crossed herself so slowly, so devoutly. She buried her face in her hands and knelt long without fidgeting on the hard, uncomfortable stool. She took holy water and held a tip of her finger to Kaethe as they went out and then to Tante Ilde and to Leo. She and Kaethe had always loved each other very much. Fanny after her wont was going through the afternoon

without stint or sloppiness. It would be, in her hands, an
'entire' matter.

As they drove along Kaethe rested her head on her
sister's warm, scented shoulder. Her eyes were dry, but
her face was haggard from the night.

No one noticed that Tante Ilde didn't say a word.
Kaethe and Leo were with their child a last time and Fanny,
who generally selected pleasant things to do, was finding
it more wearing than she had thought and was plunged
in her own reflections. At one moment she said to
herself, 'I'm not going to be able to stick it out,' and
forgot their griefs and miserably let her thoughts turn to
the man she truly loved, and if everything in the world,
every last thing, had been different . . . Then suddenly
she fell to cursing in her heart a certain predatory gentleman whom she had known in the 'beginning,' no, before
the 'beginning,' but she pulled herself up round, that
carriage was no place for curses, neither was it the
moment. Then she caught sight of her face above
Eberhardt's right shoulder. It was distinctly mirrored
in the reflecting surface of the glass at his back, formed
by the heavy black flaps of the driver's coat. It was white,
white as the coffin on Eberhardt's lap, and the eyes were
deep, dark pits, almost as if the flesh had fallen away
from them. She was horribly frightened. What was
the warm thing that went out of you and after it went
out you were put in a box? . . . She jerked her head
so that it slipped from view. But she got Tante Ilde's
instead. . . . It was just dreadful. . . . All right as long

as you lived, but there came a time when beauty, which had been so helpful, was clearly of no avail. . . . The activities of family and town were concentrated on getting you into a box, and then . . . Fanny, who believed in hell and damnation, drew in her breath shudderingly. She was thankful to feel Kaethe's warm, living head against her shoulder. She wasn't dead yet – she was suddenly sure, too, that she'd have 'time to repent.' She quite brightened up, and as she never did anything by halves was apparently entirely herself by the time they got to the cemetery.

Fanny in the bosom of her family, for once taking charge of things in person, not just paying from a distance, was really worth seeing. Fanny at last visibly the source of whatever mercies they received. Fanny, as Pauli so truly called her, the family Doxology . . . according to the mysterious permissions of God the source of their only blessings.

Fanny weeping and praying by the little grave, supporting the stricken mother – her sister, and laying on it the big wreath. Fanny taking them to the café near the cemetery and giving them hot coffee after their cold grief. . . .

It was Fanny, too, who, when some extraordinarily stubbly semmels were served with it, bearing not the slightest resemblance to the anciently far-famed Viennese rolls, scolded the shambling, flat-footed waiter and said loudly it was a 'shame' and 'disgusting,' and ended by going over to the desk and saying something in a lower

tone to the gaunt woman who sat there. The woman
had promptly produced some coffee-cake and some crescents kept only for rich grief. She was used to pale, tear-
washed faces. Every day, every day, they came in and
went out. She had seen many a strange alteration in their
looks after that hot coffee, even after ersatz coffee. People
kept on living for all they had that momentary feeling
that they couldn't. She had sat at that desk for twenty
years. Grief, she knew it, all kinds . . . and they kept
on living.

Even Kaethe, though her throat was stiff and dry
with mother-grief, even Kaethe had taken her coffee.

But Tante Ilde made no pretence at drinking hers, not
even a sip. Those little shivers had changed into a continuous trembling. She felt both hot and cold. Her eyes
were filmy. The only thing she wanted to do really
was to lie down, never to move again, to give way to
that overpowering lassitude that she could no longer
struggle against. She was only vaguely worried because
she'd lost the new bag; dropped it at the grave probably,
though when she noticed its loss, on coming out of the
cemetery, it had already vanished from the earth. After
her first dismay she had strangely not cared, and
now she was murmuring something about the alcove,
not at all what any of the others were thinking or
talking of.

Suddenly Kaethe, startled out of her own grief at a
trembling motion of her aunt's shoulders, had looked at
her in alarm.

'But what is the matter, Tante Ilde?' she asked.

'Why, she's really ill!' cried Fanny sharply, 'we've got to get her home.'

Her aunt hearing the word home muttered once more something about the alcove. Her face was ashen, but her pale, wide eyes shone strangely through the film that again threatened to veil them.

'We must go right away,' Fanny cried, and hastily paid for the coffee.

Her aunt didn't even hear her. All her strength was engaged in getting totteringly to the door, the professor's arm about her.

'I'm going to take her with me,' Fanny whispered to Kaethe as they followed out to get into the coach.

Kaethe looked at her deeply; there was much love in her glance, but she only said:

'I don't think she likes it at Irma's. Irma's so fierce and she's so gentle.'

'Sour stick,' said Fanny as usual when referring to her stepmother. 'I'll just keep her with me, for a day or two, till she's better,' she continued, thinking boldly, swiftly. 'Maria can look after her.'

It seemed suddenly the most natural thing in the world to have Tante Ilde with her for a day or two.

'Fanny, how good you are to us all,' Kaethe whispered to her sister.

'Good – nothing!' said Fanny. But virtue was, all the same, its own quite sufficient reward at that moment, though she felt horribly self-reproachful at the thought that sometimes she'd let them go for months . . . suppose they had all died!

Tante Ilde kept slipping down between her nieces in the carriage, though they were supporting her as well as they could. Her head was hanging over her breast. She wanted to sleep, even bumping along over those cobble-stones. They all watched her anxiously. Once Fanny, her nerves quite on edge, leaned out of the window and screamed to the driver in a horrible voice that the others didn't recognize: 'You, sheep's-head! Get along!'

Then somewhat restored, she drew her head in and after a few minutes, opening her immense gold bag, gave Kaethe some money. No, Fanny wasn't doing things by halves that day.

'Get something nice for supper, – for the children,' she added with sudden tears that were for the living children – no more for Carli who was really for ever safe, though they seemed to have left him alone in that chill Vienna earth, under that darkening January sky. . . .

Frau Stacher scarcely knew how they got her upstairs. Only as from a great distance she heard Maria's 'Jesus, Marie, Josef!' as they went in. She was beyond any more definite impression than that she had ceased to struggle. Fortitude, cruel virtue, were no longer demanded of her.

When she was gently laid on Fanny's bed she was conscious at first of its soft comfort under her aching body. They were taking off her clothes. She wished, but not anxiously, nor even ashamedly, that her chemise

245

had not been so old or so grey from being always washed out in her little basin, but it didn't really matter, she knew, and she quite forgot about it when something fresh and silken and scented took its place, lying smoothly against her back with its hot point of pain.

'Alcove,' she continued to mutter from time to time between stertorous breathings.

'Why's she talking so much about an alcove?' whispered Fanny to Maria as they sat by the bed waiting for Hermann, whom Eberhardt was to get and send back in the mourning-coach.

'It's where she sleeps at Frau Irma's — a sort of alcove, off the living-room. She's got her old brown divan in it, you remember in Baden, but she needs a room of her own. When you get old you need to have a door to close, and then Frau Irma is not always easy.'

'Easy? A porcupine,' Fanny whispered back, and added something about Croatians in general not complimentary to that former Crownland. Then she looked restlessly at her watch.

'Why doesn't he come? Maria, I'm afraid,' she ended with a break in her voice.

'It *is* going badly with her,' nervously admitted Maria, who had once been a great one at sick beds and who, when it was not so personal, loved to be in at a death.

Frau Stacher's breathing was indeed very noisy. It whistled through her thin chest, it came in gasps from her blue mouth.

'Do you think she's going to die?' cried Fanny suddenly

in panic. 'We'd better get a priest anyway; only the poor heathen die without one!'

Fanny had always been interested in foreign missions and was in the habit of giving propitiatory sums to the Church when she got panicky, for the purpose of conversions. . . .

A ring at the door, a firm long ring, caused Maria to jump up.

It was Hermann, Hermann of the old days, despite his right arm hanging straight, Hermann completely professional, quiet, strong, but loving too.

He gave one look at his Tante Ilde.

'Pneumonia,' he said, 'she's been ill for a couple of days,' and he started to do the little there was to be done.

'But she never said anything except that she had a bit of a cold, the angel, and going to the cemetery too!' answered Fanny aghast.

'To the cemetery in such a state!' he echoed in astonishment, 'why she won't get through the night. Fanny – I'm glad she's here.'

As the brother and sister looked at each other, their eyes filled with tears. The way life was. . . .

'I'm afraid she's already begun her agony,' he whispered a few minutes later, 'dear, good, sweet Tante Ilde.'

But he wrote a prescription for Maria to take out.

'It may last longer than we think. It's sometimes so hard for them to go, even when they've nothing to stay for, but we can try to make it easy for her.'

Fanny ran out of the room after Maria.

247

'Go to the Kapuziners and bring some one back, and quick,' she whispered imperatively.

Then she returned to the bedside. Hermann was bending over his aunt, raising her up and Fanny ran again and got some of the softest cushions from the blue divan, to put high, high under her head.

Suddenly Tante Ilde opened her eyes.

'Manny, dear, good Manny!' she cried, quite loud; then, 'Fanny, darling, you won't forget little Ferry?'

And then she called for Corinne, and called again and again. She loved them all equally, but the flavour of Corinne's being was the flavour of her own, Ildefonse Stacher's being, and that made a strange, an essential difference at the end. . . .

But at that very minute Corinne was sitting in a little restaurant with Pauli, close together on a narrow, leather bench in a corner, and Pauli's dark, small hand lay closely, hotly over hers. After they had eaten he was going to take her to Kaethe's – not to Fanny's where a more merciful Fate would have led them. And that is why stupidly, horribly, Corinne was always to think, she wasn't at home when Maria came to get her. . . .

As Tante Ilde lay calling for Corinne, with her blue eyes widely open, neither Fanny nor Hermann could know that flashingly, she was seeing, as the day before, Pauli's dark, turquoise-ringed hand clasped tightly over the slim whiteness of Corinne's, and that she was very frightened for Corinne. She closed her eyes flutteringly several times, but still she saw their hands. Then suddenly the cavities under her brow grew very deep and she gave a long, whistling gasp.

'Not yet,' whispered Hermann, seizing Fanny's hand, for at the sight she had burst into wild weeping, 'but soon, – dear, dear Auntie,' and from his voice there was momentarily released all the pent-up tenderness of his great heart. It flooded the room. It surged warmly about his sister, about his dying aunt. . . .

Then Frau Ildefonse Stacher, born von Berg, began to pluck at the sheet and talk in snatches of Baden and of Heinie, her brother, their father. Once she smiled, but they didn't know that it was because the bed was so soft and she was so comfortable, quite knowing that she would never have to move again. . . . And certainly if this was dying it wasn't at all what people thought.

.   .   .   .

Maria's key was in the door . . . Maria's voice was respectfully ushering some one into that silk-hung chamber – a dark-bearded, deep-eyed Capuchin monk. He threw back widely his brown-hooded cloak, and as he did so glanced enfoldingly at the dying woman without a single other look about the room. His work lay there. . . .

Frau Stacher had fallen into a last unconsciousness, but her breathing was still terribly loud, like wind through a vacant room. Fanny on her knees by the bed, was weeping and praying and kissing her aunt's thin hand rather extravagantly, after her way.

The monk's eyes, accustomed to the sight of death,

knew without a word from Hermann that the end was very near. On the little, white, lace-covered table by the bed, on which Maria had placed a lighted candle, a basin of water and a towel, he laid the Blessed Oils, those final oils with which he was to anoint Frau Stacher's noisy tenement, commending it to mercy. . . .

Her broad-lidded blue eyes, that through tears would look no more on misery, no more on starving children, no, never any more. . . .

Her ears, that would hear no further cries of woe, nor any unprofitable discourse. . . .

Her nostrils, that would no more weakly dilate at smell of needed food. . . .

Her tongue, that would frame no more its words of gentle, helpless pity. . . .

Her hands, that had once given so freely, would be held out no more to receive. Never again would she have to suffer humble uncertainty for the gifts of food and raiment. The body, no longer needing food, was itself become as raiment, cast off. . . .

Her feet, that had for ever fallen away from the ranks of those who in aged misery still flitted through the wintry streets of Vienna seeking their midday meal of charity . . . the Mariahilferstrasse, endless, the Alserstrasse separated from the Hoher Markt by so many wide, open places, the narrow, crowded Kaerntnerstrasse and all those other streets that had sounded a last time to her diminished step. . . .

Irma would never again give her the thin part of the

soup, and never again would she watch to see that her sister-in-law drew back the curtains of the alcove. Alcove! Ildefonse Stacher, born von Berg, in the name of Principalities and Powers, in the name of the Cherubim and Seraphim, was about to take possession of her whole heavenly mansion, her very own from all time unto all time, and big and beautiful.

. . . .

Fanny not only buried her aunt decently, but splendidly, as such things in such times were rated. A Requiem Mass was sung at the Capuchin Church. Expensive wreaths were ordered in the name of each niece for which Fanny herself paid (except for Mizzi's, Mizzi got the bill, unjustly, she considered, and she ran into the office and said some horrible things to Hermann when it came). . . .

They were but more tokens of Fanny, those many flowers, Fanny inescapably, confusingly beneficent to the end. Wet with the dew of the Church's blessing, they almost concealed Tante Ilde's coffin, as to the sound of those sable horses over the cobbly streets she was carried to her grave . . . at last to be alone behind the heaviest door known to mortals. . . .

As they drove back, each was saying in one or another tone, 'what a pity,' that Tante Ilde couldn't have been there to enjoy it in her fine, gentle way, and that if they had known she was going to die so soon they would have arranged differently. They had spoken of Baden, too, and of childhood things. They had mourned, yes, but their mourning, as would have been any cheer, was after their several and varying natures.

Anna had not gone to Fanny's to see her aunt laid out. No, indeed! She and Hermine went only to the church and cemetery, as likewise did four of Kaethe's children and Irma and her boys. Hermine had been all eyes for her veiled, but still discernibly lovely aunt, whose crisp, deep black stood out cypress-like against the greyer, cheaper hues of the other mourning figures, and she had been pleasantly conscious of a sort of pricking interest in some one in her very own family who, by all accounts, would go straight to Hell when she died.

Ferry had wept overmuch for his strength and years, but Resl in her high, true voice had sung 'In Paradise, In Paradise' about the house for days.

Liesel, after a long discussion with Otto, who was born knowing what happened to husbands who didn't look after their wives, had gone, safely and properly accompanied by him, to take a last look at her aunt as she lay in Fanny's darkened salon, candles at her head and feet and all those flowers – in January. So great was the majesty clothing the features of 'poor old Tante Ilde,' that fear suddenly entered into Liesel's rippling, shallow soul, and she got confused, and afterwards, to her annoyance, she could only remember vaguely that everything was blue and that over the divan was a silken cover picked out in what seemed to be silver rosebuds. Donkey that *she* was, she hadn't noticed the jewelled elephants either, nor the rabbits of which she had heard so much. Otto couldn't help her out in the slightest – no more than a blind man. No, Liesel decidedly hadn't had her pleasant wits about her that day and she keenly regretted not having taken better advantage of her one opportunity.

Fanny had not shown herself. Maria, robed fittingly in deepest black, the expression on her face almost as sombre as her garb, saw through, competently and proudly, the visits of the sorrowing nieces.

Mizzi had been all honey, though she thought Fanny was decidedly over-doing things, and had given Maria a present of money, which Maria considered long due and took with small thanks. She couldn't abide Mizzi anyway.

Leo and Kaethe slipped in grievingly to continue their weeping by that second bier; Kaethe was greatly comforted by thinking that Carli and Tante Ilde were, even then, together.

Hermann came no more. Beloved dead, – he couldn't bear it – the cold body – and all he knew about it. No, no.

Corinne, whose sorrow was as deep as her being, spent two nights watching by her Dresden-china aunt, now done in palest ivory. She felt as if she herself had destroyed her. When you had a fragile treasure like that and threw it literally into the streets. . . .

·But Fanny mingled her bright tears so healingly with her sister's that the last night, as they sat near their Tante Ilde, they found themselves talking softly, smilingly even, of familiar little things that once had made her smile.

The flickering light of the candles at her head and feet met the silver crucifix on her breast, shimmered on the silver hair flat above the still, pale forehead. . . . The same light caught with a greedy, leaping flame the young, living gold of the two bowed heads. . . .

But after a while, except for the memory of the splendid funeral Fanny gave her, getting dimmer even that, in the hearts of those she had truly loved, it would soon be to every one except Tante Ilde herself, busied timelessly in one of many mansions, as if she had never been.

PRINTED BY BUTLER AND TANNER LTD., FROME AND LONDON

A LIST OF VOLUMES ISSUED IN THE TRAVELLERS' LIBRARY

3s. 6d. net each

JONATHAN CAPE LTD.

THIRTY BEDFORD SQUARE

LONDON

THE TRAVELLERS' LIBRARY

*

A series of books in all branches of literature designed for the pocket, or for the small house where shelf space is scarce. Though the volumes measure only 7 inches by 4¾ inches, the page is arranged so that the margins are not unreasonably curtailed nor legibility sacrificed. The books are of a uniform thickness irrespective of the number of pages, and the paper, specially manufactured for the series, is remarkably opaque, even when it is thinnest.

A semi-flexible form of binding has been adopted, as a safeguard against the damage inevitably associated with hasty packing. The cloth is of a particularly attractive shade of blue and has the author's name stamped in gold on the back.

*

4. BABBITT A Novel
    by Sinclair Lewis

¶ 'One of the greatest novels I have read for a long time.'
H. G. Wells   'Babbitt is a triumph.' *Hugh Walpole*
'His work has that something extra, over and above, which
makes the work of art, and it is signed in every line with the
unique personality of the author.' *Rebecca West*

5. THE CRAFT OF FICTION
    by Percy Lubbock

¶ 'No more substantial or more charming volume of criticism
has been published in our time.' *Observer*
'To say that this is the best book on the subject is probably true;
but it is more to the point to say that it is the only one.'
Times Literary Supplement

6. EARLHAM
    by Percy Lubbock

¶ 'The book seems too intimate to be reviewed. We want to be
allowed to read it, and to dream over it, and keep silence about
it. His judgment is perfect, his humour is true and ready; his
touch light and prim; his prose is exact and clean and full
of music.' *Times*

7. WIDE SEAS & MANY LANDS A Personal Narrative
    by Arthur Mason.
    With an Introduction by MAURICE BARING

¶ 'This is an extremely entertaining, and at the same time, moving
book. We are in the presence of a born writer. We read with
the same mixture of amazement and delight that fills us throughout a Conrad novel.' *New Statesman*

8. SELECTED PREJUDICES A book of Essays
    by H. L. Mencken

¶ 'He is exactly the kind of man we are needing, an iconoclast,
a scoffer at ideals, a critic with whips and scorpions who does
not hesitate to deal with literary, social and political humbugs
in the one slashing fashion.' *English Review*

9. THE MIND IN THE MAKING An Essay
by James Harvey Robinson

¶ ' For me, I think James Harvey Robinson is going to be almost as important as was Huxley in my adolescence, and William James in later years. It is a cardinal book. I question whether in the long run people may not come to it, as making a new initiative into the world's thought and methods.' *From the Introduction by* H. G. WELLS

10. THE WAY OF ALL FLESH A Novel
by Samuel Butler

¶ ' It drives one almost to despair of English Literature when one sees so extraordinary a study of English life as Butler's posthumous *Way of All Flesh* making so little impression. Really, the English do not deserve to have great men.' *George Bernard Shaw*

11. EREWHON A Satire
by Samuel Butler

¶ ' To lash the age, to ridicule vain pretension, to expose hypocrisy, to deride humbug in education, politics and religion, are tasks beyond most men's powers ; but occasionally, very occasionally, a bit of genuine satire secures for itself more than a passing nod of recognition. *Erewhon* is such a satire. . . . The best of its kind since *Gulliver's Travels*.' *Augustine Birrell*

12. EREWHON REVISITED A Satire
by Samuel Butler

¶ ' He waged a sleepless war with the mental torpor of the prosperous, complacent England around him ; a Swift with the soul of music in him, and completely sane ; a liberator of humanity operating with the wit and malice and coolness of Mephistopheles.' *Manchester Guardian*

13. ADAM AND EVE AND PINCH ME Stories
by A. E. Coppard

¶ Mr. Coppard's implicit theme is the closeness of the spiritual world to the material ; the strange, communicative sympathy which strikes through two temperaments and suddenly makes them one. He deals with those sudden impulses under which secrecy is broken down for a moment, and personality revealed as under a flash of spiritual lightning.

14. DUBLINERS   A volume of Stories
      by James Joyce

¶ A collection of fifteen short stories by the author of *Ulysses*. They are all of them brave, relentless, and sympathetic pictures of Dublin life ; realistic, perhaps, but not crude ; analytical, but not repugnant.   No modern writer has greater significance than Mr. Joyce, whose conception and practice of the short story is certainly unique and certainly vital.

15. DOG AND DUCK
      by Arthur Machen

¶ 'As a literary artist, Mr. Arthur Machen has few living equals, and that is very far indeed from being his only, or even his greatest, claim on the suffrages of English readers.' *Sunday Times*

16. KAI LUNG'S GOLDEN HOURS
      by Ernest Bramah

¶ 'It is worthy of its forerunner.   There is the same plan, exactitude, working-out and achievement ; and therefore complete satisfaction in the reading.' *From the Preface by* HILAIRE BELLOC

17. ANGELS & MINISTERS, AND OTHER PLAYS
      by Laurence Housman

Imaginary portraits of political characters done in dialogue— Queen Victoria, Disraeli, Gladstone, Parnell, Joseph Chamberlain, and Woodrow Wilson.

¶ 'It is all so good that one is tempted to congratulate Mr. Housman on a true masterpiece.' *Times*

18. THE WALLET OF KAI LUNG
      by Ernest Bramah

¶ 'Something worth doing and done. . . .   It was a thing intended, wrought out, completed and established.   Therefore it was destined to endure, and, what is more important, it was a success.' *Hilaire Belloc*

19. TWILIGHT IN ITALY
by D. H. Lawrence

¶ This volume of travel vignettes in North Italy was first published in 1916. Since then Mr. Lawrence has increased the number of his admirers year by year. In *Twilight in Italy* they will find all the freshness and vigour of outlook which they have come to expect from its author.

20. THE DREAM   A Novel
by H. G. Wells

¶ 'It is the richest, most generous and absorbing thing that Mr. Wells has given us for years and years.' *Daily News*
'I find this book as close to being magnificent as any book that I have ever read. It is full of inspiration and life.'
Daily Graphic

21. ROMAN PICTURES
by Percy Lubbock

¶ Pictures of life as it is lived—or has been or might be lived—among the pilgrims and colonists in Rome of more or less English speech.
'A book of whimsical originality and exquisite workmanship, and worthy of one of the best prose writers of our time.'
Sunday Times

22. CLORINDA WALKS IN HEAVEN
by A. E. Coppard

¶ 'Genius is a hard-ridden word, and has been put by critics at many puny ditches, but Mr. Coppard sets up a fence worthy of its mettle. He shows that in hands like his the English language is as alive as ever, and that there are still infinite possibilities in the short story.' *Outlook*

23. MARIUS THE EPICUREAN
by Walter Pater

¶ Walter Pater was at the same time a scholar of wide sympathies and a master of the English language. In this, his best known work, he describes with rare delicacy of feeling and insight the religious and philosophic tendencies of the Roman Empire at the time of Antoninus Pius as they affected the mind and life of the story's hero.

24. THE WHITE SHIP   Stories
by Aino Kallas
With an Introduction by JOHN GALSWORTHY

¶ 'The writer has an extraordinary sense of atmosphere.'
Times Literary Supplement
'Stories told convincingly and well, with a keen perception for natural beauty.' *Nation*

25. MULTITUDE AND SOLITUDE   A Novel
by John Masefield

¶ 'As well conceived and done, as rich in observation of the world, as profound where it needs to be profound, as any novel of recent writing.' *Outlook*
'This is no common book.   It is a book which not merely touches vital things.   It is vital.' *Daily News*

26. SPRING SOWING   Stories
by Liam O'Flaherty

¶ 'Nothing seems to escape Mr. O'Flaherty's eye; his brain turns all things to drama; and his vocabulary is like a river in spate. *Spring Sowing* is a book to buy, or to borrow, or, yes, to steal.' *Bookman*

27. WILLIAM   A Novel
by E. H. Young

¶ 'An extraordinary good book, penetrating and beautiful.'
Allan Monkhouse
'All its characters are very real and alive, and William himself is a masterpiece.' *May Sinclair*

28. THE COUNTRY OF THE POINTED FIRS
by Sarah Orne Jewett

¶ 'The young student of American literature in the far distant future will take up this book and say "a masterpiece!" as proudly as if he had made it.   It will be a message in a universal language—the one message that even the scythe of Time spares.'
From the Preface by WILLA CATHER

**

29. GRECIAN ITALY
by Henry James Forman

¶ 'It has been said that if you were shown Taormina in a vision you would not believe it. If the reader has been in Grecian Italy before he reads this book, the magic of its pages will revive old memories and induce a severe attack of nostalgia.' *From the Preface by* H. FESTING JONES

30. WUTHERING HEIGHTS
by Emily Brontë

¶ 'It is a very great book. You may read this grim story of lost and thwarted human creatures on a moor at any age and come under its sway.' *From the Introduction by* ROSE MACAULAY

31. ON A CHINESE SCREEN
by W. Somerset Maugham

¶ A collection of sketches of life in China. Mr. Somerset Maugham writes with equal certainty and vigour whether his characters are Chinese or European. There is a tenderness and humour about the whole book which makes the reader turn eagerly to the next page for more.

32. A FARMER'S LIFE
by George Bourne

¶ The life story of a tenant-farmer of fifty years ago in which the author of *The Bettesworth Book* and *The Memoirs of a Surrey Labourer* draws on his memory for a picture of the every-day life of his immediate forebears, the Smiths, farmers and handicraft men, who lived and died on the border of Surrey and Hampshire.

33. TWO PLAYS. *The Cherry Orchard & The Sea Gull*
by Anton Tchekoff. Translated by George Calderon

¶ Tchekoff had that fine comedic spirit which relishes the incongruity between the actual disorder of the world with the underlying order. He habitually mingled tragedy (which is life seen close at hand) with comedy (which is life seen at a distance). His plays are tragedies with the texture of comedy.

34. THE MONK AND THE HANGMAN'S DAUGHTER
by Ambrose Bierce

¶ 'They are stories which the discerning are certain to welcome. They are evidence of very unusual powers, and when once they have been read the reader will feel himself impelled to dig out more from the same pen.' *Westminster Gazette*

35. CAPTAIN MARGARET   A Novel
by John Masefield

¶ 'His style is crisp, curt and vigorous.   He has the Stevensonian sea-swagger, the Stevensonian sense of beauty and poetic spirit. Mr. Masefield's descriptions ring true and his characters carry conviction.'   *The Observer*

36. BLUE WATER
by Arthur Sturges Hildebrand

¶ This book gives the real feeling of life on a small cruising yacht ; the nights on deck with the sails against the sky, long fights with head winds by mountainous coasts to safety in forlorn little island ports, and constant adventure free from care.

37. STORIES FROM DE MAUPASSANT
Translated by Elizabeth Martindale

¶ 'His "story" engrosses the non-critical, it holds the critical too at the first reading. . . .   That is the real test of art, and it is because of the inobtrusiveness of this workmanship, that for once the critic and the reader may join hands without awaiting the verdict of posterity.' *From the Introduction by* FORD MADOX FORD

38. WHILE THE BILLY BOILS   First Series
by Henry Lawson

¶ These stories are written by the O. Henry of Australia.   They tell of men and dogs, of cities and plains, of gullies and ridges, of sorrow and happiness, and of the fundamental goodness that is hidden in the most unpromising of human soil.

39. WHILE THE BILLY BOILS Second Series
by Henry Lawson

¶ Mr. Lawson has the uncanny knack of making the people he writes about almost violently alive. Whether he tells of jackeroos, bush children or drovers' wives, each one lingers in the memory long after we have closed the book.

41. IN MOROCCO
by Edith Wharton

¶ Morocco is a land of mists and mysteries, of trailing silver veils through which minarets, mighty towers, hot palm groves and Atlas snows peer and disappear at the will of the Atlantic cloud-drifts.

42. GLEANINGS IN BUDDHA-FIELDS
by Lafcadio Hearn

¶ A book which is readable from first page to last, and is full of suggestive thought, the essays on Japanese religious belief calling for special praise for the earnest spirit in which the subject is approached.

43. OUT OF THE EAST
by Lafcadio Hearn

¶ Mr. Hearn has written many books about Japan ; he is saturated with the essence of its beauty, and in this book the light and colour and movement of that land drips from his pen in every delicately conceived and finely written sentence.

44. KWAIDAN
by Lafcadio Hearn

¶ The marvellous tales which Mr. Hearn has told in this volume illustrate the wonder-living tendency of the Japanese. The stories are of goblins, fairies and sprites, with here and there an adventure into the field of unveiled supernaturalism.

45. THE CONQUERED
by Naomi Mitchison
A story of the Gauls under Cæsar

¶ 'With *The Conquered* Mrs. Mitchison establishes herself as the best, if not the only, English historical novelist now writing. It seems to me in many respects the most attractive and poignant historical novel I have ever read.' *New Statesman*

46. WHEN THE BOUGH BREAKS
by Naomi Mitchison

Stories of the time when Rome was crumbling to ruin

¶ 'Interesting, delightful, and fresh as morning dew. The connoisseur in short stories will turn to some pages in this volume again and again with renewed relish.' *Times Literary Supplement*

47. THE FLYING BO'SUN
by Arthur Mason

¶ 'What makes the book remarkable is the imaginative power which has re-created these events so vividly that even the supernatural ones come with the shock and the conviction with which actual supernatural events might come.' *From the Introduction by* EDWIN MUIR

48. LATER DAYS
by W. H. Davies

A pendant to *The Autobiography of a Super-Tramp*

¶ 'The self-portrait is given with disarming, mysterious, and baffling directness, and the writing has the same disarmingness and simpleness.' *Observer*

49. THE EYES OF THE PANTHER Stories
by Ambrose Bierce

¶ It is said that these tales were originally rejected by virtually every publisher in the country. Bierce was a strange man; in 1914 at the age of seventy-one he set out for Mexico and has never been heard of since. His stories are as strange as his life, but this volume shows him as a master of his art.

50. IN DEFENCE OF WOMEN
by H. L. Mencken

¶ 'All I design by the book is to set down in more or less plain form certain ideas that practically every civilized man and woman holds *in petto*, but that have been concealed hitherto by the vast mass of sentimentalities swathing the whole woman question.' *From the Author's Introduction*

51. VIENNESE MEDLEY   A Novel
by Edith O'Shaughnessy

¶ ' It is told with infinite tenderness, with many touches of grave or poignant humour, in a very beautiful book, which no lover of fiction should allow to pass unread. A book which sets its writer definitely in the first rank of living English novelists.'
Sunday Times

52. PRECIOUS BANE   A Novel
by Mary Webb

¶ ' She has a style of exquisite beauty ; which yet has both force and restraint, simplicity and subtlety ; she has fancy and wit, delicious humour and pathos. She sees and knows men aright as no other novelist does. She has, in short, genius.' *Mr. Edwin Pugh*

53. THE INFAMOUS JOHN FRIEND
by Mrs. R. S. Garnett

¶ This book, though in form an historical novel, claims to rank as a psychological study. It is an attempt to depict a character which, though destitute of the common virtues of every-day life, is gifted with qualities that compel love and admiration.

54. HORSES AND MEN
by Sherwood Anderson

¶ '*Horses and Men* confirms our indebtedness to the publishers who are introducing his work here. It has a unity beyond that of its constant Middle-west setting. A man of poetic vision, with an intimate knowledge of particular conditions of life, here looks out upon a world that seems singularly material only because he unflinchingly accepts its actualities.' *Morning Post*

55. SELECTED ESSAYS
by Samuel Butler

¶ This volume contains the following essays :

The Humour of Homer	How to Make the Best of Life
Quis Desiderio . . .?	The Sanctuary of Montrigone
Ramblings in Cheapside	A Medieval Girls' School
The Aunt, the Nieces, and the Dog	Art in the Valley of Saas
	Thought and Language

56. A POET'S PILGRIMAGE
by W. H. Davies

¶ *A Poet's Pilgrimage* recounts the author's impressions of his native Wales on his return after many years' absence. He tells of a walking tour during which he stayed in cheap rooms and ate in the small wayside inns. The result is a vivid picture of the Welsh people, the towns and countryside.

57. GLIMPSES OF UNFAMILIAR JAPAN. First Series
by Lafcadio Hearn

¶ Most books written about Japan have been superficial sketches of a passing traveller. Of the inner life of the Japanese we know practically nothing, their religion, superstitions, ways of thought. Lafcadio Hearn reveals something of the people and their customs as they are.

58. GLIMPSES OF UNFAMILIAR JAPAN. Second Series
by Lafcadio Hearn

¶ Sketches by an acute observer and a master of English prose, of a Nation in transition—of the lingering remains of Old Japan, to-day only a memory, of its gardens, its beliefs, customs, gods and devils, of its wonderful kindliness and charm—and of the New Japan, struggling against odds towards new ideals.

59. THE TRAVELS OF MARCO POLO
Edited by Manuel Komroff

¶ When Marco Polo arrived at the court of the Great Khan, Pekin had just been rebuilt. Kublai Khan was at the height of his glory. Polo rose rapidly in favour and became governor of an important district. In this way he gained first-hand knowledge of a great civilization and described it with astounding accuracy and detail.

60. SELECTED PREJUDICES. Second Series
by H. L. Mencken

¶ 'What a master of the straight left in appreciation! Everybody who wishes to see how common sense about books and authors can be made exhilarating should acquire this delightful book.'
Morning Post

61. THE WORLD'S BACK DOORS
by Max Murray
With an introduction by HECTOR BOLITHO

¶ This book is not an account so much of places as of people. The journey round the world was begun with about enough money to buy one meal, and continued for 66,000 miles. There are periods as a longshore man and as a sailor, and a Chinese guard and a night watchman, and as a hobo.

62. THE EVOLUTION OF AN INTELLECTUAL
by J. Middleton Murry

¶ These essays were written during and immediately after the Great War. The author says that they record the painful stages by which he passed from the so-called intellectual state to the state of being what he now considers to be a reasonable man.

63. THE RENAISSANCE
by Walter Pater

¶ This English classic contains studies of those 'supreme artists,' Michelangelo and Da Vinci, and of Botticelli, Della Robia, Mirandola, and others, who ' have a distinct faculty of their own by which they convey to us a peculiar quality of pleasure which we cannot get elsewhere.' There is no romance or subtlety in the work of these masters too fine for Pater to distinguish in superb English.

64. THE ADVENTURES OF A WANDERER
by Sydney Walter Powell

¶ Throwing up a position in the Civil Service in Natal because he preferred movement and freedom to monotony and security, the author started his wanderings by enlisting in an Indian Ambulance Corps in the South African War. Afterwards he wandered all over the world.

65. 'RACUNDRA'S' FIRST CRUISE
by Arthur Ransome

¶ This is the story of the building of an ideal yacht which would be a cruising boat that one man could manage if need be, but on which three people could live comfortably. The adventures of the cruise are skilfully and vividly told.

66. THE MARTYRDOM OF MAN
by Winwood Reade

¶ 'Few sketches of universal history by one single author have been written. One book that has influenced me very strongly is *The Martyrdom of Man*. This " dates," as people say now-adays, and it has a fine gloom of its own ; but it is still an extraordinarily inspiring presentation of human history as one consistent process.' *H. G. Wells* in *The Outline of History*

67. THE AUTOBIOGRAPHY OF MARK RUTHERFORD
With an introduction by H. W. MASSINGHAM

¶ Because of its honesty, delicacy and simplicity of portraiture, this book has always had a curious grip upon the affections of its readers. An English Amiel, inheriting to his comfort an English Old Crome landscape, he freed and strengthened his own spirit as he will his reader's.

68. THE DELIVERANCE
by Mark Rutherford

¶ Once read, Hale White [Mark Rutherford] is never forgotten. But he is not yet approached through the highways of English letters. To the lover of his work, nothing can be more attractive than the pure and serene atmosphere of thought in which his art moves.

69. THE REVOLUTION IN TANNER'S LANE
by Mark Rutherford

¶ ' Since Bunyan, English Puritanism has produced one imaginative genius of the highest order. To my mind, our fiction contains no more perfectly drawn pictures of English life in its recurring emotional contrast of excitement and repose more valuable to the historian, or more stimulating to the imaginative reader.' *H. W. Massingham*

70. ASPECTS OF SCIENCE. First Series
by J. W. N. Sullivan

¶ Although they deal with different aspects of various scientific ideas, the papers which make up this volume do illustrate, more or less, one point of view. This book tries to show one or two of the many reasons why science may be interesting for people who are not specialists as well as for those who are.

71. MASTRO-DON GESUALDO
Giovanni Verga.   Translated by D. H. Lawrence

¶ Verga, who died in 1922, is recognized as one of the greatest of Italian writers of fiction.   He can claim a place beside Hardy and the Russians.   'It is a fine full tale, a fine, full picture of life, with a bold beauty of its own which Mr. Lawrence must have relished greatly as he translated it.' *Observer*

72. THE MISSES MALLETT
by E. H. Young

¶ The virtue of this quiet and accomplished piece of writing lies in its quality and in its character-drawing; to summarize it would be to give no idea of its charm.   Neither realism nor romance, it is a book by a writer of insight and sensibility.

73. SELECTED ESSAYS. First Series
by Sir Edmund Gosse, C.B.

¶ 'The prose of Sir Edmund Gosse is as rich in the colour of young imagination as in the mellow harmony of judgment.   Sir Edmund Gosse's literary kit-kats will continue to be read with avidity long after the greater part of the academic criticism of the century is swept away upon the lumber-heap.' *Daily Telegraph*

74. WHERE THE BLUE BEGINS
by Christopher Morley

¶ A delicious satirical fantasy, in which humanity wears a dog-collar.
'Mr. Morley is a master of consequent inconsequence.   His humour and irony are excellent, and his satire is only the more salient for the delicate and ingenuous fantasy in which it is set.' *Manchester Guardian*

75. JAVA HEAD
by Joseph Hergesheimer

¶ The author has created a connoisseur's world of his own; a world of colourful bric-à-brac—of ships and rustling silks and old New England houses—a world in which the rarest and most perplexing of emotions are caught and expressed for the perceptible moment as in austerely delicate porcelain.   *Java Head* is a novel of grave and lasting beauty.

76. CONFESSIONS OF A YOUNG MAN
by George Moore

¶ ' Mr. Moore, true to his period and to his genius, stripped himself of everything that might stand between him and the achievement of his artistic object. He does not ask you to admire this George Moore. He merely asks you to observe him beyond good and evil as a constant plucked from the bewildering flow of eternity.' *Humbert Wolfe*

77. THE BAZAAR. Stories
by Martin Armstrong

¶ ' These stories have considerable range of subject, but in general they are stay-at-home tales, depicting cloistered lives and delicate finely fibred minds. . . . Mr. Armstrong writes beautifully.' *Nation and Athenæum*

78. SIDE SHOWS. Essays
by J. B. Atkins
With an Introduction by JAMES BONE

¶ Mr. J. B. Atkins was war correspondent in four wars, the London editor of a great English paper, then Paris correspondent of another, and latterly the editor of the *Spectator*. His subjects in *Side Shows* are briefly London and the sea.

79. SHORT TALKS WITH THE DEAD
by Hilaire Belloc

¶ In these essays Mr. Belloc attains his usual high level of pungent and witty writing. The subjects vary widely and include an imaginary talk with the spirits of Charles I, the barber of Louis XIV, and Napoleon, Venice, fakes, eclipses, Byron, and the famous dissertation on the Nordic Man.

80. ORIENT EXPRESS
by John dos Passos

¶ This book will be read because, as well as being the temperature chart of an unfortunate sufferer from the travelling disease, it deals with places shaken by the heavy footsteps of History, manifesting itself as usual by plague, famine, murder, sudden death and depreciated currency. Underneath the book is an ode to railroad travel.

81. SELECTED ESSAYS. Second Series
by Sir Edmund Gosse, C.B.

¶ A second volume of essays personally chosen by Sir Edmund Gosse from the wide field of his literary work. One is delighted with the width of his appreciation which enables him to write with equal charm on *Wycherley* and on *How to Read the Bible*.

82. ON THE EVE
by Ivan Turgenev. Translated by Constance Garnett

¶ In his characters is something of the width and depth which so astounds us in the creations of Shakespeare. *On the Eve* is a quiet work, yet over which the growing consciousness of coming events casts its heavy shadow. Turgenev, even as he sketched the ripening love of a young girl, has made us feel the dawning aspirations of a nation.

83. FATHERS AND CHILDREN
by Ivan Turgenev. Translated by Constance Garnett

¶ ' As a piece of art *Fathers and Children* is the most powerful of all Turgenev's works. The figure of Bazarov is not only the political centre of the book, but a figure in which the eternal tragedy of man's impotence and insignificance is realized in scenes of a most ironical human drama.' *Edward Garnett*

84. SMOKE
by Ivan Turgenev. Translated by Constance Garnett

¶ In this novel Turgenev sees and reflects, even in the shifting phases of political life, that which is universal in human nature. His work is compassionate, beautiful, unique ; in the sight of his fellow-craftsmen always marvellous and often perfect.

85. PORGY. A Tale
by du Bose Heyward

¶ This fascinating book gives a vivid and intimate insight into the lives of a group of American negroes, from whom Porgy stands out, rich in humour and tragedy. The author's description of a hurricane is reminiscent in its power.

86. FRANCE AND THE FRENCH
by Sisley Huddleston

¶ 'There has been nothing of its kind published since the War. His book is a repository of facts marshalled with judgment; as such it should assist in clearing away a whole maze of misconceptions and prejudices, and serve as a sort of pocket encyclopædia of modern France.' *Times Literary Supplement*

88. CLOUD CUCKOO LAND. A Novel of Sparta
by Naomi Mitchison

¶ 'Rich and frank in passions, and rich, too, in the detail which helps to make feigned life seem real.' *Times Literary Supplement*

89. A PRIVATE IN THE GUARDS
by Stephen Graham

¶ In his own experiences as a soldier Stephen Graham has conserved the half-forgotten emotions of a nation in arms. Above all he makes us feel the stark brutality and horror of actual war, the valour which is more than valour, and the disciplined endurance which is human and therefore the more terrifying.

90. THUNDER ON THE LEFT
by Christopher Morley

¶ 'It is personal to every reader, it will become for every one a reflection of himself. I fancy that here, as always where work is fine and true, the author has created something not as he would but as he must, and is here an interpreter of a world more wonderful than he himself knows.' *Hugh Walpole*

91. THE MOON AND SIXPENCE
by Somerset Maugham

¶ A remarkable picture of a genius.
'Mr. Maugham has given us a ruthless and penetrating study in personality with a savage truthfulness of delineation and an icy contempt for the heroic and the sentimental.' *The Times*

92. THE CASUARINA TREE
by W. Somerset Maugham

¶ Intensely dramatic stories in which the stain of the East falls deeply on the lives of English men and women. Mr. Maugham remains cruelly aloof from his characters. On passion and its culminating tragedy he looks with unmoved detachment, ringing the changes without comment and yet with little cynicism.

93. A POOR MAN'S HOUSE
by Stephen Reynolds

¶ Vivid and intimate pictures of a Devonshire fisherman's life. 'Compact, harmonious, without a single—I won't say false—but uncertain note, true in aim, sentiment and expression, precise and imaginative, never precious, but containing here and there an absolutely priceless phrase. . . .' *Joseph Conrad*

94. WILLIAM BLAKE
by Arthur Symons

¶ When Blake spoke the first word of the nineteenth century there was none to hear it; and now that his message has penetrated the world, and is slowly re-making it, few are conscious of the man who first voiced it. This lack of knowledge is remedied in Mr. Symons' work.

95. A LITERARY PILGRIM IN ENGLAND
by Edward Thomas

¶ A book about the homes and resorts of English writers, from John Aubrey, Cowper, Gilbert White, Cobbett, Wordsworth, Burns, Borrow and Lamb, to Swinburne, Stevenson, Meredith, W. H. Hudson and H. Belloc. Each chapter is a miniature biography and at the same time a picture of the man and his work and environment.

96. NAPOLEON : THE LAST PHASE
by The Earl of Rosebery

¶ Of books and memoirs about Napoleon there is indeed no end, but of the veracious books such as this there are remarkably few. It aims to penetrate the deliberate darkness which surrounds the last act of the Napoleonic drama.

97. THE POCKET BOOK OF POEMS AND SONGS FOR THE OPEN AIR
Compiled by Edward Thomas

¶ This anthology is meant to please those lovers of poetry and the country who like a book that can always lighten some of their burdens or give wings to their delight, whether in the open air by day, or under the roof at evening; in it is gathered much of the finest English poetry.

98. SAFETY PINS : ESSAYS
by Christopher Morley
With an Introduction by H. M. TOMLINSON

¶ Very many readers will be glad of the opportunity to meet Mr. Morley in the rôle of the gentle essayist. He is an author who is content to move among his fellows, to note, to reflect, and to write genially and urbanely; to love words for their sound as well as for their value in expression of thought.

99. THE BLACK SOUL : A Novel
by Liam O'Flaherty

¶ '*The Black Soul* overwhelms one like a storm. . . . Nothing like it has been written by any Irish writer.' "*Æ*" in *The Irish Statesman*

100. CHRISTINA ALBERTA'S FATHER :
A Novel
by H. G. Wells

¶ ' At first reading the book is utterly beyond criticism; all the characters are delightfully genuine.' *Spectator*
' Brimming over with Wellsian insight, humour and invention. No one but Mr. Wells could have written the whole book and given it such verve and sparkle.' *Westminster Gazette*

102. THE GRUB STREET NIGHTS ENTERTAINMENTS
by J. C. Squire

¶ Stories of literary life, told with a breath of fantasy and gaily ironic humour. Each character lives, and is the more lively for its touch of caricature. From *The Man Who Kept a Diary* to *The Man Who Wrote Free Verse*, these tales constitute Mr. Squire's most delightful ventures in fiction; and the conception of the book itself is unique.

103. ORIENTAL ENCOUNTERS
by Marmaduke Pickthall

¶ In *Oriental Encounters*, Mr. Pickthall relives his earlier manhood's discovery of Arabia and sympathetic encounters with the Eastern mind. He is one of the few travellers who really bridges the racial gulf.

105. THE MOTHER : A Novel
by Grazia Deledda
With an introduction by D. H. LAWRENCE

¶ An unusual book, both in its story and its setting in a remote Sardinian hill village, half civilized and superstitious. The action of the story takes place so rapidly and the actual drama is so interwoven with the mental conflict, and all so forced by circumstances, that it is almost Greek in its simple and inevitable tragedy.

106. TRAVELLER'S JOY : An Anthology
by W. G. Waters

¶ This anthology has been selected for publication in the Travellers' Library from among the many collections of verse because of its suitability for the traveller, particularly the summer and autumn traveller, who would like to carry with him some store of literary provender.

107. SHIPMATES : Essays
by Felix Riesenberg

¶ A collection of intimate character portraits of men with whom the author has sailed on many voyages. The sequence of studies blends into a fascinating panorama of living characters.

108. THE CRICKET MATCH
by Hugh de Selincourt

¶ Through the medium of a cricket match the author endeavours to give a glimpse of life in a Sussex village. First we have a bird's-eye view at dawn of the village nestling under the Downs; then we see the players awaken in all the widely different circumstance of their various lives, pass the morning, assemble on the field, play their game, united for a few hours, as men should be, by a common purpose—and at night disperse.

109. RARE ADVENTURES AND PAINEFULL
       PEREGRINATIONS (1582–1645)
       by William Lithgow
       Edited, and with an Introduction by B. I. LAWRENCE

¶ This is the book of a seventeenth-century Scotchman who
walked over the Levant, North Africa and most of Europe,
including Spain, where he was tortured by the Inquisition.
An unscrupulous man, full of curiosity, his comments are
diverting and penetrating, his adventures remarkable.

110. THE END OF A CHAPTER
       by Shane Leslie

¶ In this, his most famous book, Mr. Shane Leslie has preserved
for future generations the essence of the pre-war epoch, its
institutions and individuals. He writes of Eton, of the Empire,
of Post-Victorianism, of the Politicians. . . . And whatever
he touches upon, he brilliantly interprets.

111. SAILING ACROSS EUROPE
       by Negley Farson
       With an Introduction by FRANK MORLEY

¶ A voyage of six months in a ship, its one and only cabin
measuring 8 feet by 6 feet, up the Rhine, down the Danube,
passing from one to the other by the half-forgotten Ludwig's
Canal. To think of and plan such a journey was a fine
imaginative effort and to write about it interestingly is no
mean accomplishment.

112. MEN, BOOKS AND BIRDS—Letters to a friend
       by W. H. Hudson
       With Notes, some Letters, and an Introduction by
       MORLEY ROBERTS

¶ An important collection of letters from the naturalist to his
friend, literary executor and fellow-author, Morley Roberts,
covering a period of twenty-five years.

113. PLAYS ACTING AND MUSIC
       by Arthur Symons

¶ This book deals mainly with music and with the various arts of
the stage. Mr. Arthur Symons shows how each art has its
own laws, its own limits; these it is the business of the critic
jealously to distinguish. Yet in the study of art as art, it
should be his endeavour to master the universal science of beauty.

119. FRIDAY NIGHTS
by Edward Garnett

¶ Of *Friday Nights* a *Times* reviewer wrote : ' Mr. Garnett is " the critic as artist," sensitive alike to elemental nature and the subtlest human variations. His book sketches for us the possible outlines of a new humanism, a fresh valuation of both life and art.'

120. DIVERSIONS IN SICILY
by Henry Festing Jones

¶ Shortly before his sudden and unexpected death, Mr. Festing Jones chose out *Diversions in Sicily* for reprinting in the Travellers' Library from among his three books of mainly Sicilian sketches and studies. The publishers hope that the book, in this popular form, will make many new friends. These chapters, as well as any that he wrote, recapture the wisdom, charm, and humour of their author.

121. DAYS IN THE SUN: A Cricketer's Book.
by Neville Cardus ('Cricketer' of the *Manchester Guardian*).

122. COMBED OUT
by F. A. Voigt

¶ This account of life in the army in 1917–18 both at home and in France is written with a telling incisiveness. The author does not indulge in an unnecessary word, but packs in just the right details with an intensity of feeling that is infectious.

★

Note

The Travellers' Library is now published as a joint enterprise by Jonathan Cape Ltd. and William Heinemann Ltd. The new volumes announced here to appear during the spring of 1929 include those to be published by both firms. The series as a whole or any title in the series can be ordered through booksellers from either Jonathan Cape or William Heinemann. Booksellers' only care must be not to duplicate their orders.

Made and Printed in Great Britain by Butler & Tanner Ltd., Frome and London